FAKE IT TILL WE FALL

A Fake Relationship Second Chance Holiday Romance

Trickle Creek: The Lyons

Book 3

ELENA AITKEN

Chapter One

Grayson

There are two things I know for certain:

1. You can't untangle last year's Christmas lights without swearing.
2. You can't untangle your feelings for your first love, either—not when she walked back into town like she never left.

Which was why I was up to my elbows in busted light strands instead of dealing with...other things.

The front counter of the hardware store was buried under a tangle of wires and burned-out bulbs. I'd already cut the hell out of my thumb trying to fix a plug that should have been thrown out years ago.

But sorting out the mass of knots and lights was a hell of a lot easier than attempting to sort out the mess in my head.

Harper was back in Trickle Creek.

It had been more than fifteen years since I'd seen her, if

you didn't count social media posts that I tried and failed not to look at. And I didn't.

Viewing her exotic life, traveling around the world, working as a chef in beautiful locations and on super-yachts through the lens of a screen was one thing. Seeing her in person, well… that would be a whole different situation.

A situation I wasn't looking forward to.

Or maybe I was.

I still couldn't figure out how I felt about having my first love—hell, my only love—back in town.

I tugged on a twisted knot of lights, yanking harder than I should have. A plastic snowflake snapped off and skittered across the floor, landing under a shelf.

"Dammit."

I abandoned the mess on the counter and went to grab the missing snowflake, right as the bell over the door jingled. I exhaled slowly and stayed crouched a little longer than necessary when I heard the familiar, overly chipper voice call out.

"Grayson Lyons. I hope you're not hiding from me."

I sighed and stood. There was no point in trying to hide. She'd find me. "That depends. Do you have that damned clipboard again?"

Tilley Beckett grinned and waved the aforementioned clipboard in the air. "What do you mean, again? I was never without it."

"Of course you weren't." I shook my head and retreated behind the counter again, as if it might offer me a little bit of protection from the never-ending to-do list the head of the town festival committee always seemed to have for me. "What can I help you with today, Tilley?"

The older lady smacked her bright-red lips, which matched the scarf tightly wound around her neck, and wiggled her eyebrows.

I knew that my day was about to get a whole lot busier.

"It's not what you can do for *me*, Grayson." She reached up and tugged on a candy cane earring. "It's what you can do for the town."

"Of course." I tried not to roll my eyes. "Whatever the town needs."

"I'm glad to hear you say that." She lifted the clipboard and pretended to scan the list before landing on the new tasks she had for me. "The tree lighting ceremony is two weeks away, and we're already behind schedule."

"I don't know if we're—"

"The new snowflake banners we ordered are in, and they need to be hung," she said. "And most of the lights that need to be wrapped around the light poles in the plaza are still in the storage shed."

"That's because they're all a tangled nightmare." I lifted the knot of bulbs and wires in front of me. "This is just the first of many."

"Well then, you'd better get moving," she said briskly. "I told the committee you'd start hanging them this afternoon."

"You did what?" I froze, mid-tug. "Why would you say that?"

"Because you're the only one who knows how to work the lift without taking out a tree or a storefront," she said matter-of-factly.

"I don't think that's true—"

"And because people rely on you, Grayson. You know that. You're the guy who gets things done."

I blew out a breath. That much was true. Somewhere over the last ten years or so, I'd fallen into that role, whether I wanted it or not. And that was a toss-up some days.

I didn't have a chance to protest, not that it would do any good, before the bell over the door jingled again, and my youngest brother, Preston, pushed inside the store. "Hey, do you still have that heavy-duty extension cord—" He stopped, taking a second to stomp the ice from his boots and brush the snow from his jacket while he looked around. "What the hell happened here?"

"Tinsel explosion." I shrugged helplessly. "You look like you just got off the ski hill," I said. "And that maybe you wiped out a few times."

"Not the hill." He laughed. "I was in the back country."

"Of course you were."

"The powder is fresh out there, man. You should get out—"

"Don't even say it." I held up a hand to stop him before he could tempt me with some backcountry ski adventure. "As much as I'd love to join, there is literally no time."

"Not if he's going to get all these lights hung in time for the festival," Tilley chimed in.

Preston looked between us and lifted the knot I was working on. "These lights? They look like—"

"A total mess." I cut him off.

"I was going to say something else." Preston grinned. "But sure, let's go with mess."

I shot him a look. "If you're not going to help, you can—"

"I'm leaving." My youngest brother held up his hands. "Just as soon as I get that cord. Don't get your cables in a knot." He laughed at his own joke, and I clenched my teeth to keep from saying something rude in front of Tilley.

"Well, I'd better let you get to it." Tilley adjusted her scarf and tucked her clipboard under her arm. "The plaza isn't going to decorate itself."

Didn't I know it.

She started for the door, pausing long enough to throw me a look over her shoulder. "You never know who you might run into over there, Grayson."

I didn't respond, but Preston caught the exchange. His

mouth quirked. "She talking about who I think she's talking about?"

"Don't start."

He only grinned wider and wiggled his eyebrows. "Uh-huh."

"Preston, I'm—"

"Yeah, yeah. I'm going."

"That extension cord is in the back."

He saluted me and thankfully, before he could say another word, followed Tilley out the door, leaving me mercifully alone with the thoughts I hadn't been able to get out of my head since I'd heard the news.

Harper

THE EARLY DECEMBER cold bit at my cheeks as I helped Grandma cross the plaza. After more than fifteen years away from the mountains, I'd forgotten just how sharp the winter air could be. Especially because I'd spent most of that time working on super-yachts in tropical climates.

My body wasn't used to such cold.

"Your teeth are chattering, dear." Grandma squeezed my arm. "I'm going to knit you a new scarf."

"You don't have to do that."

"Harper, I'm eighty-two years old." She stopped suddenly, causing me to jerk backward. "I don't *have* to do anything. I want to do it."

I couldn't help but smile and shake my head. She might be slowing down a little bit, but she was still the same feisty, stubborn grandma she'd always been.

"And you're going to need some warmer clothes now that you're back in Trickle Creek."

I opened my mouth to correct her, but closed it again.

There was no point in reminding her again that I was only back temporarily. Just until I could get the restaurant sorted out, put in some trustworthy employees, and figure out what was going on with Grandma's health.

With any luck, I could pull off a Christmas miracle and figure all of that out before the holidays, and get on the first plane to the Mediterranean to start the new charter season.

Grandma shook my arm until I looked at her. "I won't take no for an answer, Harper."

"Don't I know it." I smiled down at her. "And you're not wrong. It's freezing out here. I can't believe how much snow there is already."

"This little dusting." Grandma waved her hand around. "You've been gone too long, sweetheart. It's only just beginning. It's going to be a white Christmas."

She wasn't wrong. Christmas garlands and wreaths already hung from some of the light poles and most of the storefronts. The only thing better than seeing the plaza lit up for the holidays was seeing all those twinkling lights through the sparkle of the snow.

We kept walking, stopping only when we reached the restaurant, still bare of decorations. I mentally added it to my list of things to get done before the festival. By the looks of the heaps of lights and decorations still piled up around the plaza, I still had time to get my own decorations up.

"Let's get inside, and you can talk to me over a cup of tea," I told Grandma as I unlocked the glass door.

"Talk about what?" she said, like I hadn't just spent an hour in the doctor's waiting room waiting for her to finish up what she tried to play off as a routine appointment.

"The doctor," I pressed.

She waved her free hand, dismissing the question like a fruit fly. "I lived a lot of years, Harper. Sometimes a woman just needs a check-up."

I tugged my parka off and hung it on the rack by the door. "Grandma, that was more than just a check-up, and you know it. You said yourself that you haven't been feeling yourself and—"

"There's nothing to discuss." Her voice held a sharp edge I hadn't heard in years. But before I could respond, her voice softened as she settled into one of the tables by the window. "Now, what is it you said about a cup of tea?"

I blew out a breath and shook my head. I knew better than to push the issue. I didn't know anyone as stubborn as my grandma. The very fact that she called to tell me she needed me to come home spoke volumes. There was no way she'd do that if things weren't serious.

Besides, I didn't need to hear her say it to see how much help she needed. The evidence was all around me. It was shocking to see how much the once bustling, vibrant restaurant now seemed tired and old.

In the kitchen, I set the water to boil and grabbed the notebook with the lists I'd started making the moment I'd arrived a week earlier. The pages were filling up quickly. Even if I worked around the clock, there was no way I was going to get everything done before I needed to leave again.

I was definitely going to have to triage a few things.

With a quick scan, I circled "hang decorations" and "hire a head chef" before the water boiled.

Her eyes were closed when I returned to the dining room with two mugs of tea and my notebook. I watched for a moment, sure she'd dozed off, before her eyes snapped open again.

"Drink your tea, Grandma, and then maybe while I get ready for dinner service, you can go upstairs and rest."

"I don't need a rest." She shook her head. "What I need is for you to go over that list of yours with me. We'll be short-staffed for the holiday season if we don't start hiring soon."

"I've got it," I said. "I'll handle the interviews, the menu changes, and the ordering."

"Menu changes?" She held a spoonful of sugar before stirring it into her tea. "Why do we need menu changes?"

I was worried she might push back on a few of the changes I wanted to make. "Nothing too crazy, Grandma. I thought maybe if we streamlined things a little, keeping the classics and a few of the old favorites, it might be a bit more manageable."

I held my breath, ready for her pushback, but it didn't come.

Instead, she stirred the sugar into her mug and nodded. "Whatever you think is best."

What I really thought was best was for her to close Willa's Whisk entirely and enjoy her retirement. Especially if she was ill. But I knew I'd have to ease her into the idea of that very gently.

"I don't want you to worry about anything, Grandma," I told her. "I'll take care of whatever I can on this list and get some good help in here for you." I lifted my mug to my lips and blew the heat off. "I'll feel better when I leave knowing you have—"

"What do you mean, when you leave?"

I set the mug down again. "After New Year's."

Her brows rose. "New Year's?"

"That was the plan," I said as lightly as I could. "I promised I'd stay through the holidays. After that, I'm hoping to get on as head chef on a new boat for the charter season. I told you—"

She waved away my explanation. "Let's just take it one day at a time."

I bit my tongue and once more picked up my tea.

"You know," she said casually, "Trickle Creek during the holidays is a busy time. You'll probably run into a lot of people you haven't seen in a long time. It's hard to avoid people in a small town."

"That's true." I didn't meet her eyes.

"I'm sure some of those people will be pretty happy to see you, too," she added, her tone far too innocent.

I lifted one brow. "Is that your not-so-subtle way of telling me Grayson Lyons still lives in town?"

"Oh. You remember him?"

"You know I do." I shook my head. "And this is where you tell me he's happily married with three kids and that it could have been me."

Grandma sipped her tea and smiled behind the mug. "I wouldn't want to ruin the surprise, sweetheart."

I rolled my eyes. "Grayson Lyons is old news, Grandma."

It had been fifteen years since he broke my heart. I wasn't that girl anymore.

Besides, that was more than enough time to get over a teenage heartbreak.

Wasn't it?

Grayson

THE LIFT GROANED as I eased it to the edge of the plaza. After working all day, the lights were now untangled and almost most of the poles were wrapped, as well as the brand-new flags Tilley wanted hung.

My gloves were stiff from the cold, and my thumb throbbed from wrestling with an extra stubborn plug earlier.

There were still a handful of poles to wrap before I could call the job done. At least until Tilley assigned me another urgent holiday task. But first, I needed a quick warm-up.

I parked the lift by the flower shop and climbed down. I

had to admit, the plaza was starting to look good, decorated for the holidays.

The gazebo, which served as the centerpiece of the plaza, held a festive throne where Santa would sit soon to meet all the kids and hear their Christmas wishes. Garlands were strung over walkways, wreaths hung on the shop doors, and pine boughs framed windows.

Most of the doors and windows.

My gaze landed on Willa's Whisk and the still-undecorated storefront.

A part of me itched to walk over and offer to help. Just a neighborly thing to do. A kind gesture. No hidden agenda. No other reason.

Only, this year, there was a reason.

I shoved my hands in my pockets and started to walk.

"Brother!"

I turned to see Ethan in the door of Peaks & Brews.

"Get over here and warm up with a cold beer."

"That doesn't make any sense," I shouted back.

"Get over here!" My twin brother, Reid, appeared next to him, his arms crossed over his chest.

I knew when I was beat. Besides, warming up in the brewery beat the alternative of sitting in the cab of my truck with a thermos of stale coffee.

"Five minutes," I called back.

Reid raised a brow, as if he knew exactly what—or who— had slowed my pace.

I shook my head, tore my eyes from the undecorated restaurant, and headed toward them.

Chapter Two

Harper

With Grandma settled into her armchair upstairs with a fresh cup of tea, her knitting, and the television remote, I was back in the dining room with my laptop and my notebook list. Happily, I'd already made quite a bit of progress.

Help wanted ads were posted on local community job boards, looking for part-time serving staff and kitchen help. I used the same job boards for a head chef, but I also expanded the search to some of the nearby cities. If we were going to get the type of chef we needed to manage things for Grandma, I knew I'd have to look further afield.

With any luck, I'd get some interest for those who were interested in moving out to the mountains in the middle of winter. Fortunately, Trickle Creek was a popular destination, and I was hopeful we'd get a few quality candidates.

I'd also grabbed a menu and a marker and had started trimming things, which was a harder task than I'd anticipated. It was a balancing act to keep the classics without upsetting the loyal customers—all while keeping things streamlined enough to cut down on food costs.

Satisfied with my progress so far, I clicked open the accounting software I'd had Grandma install a few years back to help with the bookkeeping. It wasn't my favorite job, but it was important for me to know where things were at and what exactly we were working with.

I clicked over into the vendor invoices and started to scroll.

Most things were pretty normal, but a note under an entry for Trickle Creek Hardware stopped me.

Free delivery as per Grayson Lyons.

A TWINGE HIT low in my belly before I could shove it aside.

Grayson.

High school sweetheart. First love. The boy who kissed me behind the bleachers and made me believe we'd have forever.

Until he changed his mind.

Or was it me?

It didn't matter anymore. He was the boy who broke my heart, because it turned out he changed his mind.

"Whatever."

I shut the laptop with a little more force than necessary and reached for my tea.

"Am I interrupting something?"

I looked up to see Erin, Grandma's longtime restaurant manager, breeze through the front door.

"No." I shook my head. "I was just looking over the books. But it's probably time to get into the kitchen and get organized for service."

Erin laughed.

"What's so funny?"

"We don't really call it *service* here." She held up her fingers in air quotes. "I know you're used to fancy restaurants and yachts, but…"

I shrugged. "Just a habit, I guess."

"Either way, I think we're going to have a good crowd in here tonight." Erin moved around the dining room, adjusting chairs. "Word's out that you're back in town."

I smiled wryly. "Of course it is."

"It's a good thing." The older woman laughed.

Erin was the same age my mom would have been had my parents not died in a car crash when I was a toddler. They grew up together, and Erin would often tell me how I reminded her of my mother at my age. It used to make me sad, but ever since I moved away and started traveling, she never mentioned the similarities anymore.

I'm not sure what hurt more to think about.

"Everyone's talking about how you're going to put your special flair on Willa's most popular dishes. And last I heard, there's a bit of a poll going on to see what you're going to add to the menu."

I tucked the copy of the menu I'd scribbled my changes on under my laptop. No point telling her I didn't actually plan to *add* anything at all, but instead cut our offerings.

"I don't know if—"

"Don't worry." She interrupted me. "I didn't tell anyone you're going to be taking over the Whisk." She winked at me. "Not yet."

"Well, that's a good thing." I gathered up my things. "Because it's not so much a takeover, but more of a help out." I could hear the hollowness of my own words. "And I'm definitely not here to burn things down, just make a few tweaks and freshen things up."

She smirked. "Whatever you do, Harper, I'm sure it's going

to be great. This place is a Trickle Creek staple. The locals all have their usual tables and favorite orders. Change can be a tricky thing in a small town."

She wasn't wrong. I knew what I was up against. But if it meant facing the wrath of a few townspeople to make things more manageable for Grandma, I was prepared to do what it took.

At the door, Erin flipped the lock and turned the sign to *Open*.

Outside, the winter sky was already darkening, and the plaza started to light up with the lights of the nearby shops. I took a second to look out at the bookstore, Plot Twist, and the brewery that sat next to it, both new since the last time I'd been home. Most of the shop fronts were fully decorated.

"Do you want me to get someone to put up our decorations?" Erin came up beside me. "The light-up festival is coming up, and you know how Tilley can get if all the shops aren't ready. I know Grayson—"

"No," I said, a little too sharply. "I'll get it done tomorrow. It won't take me long to hang things."

"Okay," Erin said warily. "But Grayson is really helpful and I'm sure he—"

"It's good." I cut her off. "I've got it."

I turned away and took a breath.

Grandma was right. In a town this small, it wasn't a matter of *if* I ran into Grayson Lyons, but *when*.

It might be inevitable, but what I didn't need was anyone opening the door to that meeting before I was ready.

I left Erin out front and headed into the kitchen. The moment I stepped through the swinging door and inhaled the pot of sauce I'd set to simmer earlier, the tension in my neck loosened.

This was where I felt most at home.

Slicing, stirring, measuring, mixing, and creating—the

kitchen was my safe place, where I could forget about everything else.

I grabbed the old recipe box Grandma kept on the counter. I took a moment to run my hand over the smooth wood. The box held all her special recipes that had been handed down from her mother and grandmother over the years.

She knew all these recipes by heart, and I knew most of them, too. But whatever chef I hired was going to need to be brought up to speed.

I flipped through the cards to the lasagna she was famous for. Erin was right; the locals all had their favorites. But that didn't mean I couldn't tweak things a little bit.

I got to work, adding my own touches to Grandma's classic recipe, and soon I was lost in the flow of cooking: extra garlic, a pinch of fresh basil instead of dried, and a layer of roasted vegetables between the meat and cheese.

One thing at a time.

Tomorrow I'd get to the decorations, and…everything else.

For the moment, I just needed to cook.

Grayson

"YOU'RE WORKING TOO HARD, BROTHER." Ethan slid a beer across the bar top toward me. "Do you ever take a day off?"

"You know I don't." I lifted the pint glass to my lips and took a sip. I'd reluctantly agreed to one beer before heading back out into the cold. Mostly because my brothers weren't about to take no for an answer. "Not in this town."

"I don't know what happened." Reid took the seat next to me. "Somewhere along the way, you got labeled the nice, helpful twin while I slipped under the radar."

I almost choked on my drink. "That's because up until that

sweet wife of yours came along, you *were* the grumpy twin. And not exactly open to helping out with town activities." I raised an eyebrow, but Reid only laughed. "It's not too late to change that, you know?"

"Forget it." He laughed harder. "I like things the way they are."

I grumbled under my breath and shook my head. It was true, I'd become the town's go-to guy, but I didn't mind. Not usually. I liked to help out where I could. Besides, it wasn't as if I was filling my days with much else.

"You've got to be almost done." Ethan leaned up against the bar with a beer of his own. "You've been out there all day."

"I only have a few more poles," I told them. "It won't take too long to finish them up. That is, unless Tilley unearths some more decorations she forgot about. It's incredible that there's even space out there for the things she had in storage."

I shook my head and relaxed into the warmth of the brewery, my body slowly thawing. The air was thick with the smell of hops and the low hum of conversation. Ethan hadn't been open very long, but already Peaks & Brews had become a local favorite.

"So," Ethan said, breaking my moment of quiet. "Have you seen her yet?"

I didn't need to ask who he meant.

"Nope." I took a slow sip.

"Not even a glimpse?" Reid pressed, his tone a mix of curiosity and something heavier. "Because I remember the last time you two were in the same room together. Pretty sure you didn't sleep for a month after she left."

I shot him a look. "Thanks for the reminder."

He shrugged. "I'm just saying. It might be easier to get it over with."

"You've got to eat," Ethan added. "Maybe go grab some dinner before you—"

"Or not."

"Come on, Gray," Ethan pushed. "It's not like you're going to be able to avoid her forever."

"Is she here forever?" I challenged each of them in turn. "Do you know something I don't?" When neither of them spoke up, I set my glass down with more force than necessary. "Exactly," I said. "Unless she's here permanently, I don't *have* to do anything."

"It's going to happen," Reid said. "Better you do it on your terms instead of—"

"Not going to happen." I pushed up from the stool. "Besides, I've got work to do tonight. Real work."

"More lights to untangle?"

"No," I answered my smart-ass brother. "Ollie called earlier and asked me to prepare some extra financial reports for the store."

That got their attention.

"What's that all about?"

I shrugged. "No idea. He didn't say. You know, Ollie, he's always a little short on details."

"You think he's going to sell?" Ethan asked. "If he wants reports, I bet that's it."

I agreed with my brother. The kind of reports he wanted led me to believe that's exactly what he was getting ready to do.

"He should have retired years ago," Reid said.

He wasn't wrong. A few years back, when Ollie had broken his hip, I thought he might retire then. Instead, I got a promotion to manager, and he took a big step back. In fact, he continued to step further and further back, and it wasn't unusual to go entire weeks without seeing him in the store.

But he still took a lot of pride in it, and I knew how much of Ollie's identity was tied up in his hardware store. Because it was turning out to be the same for me. I'd worked there so long, it was hard for me to imagine doing anything else.

17

"Have you ever thought of buying it?"

Ethan's question caught me off guard. Of course, I'd thought about it. A lot. In fact, it's all I'd been thinking about since he'd asked for the reports.

But I'd never mentioned it to my brothers. After all, there was no point getting my hopes up about something that wasn't likely to ever happen. There was a big difference in thinking about buying a store and actually doing it.

If I told them what I was thinking, I knew they'd be supportive. But they'd also be overbearing about it. I wasn't ready to deal with that yet.

So I lied. "I hadn't really thought about it. I've been a little busy, in case you hadn't noticed."

Reid gave me a strange look. There was a good chance he knew I was full of shit. We never could lie to each other. Thankfully, he didn't call me on it. Instead, he shrugged and said, "So, you're going to hide behind spreadsheets instead of facing Harper?"

"Exactly." I slipped my parka back over my sweater and turned to leave, throwing a wave over my shoulder.

I'd learned long ago that there were things I could control, and things I couldn't. Harper Bennett and the way she still got to me landed squarely in the second category.

Chapter Three

Harper

I'd run out of time. Despite my plan to get the Christmas decorations up, I had an unexpected response to my help wanted ads, and ultimately, interviewing and hiring had taken priority over hanging lights and wreaths.

But I'd run out of excuses, and I knew if I didn't get them up promptly, I'd be hearing from Tilley Beckett about it. Or worse, Erin would go over my head and call Grayson herself to get the job done.

Neither was an option.

It was a bright, bluebird afternoon. The type of day where you had to wear sunglasses to protect your eyes from the blinding reflection of the sun off the snow, but could still see your breath.

I dragged two boxes out front and assessed the situation.

Grandma hadn't changed much of the decorations over the years, only bothering to freshen up a few things. But we still had the pine bough that would be draped along the window, with two oversized red bows on either side and the massive wreath that hung on the door.

Easy.

I pulled the massive pine bough from the box and noticed the upgrade of twinkling lights that would require an extension cord to be strung from one side of the storefront to the other.

Okay…slightly more complicated.

But nothing I couldn't handle.

First things first. I needed a ladder.

With my hands on my hips, I turned a slow circle and took in the plaza around me. It was busy in that pre-holiday way, with both tourists and locals milling about with their shopping and steaming cups of coffee from the Bean Bag.

For a moment, I thought I saw Grayson over by the gazebo, fiddling with a strand of lights. The tall frame, the dark hair, the way he moved…it had been a long time, but…

I didn't let myself look twice. The sooner I got the job done, the sooner I could get back inside to the kitchen.

Without a ladder, my next best option was a chair from the dining room. Inside, I grabbed the sturdiest one I could find, making a mental note to double-check all the chairs, and dragged it outside.

If I could survive for years working in a yacht kitchen on the rolling seas without any major calamities, there was no reason I couldn't string a garland over the window. Even if it did require a few questionable acrobatic moves.

With the garland in one hand, I climbed up on the chair, but it wasn't tall enough to reach the hook.

I sucked in a breath, stood on my tiptoes, and stretched as far over as I could.

It was only *just* out of reach. I just needed to stretch a little further.

My fingers brushed the hook, just as the chair wobbled, the leg catching on the uneven patio stones below. The next thing I knew, the ground tilted, the garland slipped from my hands, and—

A pair of strong arms caught me moments before I hit the ground.

Grayson.

I didn't need to open my eyes to know it was him. The second I allowed myself to breathe again, my senses were overwhelmed with the fresh scent of pine and peppermint that was both familiar and brand-new.

Then I opened my eyes, looked up, and my breath caught in my throat.

Clear, blue eyes. The color of glacier water. The very same eyes I saw in my dreams for so many years.

But everything else was different. He'd filled out since I'd last been that close. A thick, muscular chest with strong arms that held me steady, as if I weighed nothing at all.

"Harper," Grayson said, his voice low and steady.

Deeper than I remembered it.

And just like that, I was back in his arms. A place I no longer belonged.

Grayson

I TRIED NOT to look her way, but it was as if a magnet kept drawing my gaze away from the missing lightbulbs at the gazebo, directly to the shop front of Willa's Whisk. And Harper.

She was balanced on a chair, of all damned things, and it looked like she was on her tiptoes, trying to—shit!

I didn't think, just moved. My boots crunched on the snow-covered bricks as I sprinted across the plaza.

The chair wobbled.

Two more steps, and I was there right as the chair tipped.

She let out a startled sound as she landed safely in my arms.

"Harper."

She felt the same. Small, warm, and *familiar*. But she was different, too. Older. Stronger. And somehow, just *more*.

And still, every woman I'd held over the years—admittedly, not that many—had been measured against her without even realizing it. None of them had ever come close.

Without meaning to, I breathed in and filled my senses with the familiar scent of the girl I'd loved for so long.

Only she wasn't a girl anymore.

She wasn't the Harper I knew.

Instead of the peach-scented shampoo she'd favored in high school, Harper smelled of fresh basil and parsley and the undeniable scent…of tomato sauce.

I didn't let go right away. I couldn't.

Her eyes opened, finding mine. Wide at first, then narrowing a little, like she was searching for something in my face. "Grayson."

I nodded.

"You caught me."

I managed a smile. "Someone had to keep you from breaking your neck."

She huffed out a breath that might have been the start of a laugh. "I had it under control."

"Balancing on a chair on the snow and ice? Is that what we're calling under control?"

She pressed her lips together, and I eased her to her feet, reluctantly and slowly. When she was safely upright, I forced myself to take a step back. The space between us was instantly too much. The familiar ache in my chest that had taken over ten years to fade to a tolerable level flared back to life with an intensity that took my breath away.

"Thanks." She turned away from me to grab the garland. "I can handle it from here."

"You know I've done this for Willa every year, since— well…for a long time." I reached for the garland in her hand, but she pulled away. "I don't mind helping, Harper."

"I think I can handle a few lights and garland."

I lifted a brow, and she laughed.

"It'll only take a few minutes," I insisted. "Let me grab my ladder. We don't need any more close calls."

She hesitated, as if she were about to argue again, but finally sighed. "Fine. But only because I have so many things to get done, and a broken bone would really get in the way."

I grinned and jogged back to the gazebo, where I'd left my ladder and the half-fixed lighting. It could wait a few more minutes. By the time I got back, Harper was untangling the garland and muttering as if it had personally wronged her.

"I don't know what it is about holiday decorations, but they all seem to end up in tangles and knots." I locked the ladder in place. "Ask me how I know."

Harper chuckled, and the sound filled me with warmth. "You really do seem to be Mr. Christmas around here." She waved to the lights and decorations in the plaza.

"I wouldn't say it's Christmas exclusive." I grabbed the end of the pine garland and climbed the ladder. "Tilley Beckett seems to have my number on speed dial whenever there's something she needs done around town."

"You're just a helpful guy, then."

"I guess I am." I looked down at her before looping the first end over the hook I'd installed for that very purpose. "I volunteered for one thing about ten years ago, and…"

"It stuck."

I laughed. "It sure seems that way."

It only took me a few more minutes to stretch the garland out, letting it hang just so before hooking it to the opposite side of the window. I trailed the cord down the side of the door, tucking it neatly behind a piece of flashing, and plugged it in. "There you go," I said when the lights flickered to life. "The only thing left is the—"

"Wreath." Harper held it out in front of her. "I think I can handle this much."

"Are you sure?" I eyed her, but I saw the flash of a smile before she turned away.

"I'm sure." She rolled her eyes and stepped toward the door, where she dramatically lifted the wreath in the air.

Right before she placed it on the hook, I sucked in a sharp breath and pretended to gasp.

Harper spun to face me. "Gray!"

Hearing the abbreviated version of my name from her lips sent a shock wave through me. "Sorry," I mumbled and bit back a laugh as she finished hanging the wreath in its place. "Nice work," I said when she stepped back. "I didn't doubt you for a second."

She shot me a look and shook her head. "Thank you for your help," she said with a small smile. "I'm happy to have this off my list before the town decorating committee comes after me. I've been pretty busy since I got back and—"

A flash of movement from across the plaza caught our attention. We both turned at the same time to see Symon Scott and his wife Charli, both of whom we'd gone to school with, watching us. I knew what they were thinking. What, no doubt, anyone who knew us when we were younger was thinking.

"Looks like we have a bit of an audience," I murmured.

Harper blew out a breath. "I guess two people hanging up decorations is pretty exciting stuff around here." She met my eyes, and again, there was a surge of something from deep inside me.

It had been so long since I'd seen her. There were so many things I wanted to say. Things I'd dreamed about saying for a long time. Things that had kept me up at night, wishing I'd said them over a decade ago.

I opened my mouth, but, thankfully for my pride, before I had the opportunity to say anything, Harper clapped her hands together. "I should probably get back inside." She turned to walk away, and it took everything in me to keep from reaching for her and making her stay. "Thanks, Grayson," she said. "I appreciate it."

I lifted my hand in a pathetic wave, but she was already gone.

Harper

THE SECOND THE door clicked behind me, I pressed my back up against it, holding still until I was sure my knees wouldn't give out.

I closed my eyes and willed my heart to slow down.

It was hammering against my ribs, the sound loud in my ears.

It had been a long time since I'd been in Grayson Lyons's arms. It was a lifetime ago. It shouldn't feel that way anymore. It shouldn't affect me. It shouldn't make me *feel* at all.

Naively, I'd assumed that time and distance would have dulled the hold he had on me. I should be able to look at him and see a boy I used to know once upon a time.

I was wrong.

So. So. *So.* Wrong.

He was broader now. Stronger. The kind of strength I felt through every cell in my body when he caught me in his arms. There was a steadiness in his touch, and the way he looked at me…like he'd been waiting all these years for me to stumble on a chair, just so he could be there to catch me.

But there was no way.

Not after all these years.

That door was closed. That chapter of our book was long over.

I dared to open my eyes and let out a shaky breath.

He was just a man I used to know. A man who helped me hang decorations. A neighbor. An acquaintance. A friend.

I was back in Trickle Creek for one reason only. Grandma.

I needed to be there for her and her only. And leave again, without my return to town meaning anything more.

No problem.

But now, with my pulse racing and my body tingling where he'd held me, it felt like a lot more of a problem than I'd initially thought.

I blew out a breath and pushed up from the door, ready to head into the kitchen and lose myself in the dinner prep, when a sharp knock sounded behind me.

My heart lurched, and my pulse immediately picked up where it had just left off.

Grayson.

I turned and took a moment to smooth my hair and straighten my coat, schooling my face into a neutral mask before opening the door.

It wasn't Grayson.

The man on the other side of the door was short and unfamiliar. His hands were shoved into the pockets of a dark coat, a tentative smile on his face.

"Hi," he said. "I'm Kevin."

I stared at him blankly, my brain working overtime trying to reconcile that it wasn't Grayson on the other side. I peered over the man's shoulder, but Grayson and his ladder were already gone.

I turned my attention back to the man in front of me. "I'm sorry, I—"

"We spoke on the phone," he said. "About the head chef position?"

"Oh." It took me a moment to shake off the sting of disappointment and place the man in my memory. "Right. Kevin. I'm sorry, I was just…come on in."

I stepped back and waved the man into the dining room.

I needed to focus. The head chef position was important. *Really* important. How had I forgotten?

This was exactly what I'd promised myself wouldn't happen. The whole reason I'd stayed away from Trickle Creek for so long and flown Grandma all over the world to see me instead. I knew this would happen if I came back to my hometown. Sure enough, it had taken all of five minutes in his presence for me to forget myself and the most important interview I'd lined up all week.

I needed to get it together. Quickly.

Kevin stepped inside, glancing around the dining room with polite curiosity. I couldn't help but wonder what he thought about what he saw. Willa's Whisk was old. *Traditional.* It was a nice way of saying that there hadn't been any updates in over twenty years.

Looking at it through a stranger's eyes brought the moment quickly and sharply back into focus.

I exhaled, shrugged out of my coat, and forced a professional smile. "Why don't we sit over here?" I waved him to the table by the window.

Fortunately, if Kevin had any opinions on my stunned demeanor or the worn-down state of the restaurant, he didn't show it. Instead, he slipped off his coat and took the seat across from me.

I managed to pull myself together, grab a notebook and get through the interview, which turned out to be better than expected. Kevin was capable, experienced, and seemed to have a calm and steady demeanor, which was necessary in the kitchen. Even better, he was looking for a change and excited about the opportunity to move out of the city and into the mountains.

By the time we shook hands and I saw him out, I was once more fully focused on the task at hand and picturing him in Willa's Whisk.

The door had only just closed behind him when the kitchen door swung open and Grandma appeared, apron on, wiping her hands on a towel.

"You were in the kitchen?"

She stared at me incredulously. "Where else would I be?"

"Upstairs?" I shook my head. "Resting? You're not well, Grandma."

"We needed pies."

I shook my head. There was no point in arguing. "That interview went—"

"I saw you outside earlier." She cut me off, clearly not interested in the potential new chef. "It looked like you had a little help with the decorations after all." She glanced from the window and back to me with a faint smile.

Her tone was light, but the gleam in her eyes was anything but subtle.

"Grandma..."

She didn't say another word. She simply gave me a knowing little wink before disappearing back through the swinging door.

Chapter Four

Grayson

By the next morning, I'd gone over the entire ten-minute interaction with Harper at least a thousand times. Each time I replayed it in my mind, I found at least one new thing I should have done or said differently, until I might as well have rewritten the whole exchange.

Well, almost.

I wouldn't have changed the way I held her in my arms. The feel of her after so many years was the best kind of memory coming back to life. The way her eyes met mine, unguarded and full of surprise, just for a moment before softening into recognition.

I wouldn't have changed any of that.

It was what I didn't *say* that I wish I could've changed.

Like, "It's good to see you." Or "You look amazing." Or "I've missed you." Or…well, a million other things.

I'd replayed all the things I should have said to her. All the things I'd thought about a hundred times over the years. But when the moment arrived, not one of them made it past my lips.

I wanted a do-over.

That wasn't going to happen. Maybe instead of a do-over, I'd have to settle for inviting Harper for a drink.

No.

Definitely not a drink. That was too much. I didn't want her to get the wrong idea.

Or any idea.

Coffee.

Coffee was safe.

Simple. Innocent. Just two old friends catching up. There wasn't any reason we couldn't be friends after all this time. Besides, if I didn't do something, the alternative was to keep avoiding her like a coward.

I was restocking drill bits when Ben, my assistant manager, leaned around the end of the aisle with a clipboard. "We've got a problem. Carly just called. She's out sick today, and if we don't find someone to cover, we're going to be short-handed."

I took the clipboard from him and scanned the schedule. "Call Tyler. He wanted some extra hours. If he can't do it, I'll watch the front counter for a few hours."

"Don't you have inventory paperwork?" Ben shook his head.

"I'll do it after close if need be." It wouldn't be the first time.

Before he could argue, my phone buzzed.

I pulled it from my pocket and handed the clipboard back to Ben. "It's the boss. I've got to take this." I moved away from the box of drill bits. "Morning, Ollie."

"Grayson." The older man's voice boomed through the line the same way it had since I'd started working for him in high school. "I got those reports you sent over last night. The numbers look good."

"Glad to hear it. Business has been good and—"

"You've done a good job over there, son."

I beamed and straightened my shoulders. It's not that I needed the praise; I *knew* I'd done a good job with the store since taking over as manager. I'd brought in new products, offered more services, and streamlined ordering and staffing so that Ollie had been able to take bigger and bigger steps into his retirement.

At times, it was hard for me to remember that I didn't own the store outright already.

Hopefully, that would change soon. It wasn't something I'd been ready to talk to my brothers about. Not yet. I wanted to be sure I could do it. But after running the reports for Ollie, I'd run some numbers of my own. And to my surprise, they actually looked good. It was doable.

At least I hoped it was.

"Thank you, Ollie," I said. "I was hoping we could talk about the reports in a bit more detail, as well as the future of the store and where you—"

"Can't right now," he interrupted. "I'm just headed out of town. But I'll be back next week. We'll talk then."

"Right. It's just that I wanted to talk to you about—"

"Gotta run, Grayson." And just like that, the line went dead.

I stared at the phone for a moment before sliding it back into my pocket with a shake of my head. That had been my opening, and he'd shut it down before I could even get the words out. But I knew Ollie well enough to know that he wanted the best for the store. Once I got the chance to discuss my plan with him, he'd see it was the right thing.

He'd never asked me for the types of detailed reports I'd run the night before. And that could only mean one thing…he was getting ready to sell it. And after seeing the numbers in black and white for myself, I planned to be the buyer.

It was the first time I'd ever let myself believe it could happen. But it finally seemed like the right time.

"Hey, Grayson?" Ben's voice called from the front of the store. "You off the phone?"

The problems never ended. With a shake of my head, I headed to the front of the store, and when I saw who was waiting for me, immediately wished I hadn't.

"Morning, Tilley." I pasted a smile on my face.

She stood just inside the door, bundled as always in her red scarf and matching lipstick, her ever-present clipboard tucked under her arm.

"Well, if it isn't the busiest person in Trickle Creek." Her voice carried a mix of cheer and purpose that usually meant she was about to add something else to my already way too long to-do list.

"I don't know about that," I told her. "But I do have a few things on the go. What can I help you with today? All the lights are up and ready. The tree is wired and ready to flip the switch. Unless you ordered some last-minute—"

"Oh no." She cut me off. "It's nothing urgent. I was just passing by and I thought I'd pop in to say hi."

I narrowed my eyes and tilted my head, but I didn't have to wait long for the real reason Tilley had stopped by.

"I heard you were over at Willa's Whisk yesterday."

Ben tried and failed to swallow his chuckle from his position behind the desk.

I worked hard to keep my expression neutral. "Harper needed a hand with the decorations."

"I heard." Tilley's smile curved up in that knowing way that made me wish I were buried in inventory at the moment. "Well, I'm sure she appreciated the help. And I must say, Grayson, it's nice to see the two of you together again."

"We're not—"

"People like seeing familiar faces together again this time

of year," Tilley continued, as if I hadn't spoken at all. "It gives them hope."

Hope?

"Especially Willa," Tilley continued. "I'm sure it does her old heart good to see her granddaughter happy again."

My head spun. *Happy? Again?*

It had only been a ten-minute interaction. I was sure I wasn't responsible for any strong emotions of any kind in such a short time.

Before I could respond, she patted my arms like she'd just passed on a vital community update, turned and headed back out into the cold.

I waited a beat after she left before shaking my head and turning around. A smirk tugged at Ben's lips.

"Don't start." I held up a finger. "If you need me, I'll be finishing up with those drill bits." I turned to go. "Oh, and Ben? Don't need me."

Harper

"WE NEED TO TALK, HARPER."

Grandma's voice was calm, but there was a weight to it that stopped me. We were upstairs above the restaurant, in the little apartment I'd grown up in. It wasn't much more than two tiny bedrooms, a small kitchen, and an only slightly bigger living room.

When I was young, I longed for an actual house with a yard like my friends had, but coming home after all those years away, the cozy familiarity of our little apartment was perfect.

Grandma sat at the table, her hands crossed in front of her. She stared at me, unblinking, with the kind of look that had me spilling the truth on whatever I'd been trying to hide from her, more times than I could count.

"About what?" I tried for casual.

"About you." Her gaze softened when I shook my head. "Yes," she insisted. "We need to talk about you, Harper, and how good it is to see you back home in the kitchen again after all these years."

"You know I love cooking, Grandma. I got that from you."

She smiled. "I've been hearing good things about the changes you've made to the menu. The specials you're creating are getting people talking. In a good way. And that's not an easy thing to do in a town like this."

I laughed, and the warm glow of pride spread in my chest. "I'm just trying out a few of my favorites from years in the charter business."

"Well, they're going to turn into favorites here, too," Grandma said. "It makes me very happy to see you here. Happier than you probably realize." She reached for her glass of water, but set it back down without drinking. "You know... I'm not going to be around forever, Harper."

The words landed hard in my chest. Logically, I knew that was true. Grandma was getting older, and this latest health *thing* or whatever it was seemed serious. Even if she was too stubborn to tell me the slightest detail about what was going on. Still, I'd been doing a good job keeping my head in the sand about the reality of an aging grandparent.

I swallowed hard, but before I could respond, she added, "Word around town is that you and Grayson Lyons looked pretty cozy yesterday in the plaza."

I narrowed my eyes. "Word around town? Or just what you *think* you saw, Grandma?"

"Oh, I know what I saw." She wiggled her eyebrows and lifted the glass to her mouth.

"And what exactly did you see?"

She took her time before placing the glass in front of her

once more. "I saw the two of you fitting together just as you always have. Just like no time had passed at all."

I opened my mouth, but she cut me off before I could explain what had actually happened.

"You know, I think he probably likes having you around, too."

My pulse sped up. I thought about the text message I'd received earlier.

It was great to see you. How about a coffee to catch up?

I DIDN'T EVEN KNOW Grayson still had my number. Of course, he was still saved in my phone…

"He…asked me out for a coffee tomorrow."

Her smile widened, and it felt like the sun coming out after a month of grey days.

"A date?"

I hesitated, the smart answer, the *real* answer, on the tip of my tongue—that it was just coffee. Two old friends catching up on time gone by, and that it didn't mean anything. Instead, seeing the hope on her face, the joy that the mere idea of me being back together with Grayson had brought her so easily, something entirely different tumbled out. "Yes," I lied. "In fact, we're going to see where things stand between us."

The words hung there, surprising me as much as they seemed to delight her.

Grandma's eyes lit up in a way I hadn't seen in years. Bright and full of hope. "Oh, Harper. I knew it."

"You knew it?"

She nodded. "I always knew things weren't finished

between the two of you. A love like the one you two shared… well, it doesn't just fade away to nothing."

My breath caught in my chest.

She leaned forward, her fingers curling around mine. "This makes me so happy, sweetheart. You have no idea."

I tried to smile, ignoring the prick of guilt beneath my ribs. "I don't want to get ahead of myself. It's just…"

But she wasn't letting me hedge. "The two of you…" She blew out a breath and nodded. "Sometimes these things take time to come back around, but I'm so happy it's finally happening." She squeezed my hand a little. "Because the one thing I know for sure is that time is precious. We don't have as much of it as we think, Harper."

There was more behind her words. My heart squeezed so tight my chest ached.

"Grandma, I…"

"All I've ever wanted is to see you happy, Harper," she said softly, her eyes shiny with unshed tears. "To be loved by someone who sees you for everything you are. I can rest easy knowing that it might finally be happening for you."

"Grandma," I tried again, but the words I needed to say caught in my throat. "I—"

She gave my hand one more squeeze and let go. "No need to say anything. That's all I need."

Later, alone in the restaurant kitchen, I tried to lose myself in the mixing and measuring of the quiche that would be the dinner special, but I couldn't focus. My mind kept replaying the whole conversation.

The big, bold lie I'd just told the most important person in my life.

But I knew why I'd done it. There wasn't anything I wouldn't do for the woman who'd given up her entire life to raise me. She'd loved me and supported every single decision

I'd ever made. She'd given me the space and encouragement I'd needed to truly follow my dreams.

The least I could do was make her dream come true, too.

Especially if she didn't have long.

She'd yet to tell me the details, but I could see it in the way she moved. The little things she said, and the things she didn't.

Would this be her last Christmas?

I couldn't bear the thought.

Yes. I'd do anything for her.

Even if it meant letting her believe something I wasn't sure could ever be true.

Chapter Five

Harper

I'd been awake almost all night, running through exactly what I was going to say to Grayson. I decided early on that I couldn't go back on the lie. Not if it meant disappointing Grandma. No way.

Which meant I needed Grayson to go along with my little fib.

Somewhere around three in the morning, I settled on a flawless plan. I'd be logical, calm, and persuasive enough that Gray wouldn't be able to say no.

He loved Grandma, too. Proved by the fact that he'd been helping out with free delivery, decorating the restaurant for Christmas, and countless other things over the years.

There was no way he could say no.

My plan was perfect.

In reality, my stomach was in knots from the moment I woke up. We'd agreed to meet at the Bean Bag for coffee at ten.

I got there early and waited in the cold outside, hoping to

spot him before he went in. I saw him before he saw me. Broad shoulders filled out his black parka; a knit toque covered his dark hair. He looked completely at ease. Like a man who had no idea he was about to be ambushed by his ex-girlfriend with an insane request. "Grayson!" I called before I could chicken out.

He turned, that familiar slow smile curling up his lips when he saw me. "Hey. I thought we were meeting—"

"I know." I cut him off. "I was hoping to catch you before you went in." My heart thumped hard enough that I almost forgot to walk. "There's something I wanted to talk to you about in…well…in private."

His smile dipped. "Is everything okay?"

I nodded, not trusting myself to speak.

"Okay." He took my arm and led me away from the coffee shop to the relative privacy of the gazebo.

People milled about the plaza, and most certainly there were eyes on us, but at least no one was close enough to hear us. Still, I glanced around one more time, double-checking that there was no one within hearing range.

"Harper? You're starting to worry me. Are you sure everything is okay?"

"Yes. No." I shook my head. "Kind of." I took a breath. Tried and failed to remember my carefully prepared speech. The words were on the tip of my tongue.

But when I opened my mouth, I said, "I need you to pretend to date me."

Grayson's eyebrows shot up. "You need me to…what?" He shook his head as if there were no way he could have heard me properly.

"Okay." I held up a hand as if to ward off his protest before he could say it out loud. Heat flooded my face. "Hear me out. Last night, I was talking to Grandma, and she mentioned how happy she was to see us together again."

"But we were—"

"I know." I nodded. "You were only helping me, but…well, anyway," I continued as quickly as I could. "She said how good it felt to know that I wouldn't be alone and that I'd be okay when she—" I choked on the words. Grayson reached for my arm and squeezed through my thick coat. His touch steadied me enough to say what I needed to. "She was just so happy thinking that we were together, that before I knew what I was saying, I kind of told her that we were going on a date today and that we'd decided to try again."

"Try again?"

I nodded.

He was silent for a moment, trying to process what I'd just said.

"Try *what* again?" Grayson finally said. I opened my mouth, but before I could say the words, he answered his own question. "You mean, us? You told your grandma we were going to try *us* again?"

"Sort of." I shrugged and nodded at the same time. "Well…yes. I mean…I know I shouldn't have said anything at all. But she's old, Grayson, and you should have seen her face. I know how much she worries about me, and she was so happy when she thought that we were… Well, I just couldn't let her down. And you know her health isn't the greatest right now. She hasn't said much, and she certainly won't tell me the details, but if a little pretend relationship will give her something to smile about, especially at Christmas…I'd be grateful if you'd go along with it. I mean, I don't know how much you know, but she's not well right now, and who knows how long she—"

"Okay."

It took me a second to catch up with what he said. "Okay?"

Grayson nodded, a hint of a smile tugging at the corners of his lips. "Okay," he said again. "I'll do it."

"You'll pretend to date me?"

My head spun. There was no way it was that easy. We hadn't seen each other in fifteen years. Hadn't even *spoken* to each other. Not so much as a text message. And without any begging or convincing, he was just going to pretend to be my boyfriend. Just like that?

"Yes."

"But what's in it for you?"

The smile fell from his face, twisting instead into a tight frown. "You really have to ask me that?"

I did.

I swallowed hard against the lump in my throat. "I do. I mean, the way things ended between us and—"

"That was a long time ago, Harper." The smile was back on his face, but it didn't quite reach his eyes this time. "I hardly remember all of that."

A lie. It had to be. The air crackled with the weight of everything unsaid between us. And yet…here he was, agreeing without hesitation. My chest squeezed tight.

Grayson

HARPER'S EYES stayed locked on mine, searching like she thought I'd take it back.

Hell, that was exactly what I should do. I had no business pretending to be in love with Harper Bennett, especially when I couldn't be sure I'd ever stopped loving her in the first place.

She blinked slowly. It was my last chance to take it back. To stop this madness before it went too far. But that wasn't going to happen. I'd been waiting half my life to be this close to her again. If this were the only way, I'd take it.

Consequences be dammed.

"Okay," I said again, firmer this time. "We'll do this. For Willa."

"For Grandma." Harper nodded automatically. "But only until the holidays are over. I'm not going to make you... Well, you won't have to pretend forever."

"The holidays? What happens then?" I was pretty sure I already knew the answer, and I didn't want to hear it.

She tugged on her knit cap that covered her dark hair, pulling it lower over her forehead. "I'm leaving after New Year's," she said. "I'm only here to get things sorted out for Grandma and the restaurant and make sure...well, make sure her health is okay."

It felt as if she'd just punched me in the gut, which was ridiculous because up until a few days ago, I'd hardly even thought about Harper—*liar.* It shouldn't matter whether she was in town for one day or one year. The two of us and my feelings for her were ancient history—*liar!*

I worked hard to keep my face neutral. "Okay. Just for the holidays, then," I said. "After that, we'll sort out some kind of believable breakup and you'll go...wherever you're going to go and I'll..." I swallowed hard. "I guess I'll stay here."

Just like last time.

Relief washed over her features, softening the tight lines around her mouth. She nodded quickly and reached for my hand. "Thank you, Gray."

When she squeezed my hand, shock waves crashed through my body, and I knew, just like when we were kids, I'd do anything for her.

Anything.

"There's just one thing," I said. "If we're going to do this, it has to look real to everyone else."

Her brow furrowed. "Everyone else? Shouldn't it look real to everyone?"

"My brothers need to know the truth." I saw a flicker of

doubt in her eyes, but it was a nonnegotiable. "Reid tried to pull this with Avery," I told her.

"Tried?"

"I knew right away," I said. "And he will, too."

"Twin thing?" Her lips twitched up into a smile.

"Twin thing." I laughed. "Only it pissed me off, and it all nearly blew up in his face. I'm not doing that. They need to know the truth. But the rest of the town? They'll believe every second of it."

Something flickered in her eyes, and she blew out a breath.

"Okay, your brothers can know. But no one else."

I nodded.

"So." I blew out a breath and let myself smile fully. "I guess we start right now."

"Now?"

"No time like the present, right?" Before I could stop myself, I stepped toward her and brushed my lips against her cheek. I barely touched her, but it didn't matter; it was enough to send a shock through me.

Harper froze, then blinked and looked up at me with parted lips. "That felt…" She shook her head quickly, as if she were afraid to say what she was thinking.

And what I was feeling too.

"Like a good start," I finished for her. "Let's go out tonight?"

"Tonight?"

"Why not? I mean, if you're only here for the holidays, we should probably get started." I took a step back, forcing a little bit of space between us. I shoved my hands in my pockets to keep from reaching for her again.

"Like a date?"

"Exactly like a date. If we're going to sell this, we'll sell it right. Dinner at Creekside. Conversation. Maybe another kiss."

I knew I was pushing it, but what the hell? I had nothing to lose.

Harper's sharp inhale told me she hadn't thought about that aspect of the arrangement she'd proposed. Hell, neither had I until right at that moment. But it was out there now, and judging by the pink in her cheeks, she wasn't about to argue.

For the first time in a long time, I felt like I stood on the edge of something dangerous, but for the life of me, there was no way I could make myself step back.

Chapter Six

Grayson

Peaks & Brews was busier than I'd expected, although I hadn't been counting on Ethan's fiancée, Delaney, hosting her monthly book club in the brewery. Delaney owned the bookstore next door to my brother's brewery, and although their love story had started a bit rocky with the two of them clashing over the construction Ethan was doing, it didn't take long for the two of them to realize they were perfect for each other.

Along with Ethan's daughter, my super awesome niece, Quinn, they were now a very happy—and very cute—little family. A family that would be expanding in a few months.

Stories like theirs—and Reid and Avery's, too—should have given me hope that I, too, would one day meet the love of my life.

The problem was, I'd fallen for the love of my life when I was fourteen. And I'd pushed her away four years later.

"Hey, brother." Brody smacked my back and pulled me from my thoughts.

I craned my neck to see my eldest brother, gave him a nod and turned back to my untouched beer.

Along with Preston, Brody slid into the seats across from me moments before Ethan and Reid arrived. Ethan put a fresh jug of beer in the middle of the table along with a stack of glasses. "You guys need to test this new IPA. Just tapped the keg this afternoon."

"Don't mind if I do." Preston reached for the jug and poured out three glasses.

I shook my head. "I'm sure it's great," I said. "Just this one for me."

"Somewhere to be, Gray?" Reid lifted an eyebrow. My twin knew me too well. It was both a benefit and a drawback of having an identical twin. When I didn't answer him right away, he prodded, "What do you need to tell us?"

"What makes you think I need to tell you anything?"

Ethan almost choked on his beer, and Brody smacked the table between us. "Maybe the fact that you called all of us in here with only an hour's notice."

I looked to Reid, but he simply shrugged. "What's going on, brother?"

"Okay," I started. "This is kind of strange, and I'm going to need you to be really open-minded, okay?"

"Ohh, is this going to be what I think it is?"

I shot Preston a look. "Almost for sure, it is *not* what you think it is."

Brody smacked his shoulder, and he stifled his chuckle.

"It's about Harper."

That's all it took for my twin's jaw to lock tight. "What about her?"

I drew in a breath. "This needs to stay between us, okay?"

I waited until all four of them nodded in agreement before I blurted out the situation. It took a minute to explain what Harper and I had agreed on earlier in the day. Despite the fact that I'd had a few hours to think it through and let it percolate, it still seemed insane and like it could be a very bad idea.

No. It was definitely a very bad idea. For all kinds of reasons.

Judging by the way my brothers all stared at me with mixed expressions of incredulousness, they all thought so, too.

"Whoa." Ethan was the first to speak. "Wait, so you mean…"

I nodded.

"You agreed to it?" Brody asked. "Just like that?"

"Of course," I told him. "It's for Willa. And you know I'd do—"

"Anything for that girl," Reid finished for me.

It was then that I dared to look at him. Out of all my brothers, I was most worried about what Reid would say. All those years ago, they'd all been there when Harper left and took my heart with her, but it was Reid who'd picked up the pieces of what was left. He was the one who sat with me on those dark nights when I wasn't sure there was a reason to keep on living. He'd seen firsthand exactly how wrecked I'd been.

I held his gaze for a few minutes before nodding. "Yes," I said. "I'd do anything for her. That hasn't changed."

"So, wait…" Preston leaned forward. "This is just like what Reid and Avery did then?"

"No."

"Not at all."

Reid and I spoke at the same time.

Brody laughed. "And how is it different?"

"Avery was a stranger, and she needed my help to keep the inn."

I grunted and shook my head. "And this is temporary," I said. "Only for the holidays. Harper just wants Willa to have a merry Christmas while she…well, she wants to make her grandmother happy. Besides," I added, "I have no plans of ending up with Harper when this is over."

"Right," Ethan said slowly. "I'm pretty sure that Reid didn't have any plans on ending up with Avery either."

"The real difference here is that you and Harper have already been down this road." Reid's jaw twitched; I could tell he had a lot more to say. "And I remember what happened—"

"It won't happen again," I said sharply, giving him a warning look. "Listen, at the end of the day, I told you all as a courtesy because I don't want to lie to you." I didn't have to look at Reid to know he'd rolled his eyes. "This is happening, and for Willa's sake, I'm trusting you all to keep it a secret."

"I'm telling Delaney."

"Obviously," I said to Ethan. "And Avery, of course." I nodded to Reid.

"What about Lauren?" Brody asked.

"Are you dating Lauren?"

We all waited to see what he'd say. The two of them had been dancing around each other for years. But neither of them seemed to be able to get out of their own way.

"You know I'm not," he said. "In fact, she recently told me she's going to start seriously looking for a partner."

It was my turn to be surprised. But as much as I wanted to dig into that, there was no time. I lifted my beer and drained the glass before setting it on the table. "I want to hear more about that, but right now I've gotta go."

"You've got a hot date, do you?"

"As a matter of fact." I stood and shoved the chair back under the table, unable to keep the grin off my face. "I do." I waved at the guys, doing my best to avoid looking Reid in the eyes. But I didn't miss the way he muttered under his breath as I walked away.

Harper

CREEKSIDE WAS BEAUTIFUL. White tablecloths, candles flickering in low glass holders, soft music drifting from a hidden speaker. The nicest restaurant in town, it was the kind of place people went for anniversaries, special celebrations, Valentine's Day, and even proposals.

And it was awful. Not the food. The steak was delicious. Perfectly cooked. And Grayson looked unfairly good, sitting across the table from me in a dark button-up, with the sleeves rolled up on his forearms like some kind of cruel reminder of how strong he'd gotten in the years since I'd last seen him.

The problem with the date was…me. Well, us. From the moment he'd picked me up, things had been awkward and stiff between us, as if we didn't know how to act around each other.

To be fair, we didn't.

There was once a time when being with Grayson was the most natural thing in the world. In high school, he was my very best friend and the only person I could truly be myself with. I never had to hedge who I was or hold back. I'd never before—or since—known someone so intimately, and had them know me the same way.

But being with him all these years later, it was like we were strangers trying to pretend we weren't pretending, and I hated it.

By the time we stepped outside into the winter air, I was wound tight with the nervous energy buzzing between us. We walked side by side through the plaza. Lights hung from every possible surface, but they were still unlit. At least for a few more days.

"The tree lighting is Friday," Grayson said. "We'll go together?"

I nodded. "That would be nice."

"It'll be a good chance for the whole town to see us," he said quickly.

I felt a flash of disappointment in my chest, which was ridiculous. Of course, that's why he wanted me to go with him. It was to make it all look real. I should have thought of that. After all, this whole deception was my idea.

"Right," I said. "And Grandma will be there, too. She'll like seeing us and—"

A burst of laughter spilled from Peaks & Brews and grabbed my attention. "Did you tell your brothers?" I asked. "About …" I waved a hand between us. "This."

"I did."

"How are they?" I asked when he didn't elaborate. "Tell me about them."

Grayson chuckled. "What do you want to know?"

"Anything. Everything. What did they say when you told them about us?" The second I asked the question, I regretted it. Did I really want to know what the Lyons brothers thought about our deception?

Grayson raised a brow. "Do you want to ask them yourself?"

"What?" I pointed at the brewery. "Like, right now?"

He nodded. "I mean…we might as well. This date has been…"

"Pretty shit?" I finished for him.

Grayson burst out laughing. "Well, I don't know if I would have said it quite like that," he said, "but yeah. It's been a little stiff, don't you think?"

"Yes." A wave of relief washed through me that I wasn't the only one feeling the tension. "And not at all like us."

I regretted the words as soon as they came out. There was no *us* anymore. There hadn't been for a very long time.

Something flickered on his face, but I couldn't be sure in the dim light.

He took my hand in his and squeezed a little. "You're sure you're ready for this?"

"Why not?"

Grayson shook his head and ran his other hand over his face. "Let's do this, then."

Inside, the brewery was busier than I expected for a Wednesday night. "Book club meeting," Grayson said before I could ask. "Ethan's fiancée owns the bookshop next door and sometimes things spill over."

"That's my kind of book club." I laughed.

"I'll introduce you to Delaney." Grayson led me through the space. "You'll love her."

Grayson took me to the bar, where his brother Ethan was pulling pints of beer.

The moment he looked up and saw me, his face split into a smile. "Harper Bennett. Welcome back!"

He left the beer and moved quickly around the bar to give me a strong hug. "And welcome back to the family," he whispered into my ear. When he pulled away, he winked and I glanced at Grayson, who only shook his head.

"Harper!" I turned to see Brody, holding out his arms for a hug as well. "So great to see you again." He squeezed me tight.

I'd already seen him a few times when he came to pick up take-out from the restaurant.

There was once a time when these men felt like my own brothers. When we were kids, they'd all welcomed me into their family as one of their own. Those years felt like a very long time ago, but seeing them again brought all those feelings rushing back.

When Brody released me, Ethan grabbed my arm again. "Harper, I want you to meet my fiancée, Delaney."

I turned to see a beautiful woman, her dark hair up in a twist on the top of her head, standing next to Ethan.

"She owns Plot Twist next door."

I held out my hand, but the woman pulled me in for a hug. "It's so nice to meet you in person," she said. "I've heard so much about you."

"You have?"

"All good things." Delaney said. "And your food is amazing," she added. "Quinn can't stop talking about the lasagna. And she's a tough critic."

"Your daughter. Wow." I turned to Ethan, who nodded. "I still can't believe you have a daughter."

"She's an amazing kid," Delaney said with a genuine smile. "You'll love her."

"I'm sure I will." I shook my head as I tried to take it all in.

"A lot has changed." Grayson slipped his hand into mine.

I turned to look at him. "It has," I said softly.

"But some things are still the same, hey?" Brody slapped Grayson on the back and gestured obviously to our clasped hands. "It's good to see the two of you together again."

My face flushed as a few heads turned in our direction.

Grayson squeezed my hand, grounding me. "Right," he said. "And with that, we're going to go. We just wanted to pop in and say hello."

"I'm so glad you did." Delaney's smile was so welcoming and warm, I liked her at once. "We'll see you soon, Harper."

"Definitely."

With a few more goodbyes, Grayson ushered me back outside into the cold December air. "Well? That wasn't so hard, was it?"

"Your brothers always were so great," I said honestly. "It's nice to see them again. I can't wait to see little Preston and Reid, too, of course."

"Little Preston isn't so little anymore." Grayson laughed. "And Reid, well…he's married now."

"Married. Wow. Things really have changed."

And some things are still the same. I looked down at our hands.

We reached the door of the restaurant, and with his hand still in mine, Grayson spun me so we faced each other.

"Thank you for tonight," I said. "For going along with all of this."

"Don't thank me yet." His voice was low, almost rough.

Before I could ask what he meant, his free hand came up to cup my cheek. The simple touch stole the breath from my lungs. His thumb brushed beneath my eye. Featherlight and hesitant, like he wasn't sure he was allowed to touch me at all.

Then he leaned in.

I closed my eyes as his lips touched mine for the first time in over a decade.

The kiss was tentative at first, his lips just barely touching mine. But the second I let myself lean into him, everything shifted. Heat pulsed through me as his mouth pressed deeper to mine. Everything about the kiss leveled up.

My knees went weak. I clutched at his jacket to keep myself upright.

Fake.

It was all supposed to be fake. Just for show, for anyone who might be looking out the window or passing through the plaza.

But as his lips lingered, soft and sure, there was absolutely nothing fake about the way my entire body lit up from the inside out.

Chapter Seven

Grayson

The last few days had been insane. I was practically running on fumes after a rush of delivery orders at the hardware store, more part-time staff calling out sick, and, of course, all the minute issues that never failed to pop up when it came to town festivals. Especially because I was the guy everyone called when they needed something.

But through all the chaos, one thing kept playing on repeat in my head.

The kiss.

The way Harper's lips felt on mine—familiar, yet so different, after all the years that had passed between us.

The way that every single buried feeling I thought I'd left behind me had rushed back and slammed into my heart with that one single kiss had thrown me. Hard.

I'd never stopped thinking about Harper.

Not really. I'd just learned how to live with the ache instead.

Even when years had passed and my brothers forced me

on occasion to try dating, and I'd taken a woman out—or even back to my bed—the memory of Harper was always there.

I'd assumed it would fade in time.

It hadn't. Not really.

And now she was back.

The plaza was packed, glowing under the dozens of strands of lights that I'd personally strung. I had to admit, it looked good. It always did. The main reason I agreed years ago to help out with this particular festival was because I had a soft spot for Christmas lights.

And the girl whose eyes used to light up every time we walked hand in hand under them.

I spotted that girl—now a woman—through the crowd.

It took me a few minutes to make my way to her. I dodged excited children darting between the fire pits, with candy canes and mugs of hot chocolate in their hands.

I circled the smores station, and joined Harper on the other side of the fire pit, where she was standing with Charli and Symon Scott as if she hadn't been gone for over a decade. Something loosened in me seeing her there, part of everything again, talking with our old friends.

I walked toward her, swallowing down the feelings that had only been growing since the last time I'd seen her.

"There you are," Charli said as I reached them. She gave me a quick hug, and I kissed her on the cheek before saying hi to Symon and booping their little girl, Poppy, on the nose. "We were just talking about you."

"Were you?" I directed the question to Harper as I slipped my arm around her and pulled her close.

She offered up a little shrug, but it was Symon who spoke up.

"We were just saying how it's just like old times," he said. "The four of us hanging out."

"Only we weren't dating back then." Charli nudged him in the ribs, and he laughed.

"True. But sometimes the best things are worth waiting for, right, Gray?"

"You're not wrong, man."

But he was wrong about it being just like high school. Not when I'd never been more aware of Harper as a woman, instead of the girl I used to sneak under the bleachers with. And when we were eighteen, it felt like we had our whole lives ahead of us. Lives that included each other. And now…

I shook the negative feelings away and squeezed Harper a little closer to me, eager to take advantage of the situation as long as I could. "Are you guys enjoying the festival this year? The tree lighting will be—"

"There you are!" Tilley Beckett appeared out of nowhere, her red scarf trailing behind her and clipboard in hand. She zeroed in on Harper. "We're short-handed at the cookie decorating station, and I can't think of anyone better to take over."

"I'm not really a baker, Tilley."

"Why does that matter?" Tilley waved her mittened hand. "The cookies are already baked. You only need to manage a little icing and some sprinkles. Besides, who better to teach the kids some skills than our very own world class chef?"

Harper shot me a look over her shoulder as she was led away, her eyes a mix of amusement and panic.

I couldn't help it; I laughed. "I'll come find you for the tree lighting," I told her, even as the disappointment settled in my chest. Tilley Beckett always did have a way of interrupting at the most inopportune time.

Harper

THE COOKIE DECORATING station was total madness, in the best possible way. The table was covered in paper, with bowls of sprinkles scattered everywhere. Kids were squishing bags of icing all over the place. A few even managed to get some of the icing on the cookies.

Craig Carlson stood next to me, holding a cookie that was so overloaded with gumdrops that it was in danger of breaking in half. His daughter, Meri, grinned up at him as she dumped a handful of green sprinkles on top.

"I don't think it can handle much more, kiddo."

"Yes, it can, Daddy." She gave her father a look and poured more sprinkles on top, making me laugh.

"She's just like you," I told my old friend. Charli and I had been close in school, but her little brother Craig had always been around, too.

"Because she's so charming?" He laughed.

"Obviously." I grinned. "But I remember you at that age. You had such a sweet tooth."

"Still do," Craig said. "That's why I opened the Sugar Shack. Now I get to be surrounded by ice cream and candy all day long."

"That's right. Congratulations on that." Grandma had kept me updated with the happenings of Trickle Creek. "It's perfect for you. And congratulations on your marriage and new baby, too."

He beamed. "Thanks, Harper. It's been pretty incredible. Life in Trickle Creek is pretty amazing."

I nodded, but the smile on my face dipped a little.

I couldn't deny that all my old friends from school did seem to be living their best lives in the town I couldn't wait to escape. But I had dreams that were too big for Trickle Creek.

At least they used to be.

Before I could say anything more, a familiar voice floated through the air toward us.

"There's my girl."

I turned to see Grandma making her way through the crowd, bundled in her thick winter coat and a wool hat she'd knitted herself pulled low over her ears. She looked good. Rosy cheeks, bright eyes, and a wide smile.

"Grandma." I reached for her hand as she reached me. "I'm so glad you're feeling well enough to come out tonight."

"Are you kidding? I would never miss this. It's my favorite night of the year." She squeezed my fingers. "Isn't it beautiful, all lit up like this? You always loved this night when you were a girl."

"Hi, Willa." Craig leaned over and kissed Grandma on the cheek. "It's always nice to see you."

"And you," she said before leaning down to boop the pom-pom on the top of Meri's toque. "And you, too, of course, Meri."

Meri looked up with an icing-covered face, and we all laughed before Craig rushed her off to clean her up.

"Are you having fun, sweetheart?"

I nodded and answered honestly, "I really am. I forgot how these town events bring everyone together. It's lovely."

"Just one of the many benefits of small-town life," Grandma said.

Thankfully, she couldn't start into a dissertation on how much I'd enjoy living in Trickle Creek again, because we were once again interrupted.

"Excuse me," the young voice said. "Can I decorate a cookie?"

I turned to look into a set of blue eyes in a young girl who looked remarkably familiar. "Of course. Have we met yet?"

"I don't think so." The girl thrust her hand out. "My name's Quinn."

"Ethan's daughter." Of course. She had the Lyons eyes. I

saw the family resemblance immediately. "It's so nice to meet you. I'm Harper. I used to—"

"I know who you are," she said matter-of-factly. "You make the best lasagna."

"Thank you." I laughed. "It's nice to meet another Lyons. You know, I used to know your dad when we were kids."

"And my uncle, too? Right?" Her eyes glinted with mischief. There was no doubt this girl knew exactly who I was. But before I could answer, she continued. "Uncle Gray is the best," she said. "Did you know he—"

"Quinn."

The voice was low, steady, and unmistakable.

I turned and there he was.

Grayson.

Tall and broad-shouldered, his dark hair was dusted with snowflakes in the glow of the Christmas lights that made him look like he'd stepped straight out of a Hallmark movie. A shadow of whiskers framed his jaw, rougher than the clean-cut boy I used to know.

My breath caught. I still wasn't used to the new version of him. So familiar, and yet, so different.

"We were just talking about you, Uncle Gray." Quinn smirked, unbothered by his warning tone.

"I noticed." Grayson gave her a look that was equal parts fond and exasperated before turning to Grandma. "It's so nice to see you out and about, Willa." He gave her a quick kiss on the cheek. "How are you feeling?"

She swatted his concern away. "Even better now. The only thing I love more than the light-up festival is seeing my girl here so happy."

Without missing a beat, Grayson wrapped his arm around my waist and pulled me close. "I would have to agree with you on that one." He pressed his lips to my cheek as if it were the most natural thing in the world.

"Eww." Quinn threw up her arms. "It's bad enough Dad and Delaney are always kissing. Now, you, too?"

Everyone else laughed.

"It's almost time for the tree lighting," Grayson said to me. "I thought you might want to see it."

"You know I do." Automatically, I turned to Grandma, who waved me away.

"Go. I have a front row seat saved for me," she said. "Quinn, would you mind helping an old lady through the crowd?"

"Nope." The girl stuffed a cookie in her mouth and held out her arm for Grandma before the two of them disappeared into the crowd.

Grayson, his arm still around my waist, turned to face me. "Ready?"

I nodded.

"Come on." His hand slipped into mine, and he led me away from the cookie table. "I know a spot."

Grayson

I DIDN'T LET GO of her hand as I guided Harper through the crowd, weaving past kids with glow sticks and couples clutching cups of cider and hot chocolate. My pulse pounded harder than it should have, considering all I was doing was walking across the plaza.

But it had nothing to do with *what* I was doing and everything to do with *who* I was doing it with.

Harper Bennett.

I never could have imagined having this moment.

I led her to the edge of the plaza, away from the crowd gathered directly in front of the town's Christmas tree. There was a small retaining wall that I helped Harper jump on before climbing up next to her.

"Is this okay?" I took her hand again once I was next to her.

She glanced down at our hands, but didn't pull away. "This is a great spot," she said. "How did you—"

"Would you be surprised if I told you that I'd helped them build this wall a few years back?"

"No." She laughed. "That wouldn't surprise me at all."

The countdown began, voices rising all around us, and for a moment, I just let myself look at her. The lights from the plaza reflected in her eyes; the snow dusted her knit cap and her shoulders. She looked exactly like she belonged there in the moment with me. As if she'd never left.

As if the last fifteen years apart had never happened.

The numbers dropped.

Five… Four…

Instinct kicked in. I slid my arm around her and pulled her back against my chest, steadying her as she looked up.

"Grayson," she whispered.

Two… One…

The tree flared to life, lights cascading up the branches in a kaleidoscope of colors against the night sky. There was a surge of emotion at the sight of it.

All around us, the crowd cheered, but I barely heard them. All I could hear was Harper's exclamations as she took in the splendor of the tree.

"It's incredible." She twisted her head to look at me. "You did this?"

I nodded, unable to speak with her lips so close to mine.

"It's amazing, Gray."

"You're amazing." Her eyes narrowed in confusion, and I regretted the slip the moment it left my lips. This wasn't real. Just because my own feelings might not have ever completely disappeared didn't mean I needed to complicate the situation more than it already was. "I mean, it needs to look real, right?" I added.

She nodded, but I could see the uncertainty in her eyes.

My throat went tight. I did the only thing I could. I lifted my gloved hand to her cheek and spun her gently until she was up against me. I bent my head and pressed my lips to hers. It was just enough to send sparks racing through me.

The band started to play, and I pulled back to see couples moving into the empty space in front of the tree to dance.

Before I could think better of it, I stepped back slightly. "Dance with me."

"Here?" She looked down at the small platform we stood on. "Now?"

"Yes," I said. "It's what people would expect, right?"

She nodded.

"Besides, your grandma will be able to see us pretty clearly if she looks over."

Harper's brows lifted, and a hint of a smile tugged at her lips. "Okay."

She slipped her hand to my shoulder, letting me draw her into the rhythm of the song.

Her body fit against mine the way it always had. But different, too. Because we were different. Time had changed us.

Moving with her to the beat of the music took me right back to the last time I'd danced with her like this. Graduation night. It was supposed to be the best night of our young lives. Our futures were so bright, and we had the rest of our lives stretched out before us. It should have been a night for celebration and excitement.

Instead, it had been the night I'd blown it all up.

I tried to push the memories from my mind and focus on the moment. I inhaled deeply, breathing in the scent of her. I focused on the feel of her in my arms, the warmth of her cheek against my chest.

Still, the memories flooded back so vividly that it was almost painful.

Her pale-blue dress made her eyes look brighter than I'd ever seen them. Her dark hair was curled and piled into a fancy twist on top of her head, with just a few strands falling over her cheeks. We'd swayed together under the gym lights all night. I'd let myself believe that she was my future. It was perfect.

Until she told me that she'd been accepted to culinary school in Paris. The school that had been a long shot for acceptance. When she'd told me she was applying, she'd also told me they only accepted a handful of international students every year, and she didn't really expect to get in.

We'd planned to go to school in the city. Together.

I hadn't given any thought to the application or what her acceptance would mean. Until that moment.

"I won't go if you don't want me to, Gray." She'd looked up at me with so much love in her eyes, and that's when I knew.

Harper had always been destined for more than the small-town life I craved. Ever since we were little, she'd dreamed about traveling and seeing the world. About working in exotic locations, cooking delicious food inspired by all the places she visited.

I'd loved her since I could remember, and I knew she loved me too. More than anything.

Which was why I'd said what I did.

"You should go," I told her, stepping back and schooling my face into an expressionless mask.

Her face was lined in confusion. "You think I should—"

"Go," I said again. Releasing her, I tucked my hands in my

suit pockets to keep from reaching for her and changing my mind completely. "Why wouldn't you?"

I knew damn well why she wouldn't go.

"Grayson." Her voice shook. "You know why. I love you. I want to be with you."

I swallowed hard, my heart shattering as I looked at the love of my life in her eyes and lied to her. "Well, I don't love you," I said, the words sour on my tongue. "Not enough that you should stay."

The confusion and hurt in her eyes almost broke me. "Grayson. You don't mean—"

"I do."

I didn't.

"Don't stay for me, Harper. I don't feel the same." I forced a rough laugh out and then said the words I knew would clinch it. "This was never real, Harper. Did you think it was?"

I would never forget the pain on her face, and the way the tears streamed unchecked down her cheeks before she tugged her promise ring off her left hand. The same ring I'd given her almost a year earlier, when I declared my love for her and promised that one day I would replace it with the diamond she deserved.

"I never want to see you again, Grayson Lyons!" She threw the ring at me; it bounced off my chest, clattering to the wooden gym floor. My heart shattered into a million pieces as she pushed past me and ran from the dance.

It was the last time I'd seen her; she'd accepted the spot in culinary school and left a few days later without saying goodbye.

Why would she?

The memory still caused me physical pain. The familiar ache in my chest was present as I danced with Harper under the Christmas lights.

"This is nice." She looked up at me, completely unaware of the memory playing in my head.

Her eyes sparkled with the reflection of the lights, and for a second, I had to remind myself to breathe.

Nice wasn't the word I'd use.

Torture, maybe. A gift I didn't deserve? Definitely.

Dangerous, without a doubt.

I cleared my throat, forcing a smile. "Yeah. It is."

Her fingers flexed lightly in mine, like she was testing the space between us to see whether I'd pull her closer or let her go.

But I wasn't ready to let her go. Not yet. Not again.

The music carried us another few beats before someone in the crowd, no doubt one of my brothers, catcalled us.

Harper pulled away with a laugh.

I shook my head and scanned the crowd, my gaze landing on Preston with a dirty look he probably couldn't see from where he stood.

"That was fun, Gray. Thank you."

I nodded, but the words stuck in my throat. Because *thank you* wasn't what I wanted to say.

Not even close.

Chapter Eight

Grayson

The morning after the festival was mercifully quiet in the store. It was the kind of quiet I needed, especially considering everything going on in my brain was so loud. I couldn't stop replaying the night before. The lights, the tree…Harper.

Pretending to be her boyfriend was too easy because, in my heart, it still felt so right.

Which was why it was a terrible idea.

Not that I didn't know that when I agreed to it, but with every day that passed and every moment we spent together, I felt myself getting in deeper and deeper. It wasn't going to end well.

But what if it does?

As quickly as the thought popped into my mind, I shut off that little part of my brain. The part that would give me false hope that things could be different this time.

I was too old to let myself believe in fairy tales or happy endings.

It wasn't in the cards. At least not for me and Harper.

I lifted the board and carefully carried it to the stack I'd been making in the loading bay. Working in the warehouse was exactly what I needed. Just me, the scent of freshly cut lumber, and the steady rhythm of picking an order in silence.

Right on cue, the back door to the warehouse banged open. With a sigh, I straightened and brushed my hands off on my jeans.

"Morning."

I turned and smiled. "Hey, Reid. You're early."

"I didn't think you'd mind." He shrugged unapologetically. "Besides, I'm excited to get these boards into the shop and turn them into a dining room table."

"A table, huh?" I ran my hand down the board I'd just stacked. "I was wondering what your latest commission was."

My twin brother was a talented woodworker and had slowly pivoted from his handyman business to taking orders for custom pieces all across Western Canada in the last few months with his growing business.

"It's a big one, too. Supposed to seat ten to twelve people, with a river rock inlay and a live edge."

"Wow," I said, suitably impressed. "I can't wait to see it."

"Me too." He laughed.

Reid started to look through the pile of wood I'd already prepared, mentally cataloging his order, as I continued to move around the shop, gathering pieces.

"You need anything else?" I asked. "Just help yourself and add it to the order."

He took his time, moving around the warehouse, before returning to where I stood with the clipboard, double-checking a different order. Reid added a few pieces of walnut to his pile and leaned back against a stack of plywood.

When I looked up, his arms were crossed as he watched me. "So."

I shook my head and looked down at the clipboard again. "So…what?"

I knew exactly *what*, but I didn't plan to make it easy for him.

My brother wasn't the type to dance around an issue for long. "What are you doing with Harper?"

I still didn't look up but kept my pen moving across the paper. "I told you already."

"Right."

He dragged out the word in such a way that I finally gave in and looked at him.

"You have something you need to say?"

"You know I do."

I set the clipboard down and crossed my arms. "Might as well say it then."

"Do you know what you're doing, Gray?"

"It's not what you think it is." I exhaled through my nose. "This is just for a few weeks. For Willa. You know Harper would do anything for her grandma."

"And I know you'd do anything for Harper," he said, without missing a beat. "But what about you?"

"What about me?"

Reid clenched his jaw and shook his head. "Do I need to say it?"

"Apparently you do, brother."

He didn't. We both knew it.

"You're still in love with her." It wasn't a question. "She's leaving, Gray."

I nodded.

"Don't you remember what happened last time?" Reid continued. "Because I do."

How could I possibly forget? I shook my head and looked away. I didn't have the time or energy to have this conversation.

"I've never seen you like that before. Or since," he continued. "She broke your heart, Gray. I won't let it—"

"It wasn't her." I spun around, cutting him off. "She didn't break *my* heart, Reid. I did that all on my own."

"You and I both know that's bullshit." Reid took a step toward me.

I opened my mouth to protest, but what was the point in arguing with him? There was no one more protective of me than my twin brother, and I knew his heart was in the right place. I also knew he'd never understand how I felt about Harper back then. Or now.

They weren't feelings that could be shut off.

"I don't want you to get hurt again, Gray. I'm just trying to—"

"Drop it, Reid." I held up a hand. "Because it's not real this time. You know that. It's all for Willa." The lie hung heavy between us. "Like I said, it's just for the holiday," I muttered with a shake of my head and turned away before he could call me out on it.

"Right," he said easily, like he didn't believe a word of it.

I know he didn't.

"I mean it, Reid." My voice came out sharper than I meant it to. "Harper and I…it's not like that anymore."

I picked up the clipboard again and walked past him, but he turned to follow me.

"Because you don't want it to be? Or because you're scared it could be?"

Something in my chest twisted, but I wasn't about to give him the satisfaction. "I don't have time for this, Reid."

"But you have plenty of time to dance with Harper in the middle of the plaza?"

That did it. I slammed the clipboard down on the workbench, the sound echoing through the warehouse. "I told you to drop it."

My brother didn't flinch. "You're still in love with her."

"Get out."

"Gray, I'm—"

"Reid." I leveled him with a look that could have splintered wood. "I don't have time to deal with this right now. Ollie's coming in for a meeting any minute, and I need to be ready. Grab your order and go."

For once, he didn't argue. He studied me for a long second. I could see there was more he wanted to say. Finally, he shrugged. "Fine. Lie to me all you want, brother. It doesn't change the fact that you're lying to yourself."

With that, he scratched his signature on the paperwork, hoisted the boards onto his shoulder, and walked out the back.

Everything he'd said, and everything he hadn't, hung in the quiet after he left.

The worst part was…he hadn't been wrong.

Harper

THE SMELL of garlic and simmering tomato sauce filled the air, a sure sign that Kevin was settling into his new role. In the days since he'd started, I already felt a lot of the pressure ease off, and I know Grandma did too. In fact, I hadn't seen her in the kitchen since right after I'd arrived.

Which was a good thing. She needed the time to rest and recover from whatever it was that was ailing her. I'd reached out twice to her doctor, but he cited privacy concerns for the reason he couldn't tell me anything about her condition. Not that I'd really expected him to. But despite my persistence, Grandma insisted she didn't want to burden me with things I couldn't change.

I wouldn't push it for the time being. But if she didn't tell me what was going on soon, I was going to have to press the issue.

With a sigh, I looked back at my laptop, where I'd been going through the numbers.

"I thought lunch services stopped a few years back?" I asked Erin, who sat at a nearby table, wrapping cutlery rolls.

"It did," she confirmed with a small shrug. "They were too hard to staff, and it took too much out of Willa to do a full day. She insisted on hanging on to the weekend breakfasts for a while, too."

"But…"

Erin shrugged. I could see that she was trying not to say too much. "It was a lot for her on her own with only a few part-timers."

I nodded, in full agreement as I looked around. "Hopefully that will turn around now." The place looked tired. Old and worn down.

I should have come back sooner. Maybe if I hadn't been so selfish and I'd come home earlier, I would have been able to help Grandma make changes before things got to such a point.

But I couldn't change the past.

The bones of Willa's Whisk were strong. "We'll fix it," I said, more to myself than to Erin. "It'll take some hard work, but we'll make it shine again." Satisfied, I smiled and looked at Erin. "Kevin's going to be good for this place."

"Oh, sweetie." Erin laughed. "It's you who's going to be good for this place."

I pressed my lips together and shook my head. "You know I'm not staying, Erin. This is—"

"Nonsense." She waved her hand, dismissing my protest. "A young woman isn't meant to travel forever, Harper. Especially when there's so much for you right here in Trickle Creek."

"I'm only here for the holidays and then—"

"You know how happy she is that you're home."

The weight of her words was heavy in my chest.

"Having you back in the kitchen has brought her so much joy, Harper. Not to mention seeing you with Grayson again after all this time. She hasn't stopped talking about it."

I stiffened. "Of course she hasn't."

"You know, Harper, all those years ago, when you went off to school and started traveling, Willa was always so proud of you. She'd talk about you to anyone who would listen." Erin laughed. "You know that, right?"

I nodded. Grandma had never been anything but supportive when it came to my career. Even though it took me farther and farther away from her.

"But as proud as she was of all of your accomplishments and where your career has taken you, I can see how much it means to have you home again."

I swallowed hard, feeling the heaviness of the lie I'd been telling her. "She knows I'm not here to stay, though…"

"I swear, she's already planning out the next few years," Erin continued, as if I hadn't spoken. "We all knew the two of you would find your way back together again someday."

"Right." I pressed my lips together and sucked air through my teeth. "Well, I guess we'll see where things go—"

The sound of my phone buzzing on the tabletop, thankfully, interrupted my next lie. I glanced at the screen, my stomach flipping when I saw the name.

Captain Howard.

"Excuse me, Erin. I have to…" I held up my phone as way of explanation.

Erin nodded and picked up her tray of cutlery before disappearing into the kitchen.

When she was gone, I swiped my phone open and read the text.

> Still looking for a chef for the upcoming charter
> season. We'd love to have you aboard, Harper.
> You come highly recommended. Six months in
> the Mediterranean, starting after New Year's.
> Let me know if you're interested.

MY THROAT TIGHTENED. It was the job I'd been waiting to hear about. Head chef on a seventy-five-meter boat for an entire season was a dream. I'd only done shorter charter seasons on smaller boats. If I took this job, it would be a huge boost to my career. And the Med…it was an amazing opportunity. It was exactly what I'd been working toward for years.

But somehow, reading Captain Howard's message, the excitement I'd expected wasn't there.

Instead, it was a crushing weight on my chest.

I couldn't breathe.

Because as much as I'd always thought this was what I wanted, for the first time, I wasn't so sure.

Not with Grandma depending on me.

Not with Grayson back in my orbit.

Grayson

I SAT across from my boss, Ollie Holbrook, in the cramped office in the back of the shop. It felt odd to be behind the desk, despite the fact that ever since the older man broke his hip a few years back, the office had become mine. First, unofficially, as I took over the day-to-day operations while he recovered, and then officially, when he gave me the promotion to manager.

Ollie hardly even bothered to come into the store anymore, trusting me to make the right decisions with the running of things. It was strange to see him perched on the folding chair across from what used to be his desk.

"I'm getting ready to retire, Grayson," he said, just like that, with no preamble.

Not that I expected anything different. I'd been waiting for this conversation.

I was ready.

"It's time for me to put this chapter behind me. It has been for a while, truth be told."

With a nod, I smiled. "You deserve it, Ollie. More time for fishing and enjoying those grandkids of yours. Sounds good to me," I said, despite the fact we both knew that's exactly what he'd been doing for the last few years while I kept things running.

"You mean even *more* time?" He laughed. "I do appreciate all your hard work all these years, Grayson," he said. "Especially the last few. Don't think I don't."

"I don't think that at all," I said truthfully. "So, what's the plan?"

"I'm going to sell."

My chest tightened, but I leaned forward, careful to keep my voice even. "I figured as much. You've never asked for that level of reporting before." He nodded, and I swallowed hard, sensing my opening. "Since you've decided to—"

"I have a few options, Grayson."

"Options?"

The word landed like a stone in my gut.

"Unwinding a business like this can be complicated," he continued, as if I hadn't spoken. "There are lots of things to consider."

"What kind of options are you talking about, Ollie? Because I was thinking—"

A crash from the store pulled my attention.

Ollie and I both turned toward the door, but before I could move, a sharp knock rattled the office door.

"Uh, Gray?" Ben's voice came muffled through the door. "Sorry to interrupt, but we have a bit of a situation out here."

I closed my eyes and counted to three before I forced a steady breath. "Can it wait?"

"Not unless you want five gallons of deck stain soaking into aisle five. Tommy dropped the cans when he tried to carry both at once."

Damn it. The kid had been told more than once not to try to carry too much in one go.

"Can you please handle it, Ben? I need to—"

Before I could finish, another voice cut through, sharper and louder. "Does anyone work here? I've been waiting ten minutes to get some help with sandpaper. What kind of place is this?"

Perfect. A spill *and* an angry customer. Just what I needed in the middle of the most important conversation of my life. I pinched the bridge of my nose and sucked in a breath.

When I turned back to Ollie, he was watching me with the quiet, unreadable expression he'd perfected over the years. I could never tell whether he was testing me or whether he was simply amused.

"You'd better go handle that," he said.

"Sorry, Ollie." I pushed back from my desk. "I really do want to discuss this with you. I have some thoughts about—"

"We'll talk," he said with a vague wave of his hand. "Take care of what you need to take care of." He gathered up the reports I'd printed out for him. "I have a lot to deal with myself."

And just like that, the conversation was over.

I strode out of the office, already bracing myself for the chaos waiting for me. But frustration burned a hole in my chest. Every time I got my foot in the door, something or someone yanked it away.

This store mattered to me. Maybe more than it should.

But it mattered.

And all I could think of was the *options* Ollie had mentioned and how they might be able to take it all away from me before I even had a chance at it.

Chapter Nine

Harper

I was running late.

It was Kevin's first full dinner service by himself. He was an experienced chef, and our menu wasn't complicated. There was no reason that everything wouldn't be absolutely fine. Logically, I knew that.

Still.

I found a million reasons to drag my feet and delay leaving until finally Erin pushed my parka at me and more or less shoved me out the front door.

By the time I got to the open field just behind the plaza, half the town was already there for the annual snowman build-off.

Rows of half-built snowmen dotted the area. Some were little more than lumpy mounds, while others loomed to be almost done, wearing scarves, hats, and, in one case, a princess dress.

Kids darted around, shrieking with laughter as their parents tried in vain to wrangle them back into focus.

Grayson was already there, standing next to a mound of snow. In his dark jacket and matching knit toque, he looked like he belonged there more than anyone else. My heart did a weird little stutter at the sight of him, but I didn't have a chance to think about it before I heard my name being called.

I turned to see Quinn waving at me. "You made it!" She stood with Delaney and Ethan, and a very tall snowman.

"Hey." I waved back. "Looking good, you guys."

"Tell Dad our snowman should be holding a book and *not* a beer." She rolled her eyes dramatically.

I laughed. "I think I'll stay out of this one." I turned back toward Grayson.

His eyes found mine, and again, there was that same little hitch in my chest.

"Hey there." He closed the distance between us and put his hand on my waist, drawing me in.

By reflex, I hesitated until he whispered, "Everyone's watching."

Of course.

I forced a smile as he pulled me in for a chaste kiss on the lips.

It may have been no more than a peck, but I felt it through every cell in my body.

"Are you ready to show off your snowman building skills?" Grayson stepped back and pulled his gloves out of his pocket. "That is, if you still have any." He wiggled his eyebrows.

I smacked him lightly on the arm. "Don't sound so doubtful. I happen to be excellent at snow sculpture arts."

He laughed. "Is that right? You mean, all these years in tropical locations, you still managed to find time to keep your skills sharp?"

He had me there.

"Okay, so I actually haven't spent any time in the snow since I—well, for a while."

We both knew when that last time was. We'd stood in this very same field, working together on our snowman.

I swallowed hard and shook my head to clear it before crouching and scooping up some snow. "We should get started."

Grayson hesitated, but only for a second, before he squatted next to me and joined me in packing snow into a ball. "I can't wait to see how this turns out."

Me too.

We worked side by side, rolling the base until it was too heavy to budge. The middle snowball seemed to be just as large, and Grayson insisted on lifting it into place while I pretended not to notice how easily his arms handled the weight.

"Teamwork." He brushed the snow from his gloves.

"More like you doing all the heavy lifting while I supervise."

"Just like the old days." His eyes glinted. "Pretty sure you've always been bossy."

"Pretty sure you've always liked it." The words slipped out before I could stop them, but the grin that spread across his face made the heat rise to my cheeks faster than the cold could chase it away.

By the time we'd stacked the head ball onto the top and started fussing with some of the accessories Grayson had brought with him, Quinn had already declared it a suitable effort.

"It actually looks like a snowman," she said. "Some of these just look like piles of laundry. And ours…" She pointed to where her dad and Delaney were putting the finishing touches on their snowman. "Can't decide between books and brews." She threw up her hands in defeat. "I give up."

"Looks pretty perfect for your family," Grayson said. "You guys definitely have a theme."

"What's your theme?" Quinn asked.

I looked at Grayson. "Do we have a theme?"

"Sure do." His lips quirked up in a grin as he reached into his bag and pulled out an apron and a whisk.

I couldn't keep the smile off my face. "But what about you? It should represent you, too."

He shook his head. "Not this year. This one is about you."

Not this year.

Would there be other years?

Not if I took the job.

The thought sent a flash of sadness through me, but before I could let it sink in, a wet snowball landed between my shoulders.

I spun around to see Ethan with his mittened hand over his mouth. "Sorry, Harper. That was meant for—"

A snowball flew past me and landed square in Ethan's chest. Behind me, Grayson howled with laughter. "It's on now, brother!"

"What the—"

"Duck!" Grayson grabbed my hand and tugged me to take cover behind our snowman, just as another snowball flew past.

I laughed, crouched beside him as we both packed snow as fast as we could.

"On three," he said, grinning like a kid. "One. Two. Three!"

We popped up together and fired our weapons, pelting Ethan and Delaney in rapid fire until they threw up their hands in surrender.

Grayson whooped in triumph. "Victory!"

And then, while he was still celebrating, I nailed him in the chest with my last snowball.

He froze, brushing snow from his jacket as his mouth dropped open. "You didn't just do that."

I widened my eyes innocently and shrugged. "Oops."

"Oh, you're in trouble now." He lunged, and I squealed, dodging him as I darted behind our snowman. He caught me anyway, grabbing my wrist and shaking the snow loose from my palm.

We were both laughing and out of breath. He held me close, and for a second, the entire world stilled. He reached up to brush snow off my cheek with his gloved hand, his fingers lingering.

"Truce?" he asked, his eyes holding mine.

"Truce," I whispered back, my heart racing.

But neither of us let go right away.

"Now that," Grandma's voice called from a safe distance, "is a snowman worth fighting for."

I startled, turning to see her bundled in her heavy wool coat. Her cheeks and nose were pink from the cold, her eyes shining. She leaned on her cane, but looked perkier than I'd seen her in days.

Grayson chuckled, stepping back just enough to wave at her, but his other hand gripped mine firmly. "Willa. Are you enjoying yourself?"

"Very much." Her smile only widened as she looked between us. "Oh, Harper. You look happy. Happier than I've seen you in a long time."

My throat tightened as guilt pressed against my ribs. She was glowing with joy, seeing something real where there wasn't supposed to be anything at all.

I hated lying to her.

But seeing her smile, so alive in this moment, made it all worth it. This Christmas might be the last one we had like this, and if pretending with Grayson made it special, I'd play along as long as I needed to.

I swallowed hard and turned away.

It was only for Christmas. That was the plan. That had to be the plan.

. . .

Grayson

"ARE YOU SURE THIS IS OKAY?"

It was the third time Harper asked me, and the third time I'd said, "Better than okay. We need to eat."

She smiled softly. It did something to me. Something I had no business feeling, so I swallowed hard and held the door to Willa's Whisk as she walked through it.

It was the first night Harper left her new chef in charge, and I knew it had weighed on her, so going to the restaurant for dinner seemed like the perfect solution. Especially because I wasn't done spending time with Harper.

It might be just for show, but that didn't mean I wasn't fully prepared to maximize every moment.

Willa's Whisk had slowed down over the years, but tonight it felt alive again. About half the tables were filled with guests laughing and eating. The scent of garlic and rosemary drifted from the kitchen, and my mouth watered as I followed Harper inside.

I took a moment to stand and watch as she moved easily through the space, chatting with Erin at the hostess stand, and stopping to say hello to diners with a smile on her face, before slipping into the kitchen to check on her new chef.

She looked like she belonged there. Like she'd never left.

"I know what you're thinking, brother."

I was startled out of my thoughts when Brody slapped me on the back.

"And what's that?" I shook my head to clear my mind, trying and failing to appear casual.

"That she belongs here."

Damn.

"I wasn't thinking that."

"Bullshit."

Annoyed, I turned to glare at him. "What are you even doing here?"

My eldest brother grinned, either unaware that he'd gotten to me, or more likely, completely aware and loving it. "Dinner, obviously," he said. "I ran into Ethan, and he mentioned you'd invited everyone for dinner."

I rolled my eyes. "I mentioned it to them after we kicked their ass in a snowball fight. But they declined in favor of a family movie night."

"Lucky for you I ran into them then. Reid and Avery are joining, too."

"It wasn't an open invite."

He smacked me on the back, laughing. "You should know by now that's not how this family works."

I shook my head because he was right and followed him to a corner booth big enough for all of us. "Where's Lauren tonight?"

Brody's face shifted; something a little too close to jealousy flashed over his features when he said, "She's on a date."

He shrugged casually, but I didn't miss the tension in his jaw. It was completely beyond me, and pretty much everyone else, why the two of them couldn't see what was in front of them and stop trying to pretend they were *just friends*.

But there was no point saying anything. Besides, Reid and Avery chose that moment to join us. Followed by Willa, who emerged from the kitchen with a broad smile. "Is it okay if I join you all?"

"I insist on it." I stood and offered her the chair at the end of the table.

"This feels just like old times," she said after getting settled. "It's nice."

"I can't speak to that," Avery said. "But I agree, it's nice."

A few minutes later, Harper arrived with a basket of warm

bread and slid into the booth next to me. I resisted the urge to slip my hand onto her thigh.

Conversation flowed easily. Reid told a story about a new client who'd commissioned an extravagant king-sized bed, and had unrealistic expectations about how long it would take. Brody added a jab about Reid's *customer service voice*, which had Avery laughing so hard she nearly snorted into her water.

Willa shook her head fondly, like she'd seen this scene play out a hundred times before.

I leaned back and let myself soak it all in. The clinking of cutlery. Harper's warm laugh beside me. My brothers, laughing and joking. It felt easy. Like this was exactly the way things were supposed to be. Like *I* was exactly where I was supposed to be.

"This is nice." Willa's eyes shone as she looked around the table. "Having Harper back, the two of you together…" Her eyes locked on me; the warmth reflected at me tugged at my heart. "Seeing you all here," she continued. "It really feels like Christmas."

"Speaking of." Reid tore into another piece of bread. "Make sure you come by the inn and check out the tree Avery set up in the main room. It's stunning. Like something out of a catalogue."

Avery rolled her eyes, but I could see the pride in her expression. She put so much of herself into the inn. "Only because you helped with the lights, Reid. I don't think I could have strung that many strands by myself. Even if you did almost knock the tree over more than once."

The table erupted in laughter, but Willa shook her head. "I'd love to see it. I haven't had my own tree in years."

"What?" My fork froze halfway to my mouth. "No tree?"

Willa waved her hand like it was nothing. "It's a lot to handle by myself, and this year, Harper's been so busy with everything…it seems a bit extravagant."

"It's not extravagant to have a Christmas tree, Willa." I shook my head and looked at Harper.

"I thought about it, but things just got—"

I set my fork down and wiped my hands on my napkin, the words coming out sharper than I intended. "That's not okay. It's Christmas. You must have a tree."

The table went quiet for a beat. Harper gave me a look, but Willa smiled softly, like my reaction had pleased her beyond measure.

"He's right," Avery chimed in. "You need a tree, Harper."

I leaned back and crossed my arms over my chest. "It's not up for negotiation," I said. "You're getting a tree."

Even if I had to drag it into the restaurant myself.

Chapter Ten

Harper

"Do we really need to go all the way out here?" I looked across the cab of the truck at Grayson, before turning my attention back to the snow-covered forestry road he'd driven us down. The windshield wipers swished back and forth in a steady rhythm that kept time with my nerves. "This road doesn't look safe, Gray."

Beside me, Grayson's mouth curved into a stubborn smile I remembered all too well. "Don't tell me you're scared of a back road, Harper? You've been gone too long."

I opened my mouth to protest, but closed it again. "I don't remember ever loving the back roads."

"Oh no?" His eyebrow quirked up, and he shot a glance in my direction. "I remember you enjoying more than one of our back road adventures very much."

Heat flamed my cheeks. Okay, he wasn't wrong.

As teenagers, more than once, Grayson had taken me to an out-of-the-way riverbank, or a quiet meadow where we would lie out under the stars and...

"Aren't there tree lots in town?" I refused to meet his eyes as I changed the subject. "In fact, doesn't your hardware store sell trees?"

"Sure," he scoffed. "If you like overpriced, half-dead pines with no meaning."

"You are talking about your own products." I laughed. "You know that, right?"

"One, it's not *my* store." He shot me a glance. "And two, it doesn't matter. They're not good enough," he said. "Your grandma hasn't had a Christmas tree in years and you… well…" He swallowed hard. "Your tree should be perfect. And I know the best spot."

"Perfect," I echoed under my breath.

Moments later, he pulled the truck off the rough road, into a snow-covered clearing. "This is the spot."

The world outside was quiet, blanketed in fresh white powder that glittered in the winter sun. It looked like something out of a postcard. It was gorgeous.

We climbed out, and I tugged my knit toque down low over my ears. Grayson grabbed a saw from the back, and we started our trek through the deep snow.

"What about this one?" I asked after a few minutes of trudging.

"Absolutely not." Grayson shook his head. "Look at the bare spot."

I tilted my head, but couldn't see the spot he referred to. With a shake of my head, I carried on after him to the next stand of trees.

"This one?"

"Harper. You're kidding, right?"

I wasn't. The tree looked pretty good to me.

"Willa deserves better than a Charlie Brown tree." He reached for my mittened hand and pulled me forward. "Let's keep looking."

I let him keep hold of my hand as we moved through the trees. We argued good-naturedly, pointing out trees and dismissing them for a variety of reasons that I couldn't make sense of.

Too bare.

Too crooked.

Too lopsided.

"This one's cute."

"Not cute enough."

"You're picky."

"I'm looking for perfect, remember?"

My breath hitched. "I remember."

Were we still talking about Christmas trees? Somehow, I didn't think so. It both scared and thrilled me.

I took a step back, my foot catching on a root buried under the snow. I lost my balance, yanked my hand free from his and, with a dramatic whirl of arms and legs, fell backward into the snowdrift.

"Harper!"

I reached for my face, using my mittened hands to brush the wet snow out of my eyes to see Grayson standing over me, concern on his face.

"Are you okay?"

I nodded as he extended his hand to help me up.

I should have thanked him and laughed it off. But I reached for his hand and, instead of letting him pull me up, I tugged. Hard. And pulled him down into the snow with me.

He landed half beside me, half over me, our laughter tangling together in white puffs of breath in the cold air that hung between us. But just as suddenly as it had happened, the laughter faded, because there was nothing funny about how close we were and how warm his body felt against the sharp contrast of the snow.

His eyes searched mine, and I stopped breathing altogether.

When his lips brushed mine, it was tentative at first, as if he were testing me—us. But then his hand slid behind my head, and I leaned into him, and it was nothing like the staged kisses we'd shared in recent days. This was different.

Raw. Aching and everything I'd forgotten I wanted.

By the time we pulled apart, my pulse was racing.

He smiled and brushed snow from my cheek. "Come on. Let's go get you that tree."

I let him help me up this time, not trusting my knees to hold me.

When we finally picked the right one, full and even, with branches strong enough to hold all the heavy ornaments, Grayson handed me the saw.

"You should do the honors."

"You're sure?" I raised a brow.

"Of course." His grin was crooked and endearing. "After all, it's yours."

I smiled and crouched beside him, our shoulders brushing as I sawed through the trunk, and he held the tree steady until finally, it toppled into the snow with a soft thud.

"Timber!" Grayson cried out, and we both laughed like kids.

By the time we wrestled it into the truck bed and climbed back into the cab, my hair was damp with melted snow, and my cheeks ached from smiling.

The heater blasted warm air, and the silence stretched between us. Not uncomfortable. But charged with everything we hadn't said...and the kiss we'd shared replaying in my head.

I reached for the radio and turned to a station playing Christmas carols.

Grayson glanced over at me and laughed when I started singing along to a country version of "Jingle Bells."

My hand rested on my thigh, fingers twitching.

Before I could stop myself, I let it slide across the seat until it brushed his.

His hand turned, palm up instantly, like he'd been waiting for me. I probably shouldn't have done it; after all, nothing good could come from blurring the line between real and pretend any more than we already had. Still, I laced my fingers through his.

The words of the song died on my lips, and I turned to stare out the window at the passing trees, my heart lodged somewhere in my throat.

I still hadn't answered Captain Howard's message. A charter season in the Mediterranean should've been an easy yes.

It was everything I'd been working for. To be the head chef on a boat that size was a dream come true. It would open so many doors for my career.

But sitting there, my hand in Grayson's, nothing about my decision felt easy anymore.

Grayson

MANEUVERING the tree up the narrow staircase to Willa and Harper's apartment was trickier than I'd expected, and more than once I considered that maybe in my quest for the perfect tree, I should have paid closer attention to the size of it compared to the hallway.

After some wrangling, I wrestled it through the doorframe and into their small living room.

"Careful with my walls, Grayson," Willa called from her chair by the window, a steaming mug of tea balanced in her hands.

"Yes, ma'am," I said, grinning as I finally got the thing

upright. I wasn't going to admit it, but we'd definitely chosen a larger tree than was probably practical for their small apartment.

But the way Willa's eyes lit up when she saw it in the stand told a different story.

Pine needles scattered across the floor, filling the air with the sharp, clean scent of Christmas.

"Oh, it's lovely," Willa whispered, clasping her hands to her chest. "Absolutely perfect."

"It's not too big?"

"Not at all, Grayson." Willa looked smaller than I wanted to admit, tucked into her chair with a blanket across her lap. Her eyes were bright as she took in the tree.

Harper held it steady as I crouched to tighten the screws in the stand until it stood straight. Well, as straight as we could manage.

Straightening, I wiped my hands on my jeans, my gaze snagging on the door down the short hall.

Harper's room.

The same door I'd slipped through more times than I could count when we were teenagers, quiet as I could manage on the squeaky old floorboards, my heart pounding in my chest, certain we'd get caught. I could almost hear a seventeen-year-old Harper's laughter, hushed and breathless as she tugged me inside.

I swallowed hard and looked away, but the memories chased me anyway.

"Everything okay?"

I cleared my throat hard and turned to see Harper watching me.

"Fine," I lied as the memory of our most recent kiss replayed in my mind.

That kiss had been different.

Grown up.

Real in a way that I didn't dare think about for too long.

She gazed at me a moment longer before turning back to the box of decorations she'd unearthed. I watched her carefully unwrap a set of glass balls one at a time, holding each one up for her grandma to see.

My phone buzzed in my pocket, dragging me back to the moment.

I pulled it out and read the text from Brody.

Family dinner tonight. Don't be late.

Wasn't that what we did last night at the restaurant? I stopped myself from sending the reply. I knew exactly what kind of response it would get. Our family was intense about our weekly dinner dates. Even when Dad passed and years later, Mom moved down South to escape the cold winters, the carryover from our childhood persisted. Somehow, the tradition we'd found annoying as kids had become something we all looked forward to.

Mostly.

I'd never had a reason strong enough to blow off the weekly date before. But then again, Harper had never come back before now. She'd never been standing in front of me, her eyes shining with happiness that I'd helped put there as she began decorating her Christmas tree.

Bring Harper.

The second text came through as if Brody had read my mind. I hesitated, the idea more tempting than I wanted to admit. But Harper was already elbows-deep in her second box of ornaments, oohing and aahing over each one she unearthed.

I stuffed my phone back in my pocket. "I should probably head out," I said. "Dinner with the family."

"Oh." Harper's head shot up. "It's family dinner night? Did you want…should I…"

My heart squeezed at the unasked question. "No," I said. "You should stay here with your grandma." I smiled. "That big tree isn't going to decorate itself."

Her soft smile hit me in the gut.

"You should stay, Grayson," Willa said. "I have a pot of soup on. We could use the help. It would be just like old times."

It was tempting. *Very* tempting.

"As much as I'd love to," I said after a moment, "I think I'll leave the two of you to it. If I don't show up to dinner, I'll never hear the end of it. Brody doesn't seem to care that we see each other almost every day—we need to sit around a table and share food weekly to be a real family."

"Never take family for granted, Grayson," Willa chided me immediately. "You never know when they won't be around."

"Grandma!" Harper's face fell, and at once, I felt the burn of guilt.

"You're right, Willa." I stooped to press a kiss to her cheek. "I'm grateful every day for them. Even when they make me crazy."

She patted my cheek and smiled. "That's better."

"Enjoy your evening, ladies."

When I turned, Harper was behind me. "I'll walk you out."

I wanted to argue and tell her to stay with her grandma and soak up the moment. But more than that, I was hungry for another minute alone with her.

The back hallway was narrow and dark as we made our way down the stairs to the back door that led out to the alley behind the plaza. I hesitated, my hand on the door handle.

"Thank you for today," she said softly. "For the tree and…"

well, for all of it. You were right. Cutting down the tree was special. I really appreciate it."

Her eyes searched mine in the dim light and for a second, I forgot how to breathe. The memory of her lips on mine in the snow slammed into me. It took everything I had in me not to pull her in close.

"Of course," I said, my voice rough. "You know I'd do anything for you, Harper."

The words hung heavy between us, but before she could respond, I cleared my throat. "I'll see you tomorrow. Have fun tonight."

She swallowed hard and nodded, her sweet smile back on her face. "Tomorrow."

I stepped out into the cold, the sound of the door clicking behind me, and wondered how the hell I was supposed to sit through a family dinner when all I wanted was to be back upstairs with her.

Chapter Eleven

Grayson

By the time I pulled into the driveway of my childhood home, which Brody bought from Mom when she moved south a few years ago, the place was lit up with over-the-top Christmas lights strung from every available surface. I smiled and shook my head as I walked up the walk. No doubt, Quinn had a say in how Uncle Brody decorated.

Warm light spilled from the windows, and the sound of laughter greeted me as I stepped through the front door.

I shook off the cold and inhaled deeply the scent of seasoned beef and peppers that told me it was taco night. My stomach growled, but my chest tightened because I knew I'd rather be upstairs at Willa's Whisk, in Harper and Willa's tiny apartment, helping them string lights on their tree.

"It's about time," Reid called from the dining room.

I popped my head around the corner for a moment to see my brother. Avery was seated by his side, a platter of taco shells in her hand.

Everyone was there. *Almost* everyone.

The door banged open behind me. I spun back into the front entry as my youngest brother stumbled in. He was covered in snow up to his thighs, looking once again as if he'd just emerged from a snowbank, which he likely had. Preston had a scowl on his face as he brushed the equivalent of a snowdrift from his shoulders.

"Don't bring that in here!" Brody yelled. "At least knock your boots off outside."

Preston shook his head, ignoring him.

"Everything okay?" I asked Preston, arching a brow.

"No," he grumbled. "Did you know the whole lower trail system out in the nature park isn't actually owned by the trail association?"

I shook my head. "Who owns it?"

"A private investor." He held up his fingers, mimicking quotation marks. "Who's looking to sell."

"What?"

"Seriously?" Brody popped his head around the corner. He cocked his eyebrow at the snow at Preston's feet, but with a sigh, ignored it. "What do you mean, they're selling?"

Preston shook his head and stepped over the puddles he'd created. "That's the rumor," he said as we followed him into the dining room. "Apparently, there's a development firm looking to come in and build a bunch of cabins that will appeal to out-of-towners."

"You know how I feel about out-of-towners," Reid piped up, earning him a playful smack on his arm from his wife, who up until recently had been considered an "out-of-towner."

"That sucks," Ethan said. "What part of the trails does it affect?"

"Way too much." Preston slumped into a chair and helped himself to some taco shells. "Mostly the current entrance to the beginner mountain biking tracks and the general access." He groaned. "If this sale goes through, the trail association will have to reconfigure everything to keep the trail system usable. I'm all for growth and progress and all that, but what the hell?"

I slid into a seat across from him and next to Delaney. I smiled a hello and waved at Quinn, who was shoveling rice in her mouth. "I have to agree," I said. "Progress is inevitable, but we should be working to protect the spaces that make this town so special."

"Who is the developer?" Brody asked. "Maybe you can ask Jess who it is?"

"Jess Anderson?" Delaney asked. "She came to ladies' night last week."

Avery nodded. "Didn't she mention a fiancé who was a land developer?"

"What?" Ethan almost choked on his taco. "Jess is getting married?"

"To a land developer?" Preston's mouth fell open. "It has to be a coincidence."

"I may have gotten it wrong." Avery held up her hands. "I just met her, and we talked about a lot of things."

Preston let out a sharp laugh. "Unbelievable. A local girl is going to marry the guy who wants to carve up the best parts of the forest. Ridiculous."

"We don't know that," Brody offered. "I'm sure that Jess—"

"I shouldn't be surprised," Preston continued. "She always was—"

"Careful, brother." I stopped him. "I know you're worked up right now. But Jess is a good woman. And if she *is* marrying this guy, I'm sure he's a nice guy. Don't jump to conclusions just because the two of you have history."

Delaney's eyes grew wide, but Ethan gave her a quick shake of his head. I'm sure he'd fill her in later when Preston wasn't around.

The truth was, there was a time when Preston looked at

Jess very differently. Before he'd convinced himself how opposite they were. He, with his mud-splattered boots and the need to be outside and living free, and she in her tailored blazers and a growing taste for the finer things in life. I remembered the day in grade school when he'd presented her with a bouquet of hand-picked daisies, hoping with his innocent heart that a young Jess might return his developing feelings.

And how, subsequently, she'd scattered those daisies at his feet and laughed at him. Sure, they'd only been eleven or twelve. But when it came to Jess Anderson, Preston had never been able to let it go.

Brody clattered a fresh platter of tortillas down in the center of the table, breaking the tension. "Well, if Jess is serious about this guy, she'll figure out the details. I'm sure she only wants the best for Trickle Creek, too. In the meantime, eat."

We all dug in, settling into the familiar rhythm of family dinner. Bowls of ground beef and chicken were passed around with plates of toppings. Quinn tested the limits of her tortilla shell with an unreasonable amount of toppings that resulted in a minor explosion that had everyone laughing, and her father rolling his eyes as he passed her a fork.

Conversation shifted from topic to topic, and no matter how much I tried to stay present, I couldn't seem to focus on anything. My thoughts kept drifting.

To Harper's smile.

To the way her hand felt in mine as we drove back with the tree.

The way her lips felt on mine. The kiss that wasn't for anyone else.

Just us.

"Earth to Grayson." Reid's voice cut through my thoughts.

I blinked. "What?"

He gave me a look, too sharp to ignore. "Fuck, brother."

"Watch your mouth," Ethan said.

"No way! Money for the swear jar," Quinn called out with glee.

While I watched, Reid handed Quinn a five-dollar bill. "That should cover what I need to say."

I swallowed hard and narrowed my eyes at my twin. "What?" I asked again, rougher this time. "You have something to say, brother? Just say it."

"What's happening?" Brody glanced between us. We both ignored him.

Reid held my gaze. "It's too late, isn't it? You've fallen for her."

The table went quiet. All eyes turned to me.

What I wasn't going to say was that I hadn't *fallen* for her, because I'd never stopped caring. I gripped my fork a little tighter, my pulse pounding in my ears. "It's not like that," I said evenly. "This is all for—"

"The holidays," Reid finished for me. "Fuck that."

"Hey!" Ethan said. "Language."

"Look," my twin brother continued. "Keep telling yourself whatever you need to believe, Gray. But you know how this ends. Her future isn't in this town. It never was."

After a second, the table carried on, laughter bubbling back up, but I didn't hear a word.

Because Reid was right.

And we all knew it.

Harper

THE APARTMENT WAS dark except for the glow of the tree, every light twinkling against the glass ornaments Grandma and I unpacked and hung a few hours earlier. I curled into the corner of the couch, glass of wine in hand, and let the silence settle around me.

Grandma had gone to bed just over an hour ago, completely exhausted from the evening. She'd looked so alive and vibrant earlier, it was easy for me to forget that she was sick at all. But then, as we'd hung the final few ornaments, a shot of pain in her lower abdomen had her clenching her stomach.

I settled her back into the couch and fetched her bottle of pills and a cup of water. It hurt to see her in pain. Especially when there was nothing I could do to help her. Except be there.

I'd finished hanging the last few decorations, showing her the salt-dough handprint I'd made in kindergarten, adorned with green glitter, most of which had rubbed off over the years. It was cracked and worn, but Grandma declared it her favorite.

Just like every other ornament we'd pulled out of the box and hung.

By the time we were done, I'd seen the fatigue in her face and the way her shoulders slumped when she thought I wasn't looking. She'd excused herself early, claiming she wanted to read for a bit before turning in.

"It was a perfect evening, Harper." She'd clasped my hands in hers, tears shining in her eyes. "Thank you."

"Anything for you, Grandma." I squeezed her as tightly as I dared, holding the moment in my heart.

I took a long sip of wine and made a mental note to reach out again to her doctor. Privacy rules be dammed. He'd known me almost my entire life; surely, he'd understand what I was dealing with when it came to Grandma. She'd been so tight-lipped about it all. Only telling me she was *sick* and *she wasn't going to live forever.*

As much as I didn't want to know, I *needed* to know what we were up against and whether I should be making longer-term care plans for her.

Or thinking about changing my own plans completely.

My phone buzzed on the table, startling me.

> Still waiting to hear from you, Harper. We'd love
> to have you aboard for the season. Are you
> ready to commit?

My stomach twisted. The job was everything I'd been working for. Head chef on a super-yacht in the Med. Captain Howard had more faith in me than I probably deserved, but it would be the career boost that some chefs waited their whole lives for. I'd be crazy to turn it down.

But…

My eyes drifted to Grandma's closed bedroom door.

> Sorry. I'll let you know soon.

I typed back, my fingers hesitating over the words before I hit Send. Noncommittal and cowardly. It wasn't a good look in my industry.

> We want you for the season, Harper. But we
> can't wait forever.

I was lucky he was waiting at all. I swallowed hard and set the phone down again, losing myself in the glowing lights of the tree, in an effort to steady myself.

I took a slow sip of my wine, but before I could swallow, my phone buzzed with another text.

> I hope the decorating went well. I had a lot of
> fun with you today.

Instantly, my worry was replaced with heat in my chest. I snapped a picture of the tree glowing in the dark and sent it back to him.

> Thank you for today. Grandma loves the tree.
> So do I.

It wasn't what I wanted to say. Not really. I wanted to tell him how much I'd enjoyed spending time with him all day and…the kiss.

Noncommittal and cowardly.

It wasn't a good look in life either.

Three dots appeared as he typed a response. I held my breath.

It's beautiful. I'm glad you both love it.

I leaned back into the cushions, my wine forgotten. Grayson had known exactly what Grandma needed this Christmas. Maybe even what I needed. He always did.

He'd been the boy who fixed all the things and showed up when no one else did. Now, he was the man who still did.

Except when it came to me.

Because when it had mattered most, he'd been the one to walk away and break my heart.

I stared at the tree until my eyes burned. What we were doing now felt easy and fun, and so help me…it felt *real*. But I couldn't let myself forget that it wasn't.

And it never had been.

He'd made sure of that when we were kids.

Only, sitting here with the glow of the tree he'd insisted on getting us, it was hard to remember why I ever thought that.

Chapter Twelve

Harper

The bell over the door of Earth's Own chimed as I stepped into the warm shop that smelled of cinnamon and cardamom. Strings of twinkle lights ran along the shelves, making the jars of tea sparkle like they belonged in a Christmas market.

"It's always so welcoming in here," I told Lauren as I scooped up a package of organic gingerbread. "I just love this store. What a great addition to Trickle Creek."

"Thank you." My new friend smiled warmly. "I've really tried to bring new and different products in."

Lauren was hardly new to town, but because she'd moved here after I left, she was new to me. But both living and working in the plaza, we'd become friendly in a short amount of time. Especially considering she always seemed to be with Brody.

Well, less so lately, according to Grayson. There seemed to be some story between the two of them, but I didn't know Lauren well enough yet to ask her about it.

From the back of the store, a customer caught her eye. Lauren turned to me quickly before going to help her. "Let me know if I can help you find anything, okay?"

"For sure. I was just hoping to pick up a few stocking stuffers."

I took my time browsing the homemade soaps and bath salts, lifting each one to my nose to find the perfect scent for Grandma. I lingered over a cedar and orange-scented bar that reminded me of Grayson.

I was about to put it in my basket when a voice stopped me.

"Harper. Hey."

I turned to see Doctor Samuels by the bulk bins, a paper bag of sliced almonds in his hand.

"Doctor." I smiled. "I was actually hoping to run into you."

His expression softened. "I hope everything is okay?"

"Oh yeah. I'm fine." I hesitated. "I was actually hoping to speak to you about my grandma. She's been pretty vague about her health lately. I'm concerned that there's not more I can be doing for her while I'm…well, while I'm home," I continued quickly. "I want to make sure that she's got every-thing she needs and help in the restaurant and…well, I guess I just want to know what the prognosis is." I blew out a breath. Now that the question was out there, I wished I could take it back.

Was knowing the truth of the situation really going to make it any better?

The doctor smiled kindly as he shook his head. "Harper, you know I can't talk about her case without her permission. Patient confidentiality."

I knew that. Still, the words felt like defeat.

"I understand," I said. "It's just that Grandma is from a generation that doesn't like to talk about these things. All she's told me is that she's sick. I'm sure I don't have to tell you how difficult it is for me to be far away and not know exactly how much…" I let the sentence drift away.

Doctor Samuels nodded and took a step closer. "I'm sure it's very hard," he said. "You're planning on leaving for work again, I take it?"

I started to nod, but finished with a shrug.

"Your grandmother is a strong woman, but time does have a way of catching up with us all. Perhaps we can set up a time for both of you to come in together. That way, we can discuss any concerns you might have with her present and won't be in breach of any confidentiality issues. Would that help?"

"Yes." I blew out a breath. "I would really appreciate that. I'll talk to Grandma and call the clinic to set it up." I shook his hand. "Thank you, Doctor Samuels."

He returned to his shopping, and I took my soaps up to the counter to pay.

"That looked serious," Lauren said as I dropped my purchases in front of her.

"I sure hope it's not." I didn't want to get into my concerns about Grandma's health. At least not until I knew more.

Lauren clearly understood. She grinned and made small talk while she rang everything up. "Am I going to see you tonight at the community skate night?"

I laughed. "You're going to see exactly how long it's been since I've skated," I told her. "Living in the land of sun and sand hasn't given me many opportunities to get out on the ice."

"I'm sure Grayson will be more than happy to help you out." She winked.

I shook my head. Grayson told me that his brothers all knew the truth about our relationship, but I didn't know if that extended to Lauren as well. To be on the safe side, I assumed she didn't know anything.

"Oh," I smiled, "I'm sure he will. He's been on a personal mission to make me fall in love with winter again." *And him.* The thought flashed through my mind, but I dismissed it just as quickly.

"The two of you are so sweet together," Lauren said wistfully. "Seeing you together, you both look so happy and…well, hopefully, one day I'll find that kind of happiness, too."

So, she didn't know the truth.

"I'm sure you will." I handed over my credit card. "Grayson said you're dating?" It was actually Brody who'd said it, but something told me not to mention that particular detail. Or the fact that Brody hadn't seemed all that happy about it. "How's that going?"

Lauren waved my question away. "It's a process," she said after a moment. "But I'm not losing hope. Not yet." She handed me my card and a paper bag with my wrapped soaps. "I've hit a point in my life where I have everything I've ever wanted and things are really good, you know?"

I nodded.

"Now, I'd really like someone special to share it all with. I'm not getting any younger and lately, I've been feeling a pull for more."

I could see the longing in her eyes. I had no doubt she'd find it, too. I told her as much.

"Well," Lauren laughed, "I guess we'll see if I can be as lucky in love as you."

I laughed along with her, but as I stepped out into the cold December day, the laughter died on my lips.

My new friend was chasing the kind of love she thought I already had. If only she knew the truth, that what she thought she saw between me and Grayson was nothing more than borrowed time.

Grayson

THE SCENE in front of me looked like it had just been ripped out of a Hallmark movie. Pretty much like everything this town did. I had to laugh at it, but I also kind of loved it.

The air was filled with the scent of woodsmoke and pine from the giant bonfire next to the creek and the frozen skating rink that had been created for the season, and the town skate night.

White twinkling lights were hung from the low tree branches nearby, and someone had a tinny speaker blasting out carols, enhancing the whole Christmas card effect.

All the festivals and over-the-top events that Trickle Creek hosted were part of what made my hometown so special. They were also a big part of why I'd always wanted to make a life there and raise a family one day.

Of course, those were dreams of a much younger Grayson. Dreams that had only ever been about one person and had faded over the years.

I should have moved on years ago, but something had always held me back. What if I couldn't ever find someone who would come close to making me feel the way she had? Even if all those feelings were based on the naivety of youth.

But now…

Harper.

I spotted her before she saw me. She stood near the hot chocolate booth, laughing and talking with Charli. Every single time I saw her, I was struck by how natural she looked back in Trickle Creek. Like she never left.

And maybe she'd stay.

Reid's words kept replaying in my brain.

Keep telling yourself whatever you need to believe, Gray. But you know how this ends. Her future isn't in this town. It never was.

Of course, there was a part of me that believed that he was right, but there was a growing piece of me that was certain my twin brother was wrong. We weren't kids anymore. Things changed. And even if they hadn't, they still could.

"You look beautiful tonight," I said as I approached, sliding my arm around Harper's waist and pulling her in for a quick kiss on her cheek. "Hi, Charli. You look great, too."

My old friend laughed and waved away the compliment. "You're a charmer, Gray. But I know you only have eyes for this one."

She wasn't wrong.

"Hi." Harper's eyes flashed with warmth as she turned to greet me. "I'm still not sure about this skating thing. Charli says it's like riding a bike, but I have to admit, it's been a while since I've done that, too."

"What?" I pulled back, pretending to be surprised. "What *have* you been doing?"

Harper shrugged. "Cooking."

"I'll see you guys out there," Charli said with a laugh before slipping away into the crowd, leaving us alone.

"I promise, you'll be fine," I told Harper. "I won't let you fall."

"I know."

She looked up at me with so much trust, my heart clenched in my chest.

It was ridiculous the way I was letting her affect me. But I was powerless to stop it. I wasn't even going to try.

"Come on." I tugged her hand. "Let's go get laced up."

We found a spot on the bench by the ice, and I quickly pulled on my skates and laced them with practiced ease while Harper struggled with the laces of her borrowed skates.

"This is ridiculous," she grumbled. "Why do they make them so long?"

She held out the excess string, and I laughed. "Here." I crouched in front of her, brushing her hands away. "They're so long, so you can wrap them around your ankle like this." I wrapped them snugly and tied them in a neat bow before looking up.

Her eyes caught mine, and for a moment, it was just us. "Some things never change," she said softly.

I forced myself to look away and move on to the second skate. "What do you mean?"

"You taking care of me."

Her words caught me. I froze, the laces in my hand for a moment before I swallowed hard and finished the job. "Ready?"

She clung to my arm as we stepped onto the rink, wobbling just enough to make me grin. "I warned you," she said. "It's been a long time."

"I've got you."

"I know."

Dammit if she didn't have a way of getting right to my heart with a few simple words.

We glided slowly at first, her steps cautious. I kept my hand firmly in hers, steadying her every time she slipped.

Soon, muscle memory returned, and Harper gained a bit more confidence.

"So," I said, steering us around a cluster of kids. "Tell me all about it."

"All about what?" She almost lost her balance when she looked over at me, but quickly regained it.

"Your life. The yachts. The fancy restaurants. All the places you've been. You've probably got a story for every stamp in your passport."

"That's a pretty long list."

"I've got all the time in the world," I told her. "I want to hear about it all." I spun her around, so she was facing me and I could hold her in my arms.

"You really want to know?"

I nodded. "All of it."

Her lips curved, but there was something in her eyes…hesitation, maybe. "It wasn't all glamorous," she started. "Long hours. Demanding guests. Half the time when I'm on charter, I hardly even know what port we're in, or what country. I'm always belowdecks in the galley. But the food…the creating… it's amazing, constantly striving to be better."

"Why doesn't that surprise me? You always were chasing more."

She shrugged, but didn't deny it.

"What about boyfriends?" I hadn't meant to ask. I didn't want to know. Not really. "Did you leave anyone special in any of those ports?"

Her smile dimmed. She shook her head.

"No one?" I pushed, aware that I was only going to be torturing myself if she told me what I didn't want to hear.

"No," she said softly. "Nothing serious. It's not really the kind of life that's conducive to a relationship."

Her admission probably shouldn't have made me so happy, but I couldn't help it.

"And you?" Harper turned the question around on me. "You stayed here. I'm surprised you're not married yet."

"Are you?"

Before she could answer, I spun her away again and once more started gliding easily on the ice. After half a lap, she finally spoke. "Grayson, I—"

"Hey!"

We were jostled by two other skaters.

"Sorry, I didn't see…oh, Grayson." Mike Dobson, a local contractor, and his wife bumped into us. "How are you?" He stopped, clearly expecting a conversation.

"Good. I was just—"

"Heard that Ollie is selling the shop," he said. "That true?"

"Word certainly travels fast," I said carefully.

"To be honest, I'm surprised it took him so long," Mike continued. "I've heard he's had offers already."

That was news to me. The *options* Ollie had mentioned.

Damnit. I still hadn't been able to find the chance to discuss my thoughts about buying the store from him. Had I missed my chance?

I worked to keep my face neutral, not wanting my reaction to show on my face.

"I hope it stays local," Mike said before I could respond. "You've done great things with that place. It would be a shame to see a big corporation buy it up."

"I can't disagree with that." I nodded. "Have fun tonight."

Mike and his wife skated off.

Beside me, Harper glanced up. "Ollie's selling? Really?"

"He is." I shrugged. "I've barely had a chance to discuss it with him myself, but of course, everyone already knows about it. Small town and all." I shook my head. "I didn't know about the offers already, though," I muttered, jaw tight. "Not that I should be surprised."

Her brows lifted. "Have you ever thought about doing anything else?"

I studied her for a beat before turning it around on her. "Have you?"

Her lips parted, but she didn't answer right away, and I found myself wanting that answer more than I should have.

Harper

HIS QUESTION LINGERED in the air between us.

Have you?

How could he know that I'd been thinking of it? More than I wanted to admit.

It should have been easy to laugh it off and tell him, *Of course not. My life is elsewhere, in galleys on super-yachts in exotic locations halfway around the world. Far from this small-town, basic life.*

I was living the life I'd always wanted. The one I'd given up everything for when I was a kid. The life I'd given *him* up for.

But I couldn't say that.

Because the truth was, the longer I'd been back in Trickle Creek, the harder it was to ignore the tiny voice inside me whispering, *Maybe.*

So I pressed my lips together and let him lead me around the rink again. I studied him as we circled the ice together. His jaw set against the cold, his hand firmly in mine. How had he never had a relationship after I left? A man like him?

Grayson had been the boy every girl wanted in high school. Handsome, athletic, and smart. Unlike his twin brother, who seemed to have a chip on his shoulder about everything, Grayson was warm and friendly to everyone.

Now, he was the man everyone depended on. One everyone respected. Solid. Reliable. And somehow, even more handsome. He was a catch by any standard.

It was a mystery how he hadn't been snatched up yet.

But then again…would he have been enough for me all those years ago? If he hadn't pushed me away, would I have stayed? Would I have been happy with the small-town life?

The life he loved so much.

The thought made my chest ache.

I opened my mouth, the beginnings of a: *Maybe I have thought about staying* on my tongue—

"Grayson! Harper!"

We both turned as Tilley Beckett swooped wildly and dangerously toward us. Grayson reached out with his free arm just in time to keep her from crashing into us.

Her sparkly red scarf flew out behind her; gaudy glittery Santa hat earrings dangled from her ears, catching the twinkling lights. Somehow, Tilley's ever-present clipboard was tucked under her arm, even out on the ice.

"Just the happy couple I've been wanting to run into," she said as she found her balance. "Are you two having fun?" She wiggled her brows.

I couldn't help but laugh.

"Another great event, Tilley," Grayson said. "I don't know what this town would do without you."

"It certainly wouldn't be nearly as festive," I added.

"You two are way too kind." She flipped open her clipboard and produced a small white envelope. "But you are equally responsible for the Christmas cheer in this town," she said. "Which is why I'm so pleased to present this to you."

She pressed the envelope into Grayson's hand before he could protest.

He frowned, glancing down at it. "What's this?"

"It's nothing." Tilley waved her hand. "Just a little token of appreciation from the festival committee."

"I thought you *were* the committee, Tilley?" He eyed her, but she only shrugged.

"You've been working so hard for us that the committee agreed you deserved a little something for all your efforts. Lord knows the light-up could never have happened without you."

Grayson blinked, clearly caught off guard. "I don't usually get things like this," he said. "I've been helping for years."

"Which is why this is long overdue," Tilley said gleefully. "And the committee won't take no for an answer."

He shook his head and slid the card from the envelope. "A gift certificate for a night at Trickle Creek Lodge? Tilley! This is too much."

"Nonsense." Her eyes twinkled as she looked between us.

"A romantic getaway for two at the lodge? I can't think of anyone more deserving."

Heat climbed up my neck. I couldn't help but wonder if our *relationship* had anything to do with this gift of appreciation for Grayson.

"Enjoy yourselves," Tilley added with a wink. "Nothing like a cozy night in front of a roaring fire with a bottle of wine to fan the flames of a newly rekindled relationship."

Yup. Our *relationship* had everything to do with it.

Grayson cleared his throat, tucking the envelope quickly into his coat pocket. "Well, thank you, I guess."

"No thanks needed." She once again wiggled her eyebrows. "I can't wait to hear all about it."

Before either of us could protest, Tilley turned and skated away, her scarf waving behind her as she set her sights on someone new.

Grayson shifted beside me. "You don't have to come," he said, his voice low, almost gruff.

I arched a brow. "To a luxury lodge with a roaring fire and someone else cooking meals for me? You think I'm passing that up?" I laughed. "Besides, it didn't feel like I had much of a choice there."

A smile tugged at the corner of his mouth, but his eyes remained serious. "I'm just saying, I don't want you to feel like you've been forced into something where you're not comfortable. I know this is all for…"

"Grayson." I touched his arm. "If Tilley wants to believe we're the kind of couple who spend a romantic night away together, then maybe we shouldn't disappoint her."

His gaze held mine. "Maybe not," he said softly.

Heat traveled through me, landing low in my belly at the idea of spending a night together with Grayson. "It'll be hard." I forced a lightness into my voice. "But if I have to suffer through a night of luxury to make the town happy, I'll do my very best." I held my arm up over my forehead dramatically, and almost fell on my ass in the process.

"Careful there, sweetheart." Grayson caught me easily. "I know you're falling for me, but there's no point in getting hurt while you're doing it. At least not before our night together."

His voice was laced with an undeniable heat, and suddenly I wasn't so sure where the lie ended and the truth began.

Chapter Thirteen

Harper

I tossed another sweater on the bed and then immediately grabbed it back. Too casual. Too warm. Too...*ugh.*

Why was I overthinking this? It was a simple overnight trip with Grayson. It's not like it was a real romantic weekend.

One night.

Just for show.

I reached for the sweater again. It had a high neck, long sleeves. I shoved it in the bag.

Behind me, Grandma's voice carried from her chair in the living room by the window. "You've folded and unfolded that sweater at least three times now. Just put it in the bag."

I glanced over my shoulder. She looked small, wrapped in her blanket; the December light made her look extra pale and frail, but her eyes were sharp as ever.

"Maybe I shouldn't go," I blurted, shoving the sweater back in the bag. "You seem extra tired today, Grandma, and I hate to leave you when—"

"You're going." She cut me off firmly. "Besides, when you go back to work, I'll be on my own then, too, won't I?"

She was searching for answers that I didn't have yet.

She wasn't the only one good at avoiding uncomfortable questions. "It's only a few days before Christmas, Grandma." I changed the subject. "Are you sure you'll be—"

"You're going. That's final."

I pressed my lips together. "Grandma, I'm just—"

"Harper." She wagged her finger at me. "Don't argue. Erin will be here, and that chef you hired is fabulous. Besides, half this town pops in to check on me every time they walk past the restaurant. I'll be fine for one night. You deserve this, Harper." Her tone softened. "You and Grayson need this time together."

We didn't. But I couldn't tell her that. Guilt for lying to the most important person in my life flooded through me. It was for her own sake, though. More than anything, I just wanted to make her happy.

Which was exactly why I was going to go.

Never mind the fact that the idea of spending a night alone with Grayson filled me with conflicting feelings that I wasn't sure I was prepared to handle.

I smiled despite myself, but the worry still gnawed at me. "Okay," I conceded. "But you just seem so tired, Grandma. I'd really like to have an appointment with Doctor Samuels and discuss what we can—"

"I'm an old woman, sweetheart. And I'm unwell. Of course I'm tired. But you can't let that keep you from living your life. Not now."

I swallowed hard, my throat thick.

"Okay. It's only for one night." I wasn't sure who I was trying to convince. "I'll be just a phone call away if you need anything."

"I won't." She winked then, her smile turning just a shade too knowing, like she was in on a secret I hadn't been told.

. . .

Grayson

THE SUITE TILLEY had gifted me was way over the top. It was the kind of room that people booked for honeymoons, wedding nights, or special anniversaries. It was *not* the type of room you would gift a volunteer as a thank-you.

"This is unreal." Harper stepped inside the room and took in the vaulted ceilings with the floor-to-ceiling windows looking out over the ski hill and beyond, down the valley. The views were breathtaking.

I stood back and watched while Harper walked slowly around the room. She trailed her hand along the stone fireplace with large rock work that stretched all the way to the ceiling. She stopped at the bar and the bucket of ice with a bottle of bubbly and two glasses, waiting for us. "Interesting." She raised her eyebrows, and I laughed.

When Harper disappeared into the attached bedroom, I forced myself to stay back, eyeing up the overstuffed couch in front of the fireplace as my potential bed for the evening. As much as I wanted to share what was no doubt a plush, king-sized bed with Harper, I needed to keep reminding myself that even if Tilley and the entire town thought so, our relationship wasn't real.

"Grayson," her voice came from inside the bedroom, "you've got to see this bathroom. This tub is unreal."

I shook my head and grinned. "You always were a sucker for a bath."

"Right?" She reappeared in the living room. "A bathtub is hard to come by on a yacht," she said. "At least, it is if you're not a paying guest."

"I would imagine." I dropped our bags next to the closet.

"You'll have to enjoy a bath. Later," I added. "First, I want to make the most out of this whole thing."

"Oh?" She leaned against the counter, looking so damn cute. "What did you have in mind?"

My thoughts flashed to all the dirty things I definitely couldn't get out of my mind. I swallowed hard and moved my line of thinking to a much more PG-rated track. "Snowshoeing?"

Harper burst out laughing. "Seriously? I think you're trying to torture me with all these cold outdoor activities."

"Hardly." I reached for her. "But maybe I am trying to remind you just how much fun the mountains and small-town life can be."

Something in her eyes flickered, but before I could let her think too much about it, I added, "Besides, we need people to see us, right? After all, won't your grandma be happy to know how much we're enjoying this little romantic getaway?"

She hesitated.

"That was the point of all this, after all, wasn't it?"

She inhaled slowly, and when she blew out her breath, the smile was back on her face. "Of course. And you're right. Grandma will love hearing about every detail. We can send her a photo."

SHE HELD UP HER PHONE, framing the two of us in the shot. "Smile. Let's give Grandma proof we're making the most of it."

I leaned in close enough to catch the faint scent of her shampoo and grinned. There was nothing fake about the smile on my face. Every minute with Harper was fun and easy.

She clicked the button and flipped the phone around to look at the shot. "We're so cute."

"We always were," I said before I could stop myself.

Her smile faltered, but only for a second.

I was doing a terrible job hiding my growing feelings for Harper, and I wasn't sure I cared anymore.

She sent the picture to Willa and tucked her phone back in her pocket.

"If we're done with the photo shoot, let's go." I pulled my toque down low over my ears. "Before we lose the light."

I'd forgotten how hard it could be to maneuver on snowshoes, but it didn't take long to remember when my heart was beating fast, and I'd unzipped my coat in an effort to cool off.

"Slow down!" Harper called out behind me. "It's not a race."

Maybe it wasn't. But part of me hoped that by getting my heart rate up, I could run away from the conflicting feelings crashing through me.

It wasn't working.

"Grayson!"

I turned around just in time to get a snowball square in the chest.

I stopped in my tracks and brushed the snow off my chest. "Did you just do that?"

She grinned. "Sure did." Harper bent over laughing, another snowball already packed in her mittened hands. "If you're not going to slow down, I'll slow you down."

"Oh yeah?"

She nodded. "Yup."

"Maybe I should just speed you up." I took off, running in her direction as awkwardly as I could in my snowshoes.

Harper squealed and tried to backpedal, but snowshoes aren't built for speed.

Snow crunched under my snowshoes as I quickly closed the gap. It didn't take long before I had her cornered between two trees, her cheeks flushed and her breath coming fast; she looked adorable.

"You surrender?"

She straightened her shoulders. "Never."

For a moment, we stood there, only inches apart, both of us smiling too wide. Her eyes met mine, and something flickered between us.

I almost leaned in. God help me, I wanted to kiss her more than anything else.

But Harper blinked, stepping past me with a playful shove. "Come on, tough guy. I'm ready for a hot drink."

I laughed, even as the ache in my chest twisted tight, and I followed her down the path back to the lodge.

There was no way she hadn't felt whatever that was between us.

But even if she had felt it, that still didn't mean anything.

At least not the way I wanted it to.

Chapter Fourteen

Harper

The dining room was lit almost entirely by candles, flames flickering against the tall windows that looked out over the snowy slope, lit up for night skiing. Soft flakes of snow fell around the strings of lights that twinkled in the pines outside, reflecting off the glass, giving the whole place the effect of being inside a snow globe.

Trickle Creek did like their Christmas lights, but I had to admit, they really did add to the overall atmosphere and turn everything into a scene right out of a movie.

It was perfect.

I sat across from Grayson, happy I'd packed a dress suitable for the occasion. It was form-fitting, skimming my body, with just enough cleavage, but not too much. I'd curled my hair into loose waves that hung over my bare shoulders, and even applied a little makeup.

I held a glass of wine in my hand and tried to focus on the delicious-looking food. Tried and failed.

Truthfully, the food was exquisite, but that's not what had my pulse tripping. It was *him.*

Grayson.

Dressed in a button-down grey shirt with the top two buttons undone, his shirtsleeves rolled up just enough to showcase his strong forearms, flexing every time he lifted his own glass, he'd never looked sexier.

But maybe it was the way the candlelight softened the hard lines of his jaw, or the slightest bit of stubble he'd let grow in over the last few days. Or maybe it was the way his gaze lingered on me just a little bit too long when he thought I wasn't looking. The way he smiled at me had my stomach flipping like I was eighteen again.

And more than anything, it was how easy it all felt with him. Laughing, teasing, and talking about nothing and everything all at the same time. It was like no time at all had passed between us. Even better, it was just us. No Tilley. No Grandma. No one watching to see what we were going to do or not do.

I wanted to lean into the feeling with him. I wanted it so badly, it ached.

I forced myself to focus on the plate of steak and mashed potatoes in front of me. It was cooked perfectly, the mash creamy and flavorful. The medium-rare beef melted in my mouth. "This is delicious. I'm impressed."

"Trickle Creek is turning into quite the destination," he said. "We're attracting all kinds of talent now." He put his fork in his mouth thoughtfully. "Including some very talented chefs." He eyed me knowingly as he chewed.

"I can't disagree," I said, noncommittally. "Trickle Creek really has changed since the last time I was here. A lot of things have."

"Oh yeah?"

I set my fork down and reached for my wineglass again,

buying myself a second to avoid his question. "Why didn't you ever date anyone, Grayson?"

"Excuse me?"

I shrugged, trying to appear casual when I felt anything but. "Seriously? How are you single after all this time?"

He leaned back, studying me in the low light, then finally shook his head. "I guess, no one else ever felt right after you."

The words hit harder than they should have, rattling something loose inside me.

I tried to laugh and lighten the moment. "You're serious?"

He nodded. "Very."

"No one in fifteen years measured up to silly, eighteen-year-old me?"

His mouth curved slightly, but his eyes were serious. "Not even close." He let that sink in before he added, "And for the record, you were never silly."

My heart stuttered, and for a second, just one, I let myself believe him.

And then the old wound opened. The one I'd worked for years to heal and put behind me. He'd walked away from me once before. He'd looked me in the eyes and told me he didn't love me.

He'd crushed me.

Even if this—whatever it was that we were doing here—felt real...It wasn't.

He was doing me a favor because that's what he did. He helped people.

His words didn't mean anything more. His touches, no matter how they lit me up inside, weren't real.

He didn't love me then. Why would he love me now, after all this time? He didn't even know me.

I forced a smile to my face, in an effort to pretend that the fact he'd stayed single all this time didn't affect me.

"You know, Harper?" Grayson lifted his wineglass. "You still show every single thing you're thinking on your face."

Grayson

WE WALKED BACK to the room hand in hand. I could lie and say it was because we didn't know who was watching, and it was important to keep up the ruse of being the *happy couple*, but there was no need. When I'd reached for her, Harper slipped her hand in mine as if it were the most natural thing in the world.

And maybe it was, because it sure as hell felt like it.

Neither of us let go as we passed through the impressive lobby with the spiral staircase and the massive river stone fireplace that rose up through the center of the room. We took the elevator up to the top floor, and by the time we'd reached the door of the suite, I knew I wasn't ready for the night to end.

A fire had been set while we'd been away. Frames crackled behind the glass, warming the room. On the bar, a fresh bottle of red wine and two glasses, along with chocolate-dipped strawberries, waited for us.

"They've really gone all out for you, haven't they?" Harper crossed the room and plucked a strawberry off the plate. "You must be one hell of a volunteer."

I shook my head with a chuckle. "Like I said before, I've been helping out with all kinds of things for longer than I can remember, and I've never once been thanked so...well, not with anything more than a card. This is next-level."

"I'm not complaining." She placed the berry between her lips. "Oh." Harper closed her eyes while she enjoyed the treat.

I had to look away. It had been torture enough sitting across from her in that tight black dress all night, with her tits straining against the fabric, and cleavage so deep, it was all I could do to keep myself from imagining getting lost in it.

But to hear her moan with pleasure from a simple strawberry and not pull her up against me so I could taste the sweetness on her lips for myself? It was more than could be expected of me.

I distracted myself by removing the cork from the bottle and pouring two glasses.

"Not ready for bed yet?" Harper asked.

"Not even close," I admitted. "You?"

She shook her head as she took a glass from me and curled up on the couch, her legs tucked up under her.

I sat next to her, close enough to feel the warmth of her leg against mine. For a while, we didn't talk, but simply stared into the fire, letting the silence stretch out between us. It wasn't uncomfortable. Quite the opposite. Just like everything with Harper, it felt easy.

Finally, I turned toward her. "Are you happy, Harper?"

"Right now?" She tilted her head back and laughed a little. "Yes."

"I'm glad," I said honestly. "But I meant in general. In life."

Her brows lifted, and her lips pressed together as she thought about the question. After a moment, she set her wine down on the coffee table and clasped her hands together. "With my career? Yes," she answered herself. "All I've ever wanted is to learn and grow in my craft. I've wanted to challenge myself and push myself every day to be better, and I've been able to do that." She looked up at me. "And living on a yacht in some of the most beautiful places in the world has been pretty amazing, too."

"I bet." I couldn't help but smile, but I hadn't forgotten that she'd also confessed to not having a serious relationship in years. "What about everything else?"

"Everything else?" She reached for her glass again.

"Family," I said slowly. "A home. A relationship." I added the last part quietly.

She toyed with the stem of her glass. "It's complicated, Grayson."

"I don't think it is." When I let her go all those years ago, it had destroyed me. But I'd done it for one reason: so she would be happy. I needed to know whether it was all for nothing. "There's more to life than a career," I said carefully. "I'm not trying to downplay the success you've had as a chef, Harper. It really is impressive. I'm very proud of you."

"Thank you." She lifted her eyes to meet mine. "But?"

"What about everything else? Is there anything missing?" My voice was low, but steady. I knew I was pushing her, but I couldn't stop myself.

Something unspoken flickered in her eyes. "Maybe," she said softly.

I set my glass down and leaned closer to her. "What about Willa? She seems happy to have you home."

Her face softened. "She is. More than I could have expected," she said. "I mean, of course, I knew she always wanted me to come home, but…it was so special to have her fly out to see me, too. I got to show her the world."

"You sure did." The pride in her eyes was clear. "But there's no place like home, right?"

"You're not wrong," she agreed. "Maybe I shouldn't have stayed away so long."

"Why did you?"

I was almost afraid of the answer, but Harper only shrugged. "It was easier that way. I guess selfishly it was easier to pretend that Grandma wasn't getting older and things were changing here, if I didn't see it for myself."

"And now?"

"It's hard to see," she admitted. "But I'm glad I did. If I

hadn't come home, I wouldn't have been able to hire Kevin and set things up so Grandma doesn't have to work so hard."

I swallowed back what I really wanted to say. That she wouldn't have to work at all…if Harper stayed.

"And us?"

Her jaw fell open.

"The pretending," I clarified. "Is it worth it? Do you think she's buying it?"

"Oh." She swallowed hard. "I think so," she said after a moment. "She wants to. And if it's her last… Well, I appreciate you playing along, Grayson. I know that lying probably isn't the best thing, but honestly, I just want Grandma to be happy. She deserves it. And this seems like just a small thing I can do. Even if it isn't exactly *right*." She blinked back a tear.

I couldn't help it; I reached for her then and brushed a strand of hair back from her face. My hand lingered, my fingers tracing the curve of her jaw. "Of course," I said roughly. "I hope you know I'd do anything for you, Harper. I always have and I always will."

She swallowed hard. For a moment, I thought maybe I'd gone too far. But at the same time, I didn't care. I was tired of pretending.

Before she could say anything, I leaned in, slow enough to give her the chance to stop me.

She didn't.

The first brush of her lips was soft, tentative. But the second, when she let out a breath and leaned into me, that wasn't tentative at all.

It was everything I'd been holding back. Everything I hadn't let myself admit until that very moment.

And God help me, it was everything I'd been missing for the last fifteen years.

Harper

IT MIGHT HAVE BEEN the wine, or the way the firelight painted him in a warm glow, but when Grayson kissed me, I didn't stop him.

There was no one watching. No one we needed to pretend for.

This was for us.

And if I were honest with myself, something I'd been actively trying *not* to do, I'd been waiting for *this* kiss from the moment I'd seen him again.

Probably longer.

I opened to him, my lips parting as his tongue slid against mine, slow and deliberate, stealing the breath from my lungs. Heat coiled low in my belly, spreading through me until I was trembling in his arms.

It was different from before. Different from when we were kids, or we kissed for show in front of the whole town. Or even when we kissed in the snow the other day.

This kiss held a promise of more.

So much more.

It was exciting and terrifying all at the same time.

But I couldn't let myself think about what it might mean. Or more importantly, what I *wanted* it to mean.

Instead, I closed my mind and shifted closer, pressing myself against him. His answering growl rumbled through his chest, vibrating against me.

His hands were everywhere—cupping my face, skimming down my back, pulling me onto his lap, rucking my dress up enough so I could straddle his lap.

The thick ridge of his arousal pressed against me through his pants and the thin scrap of my panties. A shiver tore through me at the reminder of what we were doing.

What we were about to do.

"Harper," he whispered, his forehead pressing against mine. "Tell me to stop."

"No." My voice shook, but I'd never been more sure of anything. "I don't want to stop. Not tonight."

His mouth claimed mine, harder this time, and I clung to him, needing to be closer.

Grayson's hands skimmed down my sides, his fingers splayed as if he were trying to capture me in his memory.

He found the zipper for my dress and slid it down until he could pull the tight fabric from my body.

He sucked in a breath and sat back, his eyes hot on my skin as he took in the sight of me.

The fire crackled behind us, the heat of it licking over my bare skin as Grayson's mouth moved down my throat. Every scrape of his stubble sent sparks racing through me.

"Grayson," I gasped, threading my fingers through his hair, needing more.

He groaned low in his chest, his hands sliding beneath the lacy cups of my bra to cup me fully. His thumbs teased over my nipples until I arched against him, desperate for more.

"Beautiful," he murmured, his voice reverent, as if he couldn't believe I was real. That this moment was real.

And for a second, neither could I.

He'd seen me before, of course, but this was different.

I was different.

The last time we'd been together, we were eighteen. Young, inexperienced, fumbling in the dark. I'd been all sharp edges and nerves, and he'd been a boy with too much intensity in his eyes, and not enough patience in his hands. It had been urgent and sweet and clumsy in ways that only a first love could be.

But this…

This was different.

I wasn't the same girl I'd been at eighteen. My body had softened, curved in new ways. His hands mapped each line as they traveled over my skin, releasing the clasp of my bra, freeing my breasts.

The way he touched me made me feel beautiful in a way I never had back then.

And he was most definitely not a boy anymore.

My hands fumbled at his shirt, desperate to feel him. When I finally managed to pull the fabric back off his strong shoulders, and touch the warm skin and hard muscles under my palms, I, too, took a moment to take in everything he'd become.

A grown man. Broad and strong with steady hands and a body that made me ache just to look at. There was nothing hurried or impatient about him now. Every kiss, every touch was deliberate and confident.

The rest of our clothes fell away, careless and fast, until there was nothing left between us but need.

"I should take you to bed," he murmured as he lay me down on the rug in front of the fire, making no attempt to move to the other room. "But the way you look in the fire-light…" He groaned and kissed a path down my neck to my chest. "Delicious," he whispered against my skin before pulling one aching peak between his lips.

His tongue swirled and teased until I cried out, my back arching up off the floor.

He moved to the other nipple while his hand slid lower, over the curve of my stomach, between my thighs.

"Grayson," I whispered, already trembling.

"Let me," he murmured, and then his fingers were on me, stroking and circling my hard bud until I came apart under his touch.

"So, fucking, beautiful."

His lips were on mine again, kissing me through the climax, his fingers unrelenting.

I barely had a moment to recover before he shifted, his

mouth replacing his fingers on my clit. I gasped, oversensitive, but Grayson's hands clamped down on my thighs, holding me firmly in place as the flat of his tongue lapped against my core.

My head tipped back, a moan of pleasure slipping from my throat as I arched up into his mouth.

He was relentless. Licking and tasting every inch of me until, once more, I began to unravel under his touch.

I cried out, my hands clutching at his shoulders while the sensation crashed over me. The fire roared, but it was nothing compared to the heat flooding my body. My release hit hard and fast, my body arching as the pleasure rushed through me. I called out his name, clinging to him as the waves took me under.

By the time I came back to myself, Grayson was watching me, his face raw with hunger and something deeper.

"Harper, you—"

I pulled him to me, desperate for more and unwilling to wait long enough for him to say whatever he needed to say.

I kissed him slow and deep, traces of wine and myself on his tongue. His hands gripped my hips, rolling me over until I was astride him, his thick, hard cock throbbing against me.

His hands gripped my hips, guiding me down against the thick length of him, gasping at the fullness, the rightness of the moment.

I rocked against him, bracing myself against his chest as the pressure built, delicious and unbearable at the same time.

My head fell back, a moan tearing from my throat. "Oh my God," I whispered. "I forgot how—"

"Don't say that." He cupped my face, pulling me down for a kiss that silenced me. "I never forgot."

We moved together, slowly at first, learning each other again, learning each other for the first time as adults. His hands steadied me, worshipping me and coaxing me higher.

I clung to him, chasing the rhythm until the ache built

inside me. I pressed back, my hands flat on Grayson's chest as yet another orgasm flooded me.

There was no holding back my release. I cried out his name as I shattered. Beneath me, Grayson gripped me tight and pulled me down to him, kissing me through it, his body shaking as he followed me over the edge, burying his face in my neck as he came undone, his own climax consuming him.

Completely wrung out, I collapsed into his arms. Skin damp, pulse racing, Grayson wrapped his arms around me, our breathing ragged as we lay on the rug, firelight dancing over us.

Grayson

HARPER LAY CURLED AGAINST ME, her cheek resting on my chest, her body a perfect fit in my arms. Her breath was still uneven as the firelight flickered over her skin. I tightened my arms around her, not ready to let her go.

I was in trouble.

It didn't take a genius to see that.

All of this was supposed to be for show. For Willa. A Christmas gift of sorts, seeing her granddaughter happy and in love.

But there was nothing pretend about this.

The way Harper had come apart in my arms. The way her body fit mine, like it always had. Only better now. The way her eyes had locked on mine like she was feeling every ounce of what was racing through me.

I'd tried to deny it.

I'd tried to ignore it.

But I couldn't help it.

I was in love with her.

I always had been.

For years, I'd told myself letting her go—pushing her away

—was an act of love. I told her I didn't care. I pretended I didn't want her so she'd leave town and chase her dreams. I'd been young and stupid and full of bravado. But even at eighteen, I'd known that if I hadn't done it, Harper would have given up her dreams for me.

It had damn near broken me, but at the time, I'd been so sure I was doing the right thing.

Now, lying with her in my arms again, something I never dreamed I could have, I no longer knew whether I'd done either of us any favors.

I also didn't have any idea how it was going to end this time.

The one thing I *did* know was that no matter how many times I'd tried to tell myself it wasn't real, I knew with certainty that, at least for me, it was.

She shifted against me, sighing softly. I let the sound sink deep into my bones. If this was all I got, I'd damn well make it last as long as I could.

Chapter Fifteen

Harper

I woke before dawn, my head on his chest, right where it had been when I drifted off to sleep the night before. At some point, we'd moved from the rug in front of the fire to the luxurious king-sized bed.

I could remember not wanting to close my eyes, not wanting the night to end, unsure what the new day would bring.

Had we made a mistake and gone too far?

Being with Grayson never felt like a mistake, but...

For a long moment, I let myself lie still, listening to his steady breathing, feeling his heart beat beneath me, before I moved out from under his arm to look at him properly.

He slept on his back. His features seemed softer in sleep. Almost boyish again. The same boy I'd fallen in love with all those years ago. Only he wasn't a boy anymore.

My chest ached as I studied him, letting myself imagine what might have been if I'd never left all those years ago.

Would we still be happy in Trickle Creek together?

Would we be married? Have children?

Would I have gone to culinary school?

Would we have traveled together? Or stayed and put down roots?

I knew the answers to some of those questions; others I could only guess at before my thoughts shifted to what *could* be if it were real *this* time.

What would it be like waking up to Grayson every morning?

Having coffee in bed before he went to the store, and me to the restaurant.

Would we spend our weekends curled up together, content with a simple life? Or would we be planning adventures, eager to travel together?

Would a small-town life be enough after all this time? Or would I always yearn for more?

Careful not to wake him, I slipped from the bed. In the living room, I found his shirt in a ball on the floor. I pulled it over my arms, inhaling his scent as it surrounded me like a hug.

I started a pot of coffee in the attached kitchen before I crouched in front of the fire, coaxing the embers back to life with a few fresh logs. Sparks crackled, and the smoke curled as the fire caught once more.

Outside, grey predawn started to creep across the sky. I grabbed a fluffy blanket from the couch and wrapped myself in it, before pouring a mug of coffee and settling into the couch.

It was the perfect morning.

And it scared the hell out of me.

What if I was being naive? What if last night had been nothing more than nostalgia and the wine and years of loneliness catching up with us? What if we'd gotten caught up in the pretending and gotten carried away?

What if I let myself believe it could work out between us, only to be broken in two again?

Did I even want to stay?

I lifted the mug to my lips and blew on the hot liquid.

There were more questions than I had answers for.

The job offer still sat on my phone unanswered. Six months in the Mediterranean as a head chef. It was everything I'd ever worked for. It was a dream come true.

At least, it *had* been.

The longer I hesitated on accepting the offer, the further away that dream felt.

And then there was Grandma. She tired so easily now, even when she tried to hide it. I still didn't know what was going on with her health, but I didn't need the details to know that she wasn't getting any younger. She'd worked so hard her entire life. For me. She deserved to rest and enjoy her retirement.

But I knew the only way she would step away from the kitchen completely was if I stayed.

For her, I'd stay.

But would it be enough?

I wrapped my hands around the mug of coffee and stared into the flames, searching for answers.

"Good morning." Grayson's voice, still rough from sleep, came from behind me. A moment later, his arms slid over the couch and around my shoulders as he pressed a kiss to the top of my head. "The bed felt empty without you."

I turned to give him a half smile but held onto his hand. "I didn't want to wake you."

"I wouldn't have complained." He gave me a sexy smile and kissed my hand. "Mind if I join you?"

Grayson

IF IT WERE UP to me, I would have stayed tangled up in Harper all morning—her legs around mine, her hair spilling over my chest, the warmth of our bodies keeping the real world at bay.

Waking up to an empty bed had given me a jolt. For a moment, I panicked and thought maybe I'd dreamed the night before.

Instead, I found her by the fire, wrapped in a blanket, holding a cup of coffee and staring into the fire. She'd stoked the flames back to life, and they painted her in a warm glow. For a second, I'd just watched, letting myself believe that this was really my life. And it was all real.

Maybe it wasn't a bad thing that she'd slipped away before I could wake up to see her lying there next to me. I needed whatever reminders I could get that this wasn't permanent.

I took a moment to pour myself a cup of coffee and top up Harper's before joining her on the couch in front of the warm fire. She leaned into me, and I wrapped my arm around her, pulling her close.

"So…" I tipped my head toward her. "About last night."

Her face flushed. She bit her bottom lip. "What about it?"

"We got a little carried away, didn't we?" I chuckled a little and took a sip of the hot coffee.

"I don't regret anything, Grayson."

"Good," I said. Her words loosened the knot in my chest. "Neither do I." That was a lie. I regretted the fact that I hadn't told her exactly how I felt. But I'd have to live with that particular regret, because there was no way I was going to tell her that my feelings were far from pretend. It wasn't fair. To either of us.

We sat for another beat. I gestured to the pile of clothes still lying on the floor. "Although, I guess we should address our… well, our lack of planning. Are you…"

"I'm on the Pill," she said. "It's fine."

I relaxed a little more. "Well, I guess this means I'm fully committed to the deception we have going here."

"It would seem so." She laughed. "I hope you know this wasn't some big ploy to get you back into my bed."

"I hope not." I kept my voice light, going along with her teasing. "Because, for the record, there are easier ways to seduce me."

She burst out laughing.

Careful not to spill either of our coffees, I wrapped an arm around her waist and pulled her close to kiss her. "Might as well fully embrace my role, right?"

Harper licked her bottom lip and nodded a little before kissing me back.

Fuck, yes. I'd fully commit to my role as her fake boyfriend for as long as she'd let me. Especially if these were the perks.

I should have left it there, but the words slipped out before I could stop them. "It does make me wonder, though…"

Her brows lifted a little. She pulled back. "Wonder what?"

"What's the end game, Harper? I mean, what's next for you?" I tried to keep the question casual, but there was a weight behind it I couldn't deny. "When the holidays are over, I mean."

Her smile dimmed, and for a moment, she didn't answer. She turned to gaze into the fire as if the flames held the answers. "I don't know yet."

It wasn't a lie, but it also didn't feel like the truth.

Before I could push, she shifted the conversation. "What about you? If Ollie's selling the store, what does that mean for you?"

I rubbed the back of my neck, grounding myself in the somewhat safer topic. "I don't know yet," I said. "There hasn't really been much time to talk to him about it with the Christmas season and…well, everything."

She smiled sympathetically. "So what does that mean for

you? I mean, you've been there for so long and from what I can gather, you already run the place. If he sells…"

I blew out a breath. "Can I tell you something I haven't told anyone else yet?"

"Of course." She turned so she faced me head-on.

"I want to buy it." Saying the words out loud concreted it within me. "I've actually been working on a plan for a while now."

"Really?" Harper lit up with enthusiasm so genuine, I couldn't help but smile. "That's amazing. That would be so perfect for you. What did he say when you told him?"

The smile fell from my face. "I haven't had a chance to tell him yet. It's been…"

"Grayson! What are you waiting for?"

"I told you, it's been so busy."

"No." She shook her head firmly and set her coffee cup down. "This is too important to wait. Text him right now."

"What?"

She tilted her head. "I mean, why are you waiting?"

"Because…well…it's Christmas."

She laughed. "Tomorrow is Christmas Eve," she challenged. "Today is only Christmas Eve Eve. So tell him you want to talk on the twenty-sixth. Let him know you're interested. What's the worst that could happen?"

She had a good point. I shrugged.

"Well…what are you waiting for?"

"Oh. You mean right now?"

Harper laughed. "Right now, Grayson."

I shook my head and pushed up from the couch to go in search of my cell phone. I found it in the back pocket of my pants, still crumpled on the floor, before I rejoined her on the couch.

With a breath, I typed the message before I could talk myself out of it.

Merry Christmas, Ollie. I should have said something earlier, but I'd like to have a serious conversation about me buying the store from you. Please text or give me a call when you can so we can discuss.

"There." I hit Send and sat back. "Happy?"

Her smile widened, and she leaned forward to wrap her arms around my neck. "Very."

As I sank into the familiar warmth of her embrace, I realized that for the first time in a very long time, I was, too.

Chapter 16

CHRISTMAS EVE

Grayson

A day later, and I was still riding the high of my night with Harper. Every time I let my mind drift, I could see her sprawled out in front of the fire, the flames dancing over her glowing, bare skin, her satisfied smile hazy, and her body wrapped around mine.

Every time my phone buzzed, I half expected it to be her, even though what I was really waiting on was a reply from Ollie.

Nothing yet.

Although the old man wasn't known for his prompt replies, and it was Christmas Eve, his silence still made me nervous. I tried to distract myself from worrying about it with more thoughts of Harper.

Her kisses. The feel of her coming undone around me. Her smooth, bare legs sticking out of my shirt as she relaxed on the couch, comfortable in her own skin with me.

The easy way we talked about anything and everything.

Well, *almost* everything. I still didn't know what her plans were for after the holidays. She'd managed to dodge the subject every time it had come up. But that didn't mean she was leaving again. In fact, not once had she talked about a new contract or a job she was going back to.

If I wanted to believe that meant she was staying, that's what I was going to believe.

At least until there was a reason not to.

Even if it made me seem delusional.

I set my phone down and reached for another roll of wrapping paper. The community center gym was alive with chaos. Next to me, there was a stack of gifts ready to be wrapped, tape stuck to tables, kids' names written on tags, and a pile of bows toppling over every time I moved.

My brothers were scattered around the room, recruited by me, each one attempting with varying degrees of success to wrap presents without leaving jagged edges and bald corners.

"That does *not* look like it was wrapped in Santa's toy shop." I took the sloppily wrapped gift from Preston and pulled back the tape in an effort to fix it.

"Who are you, Santa?"

"Actually," I grinned, "I am. At least for a few hours when I deliver all these later tonight to the kids in need, I am."

"Well, I am *not* an elf," Preston said. "In fact, what I really need to be doing is putting together a petition to save the trails."

I shook my head. "Still no luck with that, hey?"

A flicker of guilt hit me. The new development was still a sore spot with Preston, and I'd been so wrapped up in my own stuff and Harper, I'd forgotten to ask him about it.

"No." He gritted his teeth and shook his head. "I've been trying to pin down Jess to find out who exactly this developer fiancé of hers is, but she's not returning my calls. Yet. If she doesn't get back to me soon, I'm going to end up showing up at her house on Christmas morning."

"You are going to do no such thing." I tried to give him my best big brother look. "It's Christmas. I'm sure she's got a lot going on. Wait until after the holidays. It'll work out. But for now..." I shoved a box of LEGO at him. "Work on your wrapping."

I felt for him; I really did. And I respected how much he cared about the trails and Trickle Creek. Where Preston focused on the natural spaces in this town, I spent my energy on the people. Especially at this time of year. Which was why I needed these gifts wrapped. And wrapped properly.

I'd been playing the role of Santa long enough in this town that it was only natural that I'd developed a certain level of standards. All the kids of Trickle Creek deserved perfectly wrapped gifts. Even if they were going to shred the paper in seconds.

"Grayson Lyons, you are a saint."

I didn't even have to look up to know who it was. Sure enough, Tilley Beckett strode toward me, wearing a bright-red, glittery sweater with candy canes embroidered all over it, complete with matching candy cane earrings and, of course, her clipboard.

"I'm not sure about saint." I winked at her. "But you can call me Santa. At least for another few hours."

"Saint Santa." She patted my arm. "Year after year, you show up, put on the suit and hand out gifts, Grayson. And that's after weeks and weeks of stringing lights and hanging half the decorations in this town. I'd say that qualifies for sainthood, don't you?"

I laughed and shook my head. "I appreciate it, Tilley. And I really appreciated the night at the lodge," I added. "It wasn't necessary, but I have to admit, it was very nice."

I wasn't about to tell her exactly how nice it was.

"Oh? You had a good time with Harper then?" Her eyes lit

up. "I heard the two of you took full advantage of everything the lodge has to offer."

My head jerked up. "Where did you hear that?"

"Oh, I have little elves everywhere." She winked. "And I'm so glad to hear it. That girl has been gone from this town far too long. Whatever it takes to get her back here and keep her here, right?"

I tilted my head, ready to question exactly what she meant by that, but then someone called her name from across the room.

"Keep up the good work, Santa." She waved her clipboard in the air before sweeping away.

As soon as she was gone, Reid dropped into a chair beside me, a wide, knowing grin on his face. "So," he wiggled his eyebrows, "how *was* your night at the lodge?"

"Not you too," I groaned.

"Obviously, me too," he said.

"You don't know what you're talking about," I said without looking at him.

"Oh, I think I know exactly what I'm talking about. You've been walking around all day with that stupid grin on your face. The one that tells everyone who's paying attention that you and Harper got—"

"Okay." I whipped around to give him a warning look. "Enough."

There was no point denying it. Not with Reid.

"It was amazing," I admitted quietly.

Reid's eyebrows shot up. "Just like old times?"

"No." I shook my head. My chest tightened, remembering the fumbling sweetness of those early days with Harper. "Better. So much better. It was different. More real."

"Real?" Reid blew out a breath. "Interesting choice of words, brother."

Maybe it was, but there was no way to explain to him how

145

things were with Harper. True, it had all started as a little lie, but that didn't mean the feelings behind it weren't genuine.

When I didn't reply, he added, "So when are you going to stop pretending it's not more?"

I folded the paper over the box and reached for the tape. "What do you mean?"

"I tried to warn you away from all of this." My brother sighed. "But since that clearly isn't going to happen, I'm just going to say one more thing."

"Why do I doubt that?"

He ignored me. "Just shoot your shot, Gray," Reid said. "I mean, we're not kids anymore. What's the worst that could happen? She doesn't feel the same way?"

"No," I said after a moment. "Worse would be telling her, and she leaves again." I yanked a piece of tape from the roll and stuck it down with more force than necessary.

"Right," Reid said. "But what if she stays?" He waited a beat before grabbing a bow and sticking it on the box I'd just wrapped. "Think about it, brother. But nothing changes if nothing changes." He gave me a knowing look, grabbed the present and left, leaving me staring after him.

And thinking.

Because, as much as I hated it. He wasn't wrong.

I'd already put it out there when it came to the store and Ollie. Why not go all in?

Later, when the last gifts were wrapped and stacked and the suit and beard were ready for me to change into, I slipped out of the community hall and headed down the street toward my house.

At home, I went straight for the top drawer of my dresser.

Behind my socks, it was still there. The little velvet box I'd never been able to part with.

Inside, the promise ring glinted in the dim light. Simple silver with a small amethyst stone. I could still see Harper's tears of happiness when I'd given it to her, and then the tears of her heartbreak a year later when she'd hurled it at me after I told her I didn't love her. After I'd told the worst lie of my entire life.

After she'd fled the gym, I'd dropped to my knees and scooped up the ring, unwilling to leave it there.

Now, I turned it over in my fingers, my chest tight.

Maybe it was foolish. Maybe I was setting myself up for even more heartbreak.

But I wasn't eighteen anymore. I'd lied to her once, to make her go and live her dreams. Maybe this time, if I told her the truth, she'd stay?

I put the ring back and snapped the lid shut.

There was only one way to find out.

Harper

THE KITCHEN WAS alive with noise and motion: The scent of sage and butter thick in the air. Pots clattering; steam rising from the stove top. Christmas carols playing from a speaker in the corner. And laughter and easy chatter on top of it all.

Kevin manned the carving station, slicing turkey with laser focus while Erin and two high school volunteers assembled take-out boxes down the line.

Grandma and I worked side by side at the big prep table. We stuffed dinner rolls into bags and scooped cranberry sauce into tiny containers. It felt like the old days, the two of us moving together in rhythm without even trying. It was moments like this as a teenager that made me want to be a chef in the first place. I'd forgotten.

"This reminds me of when you were little," she said, her cheeks pink from the heat of the kitchen. "Always underfoot, stealing cookie dough from the bowl, and wanting to stir the pots."

I laughed. "I still want to taste everything," I said. "But I don't think I'm quite as in the way as I once was." I reached for a finger full of cranberry sauce as she swatted me away with a spoon.

It felt good. Really good.

For the first time in years, I wasn't trying to build a menu among wild guest requests and dietary restrictions, trying to balance in a rocking galley as a boat rode the swells, or trying to source rare ingredients in exotic ports. I was at home, in the kitchen, cooking familiar dishes with my grandma.

And for the first time in a long time, it was enough.

More than enough.

I swallowed, lowering my voice as I reached for another tray. "How do you think it's working out?" I used my head to gesture to Kevin, who was pulling another roast turkey from the oven. "He's pretty great, isn't he?"

Grandma pursed her lips together and nodded. "I have to admit, he's okay."

"Grandma." I rolled my eyes. "He's better than okay."

"He's not you, Harper." She eyed me sharply. "You know you're the best person for this job."

I sucked in a breath. It was the first time she'd said anything directly about me coming back to run the restaurant

I set my spoon down and turned to her. "Grandma, do you want me to move back to Trickle Creek and run the restaurant?"

She hesitated for a second before shaking her head slowly. "I want the only thing I've ever wanted, Harper. For you to be happy."

"That doesn't answer my question."

"You know how proud I am of all you've done with your career."

I nodded. She told me every chance she got how proud of me she was of what I'd achieved.

"This place was never your dream," she continued, a layer of sadness in her voice. "It was mine. And I've loved every minute of running Willa's Whisk. And yes, there was part of me who hoped you'd come back on your own, take over the kitchen and maybe put down some roots in Trickle Creek."

My heart clenched. "Grandma, I didn't say—"

"Speaking of happy." Grandma's voice shifted, and she looked over my shoulder. "There's the happiest baby I've ever seen."

I turned around, spoon in hand, to see Charli, with baby Poppy strapped to her chest, enter the kitchen. Just like always, the baby was grinning and giggling.

"Sorry I'm late. This little one decided she didn't want to put her coat on." Charli shook her head. She lifted the two big bags she was holding. "I have the cookies."

"Thank you, dear." Grandma pointed to the counter. "Set them over there. We'll box them up next."

"I don't believe for one second that this one gave you any trouble at all." I wiped my hands on a towel and reached for the baby, whose grin only got wider. "Let me have her."

"Gladly." Charli unclipped the Snuggly and handed me the baby.

I tucked Poppy against my chest, her tiny hands patting at my chest, her sweet laughter bubbling out. My heart softened instantly.

"See?" I nuzzled her soft hair. "This little sweetie pie was born smiling."

"Don't let her fool you." Charli laughed. "She knows how to work a crowd. But you should see her at three in the morning."

Grandma chuckled, shaking her head. "She reminds me of you at that age, Harper. Always soaking up all the attention."

Charli grinned. "I could see that."

I rolled my eyes and focused on the baby. She really was a doll. I'd never had the baby fever that other women my age spoke about, but then again, I hadn't been around a lot of people having babies in the last few years.

Charli looked so at ease with her little girl, like she was born to be a mother. With her husband and flower shop business, she'd built a solid life in Trickle Creek. I, on the other hand, had been living out of a suitcase for more than a decade, chasing seasons and contracts, never staying anywhere or with anyone long enough to feel like I truly belonged.

Poppy's little fist closed around my finger, squeezing tight, and something twisted in my chest.

"Looks like she likes you," Charli said warmly.

"She's such a cutie."

Charli tilted her head, studying me for a beat. "Feels good, doesn't it? Being back?"

I hesitated, my throat tight. "Yeah," I admitted. "It does."

Her smile was warm as she nodded. "It looks good on you."

"It sure does," Grandma said with a wink as she tickled Poppy's cheek.

I turned to look at Grandma. "The baby or the kitchen?"

"Both, sweetheart." Her eyes gleamed, a little too bright. "But for now, I'll settle for having you back in the kitchen. Now, let's get these dinners packed up before we get too sentimental. There are a lot of seniors and people in need who are waiting for their dinners."

"Okay, okay." A little reluctantly, I handed the baby back to Charli, who strapped her into the carrier.

"Symon will be here to start deliveries in thirty minutes," Charli said. "He said the whole town smells like turkey today."

"Good." Grandma nodded. "That's how it should smell.

We're going to make so many people happy with these dinners."

"You always do, Willa."

Grandma waved away the compliment. "You two keep working here. I'm going to go check on that gravy."

"She insists that she's the only one who can get it just right," I told Charli as Grandma moved to the other side of the kitchen.

The moment she was gone, Charli spun to face me. "Spill, woman. I want all the details."

My face flushed hot. "Details?"

"You and Grayson," she said impatiently. "I mean, I love seeing the two of you together again. *Finally.* But how was the lodge?"

"You heard about that?"

She gave me a look.

"Right." I laughed. "I forget how small this town is sometimes."

"So? How was it? A romantic night away. I bet the two of you needed some alone time." She wiggled her eyebrows, and I groaned. "What does this mean? Like, for the future?"

They were questions I wished I had answers for.

I sighed and put my spoon down. "The lodge was incredible. Every minute of it. As for the future…" I glanced over at Grandma, who fortunately wasn't paying attention. "We're still trying to work it all out. It's complicated."

Thankfully, the ding of the timer, alerting us to the fresh batch of buns done in the oven, distracted us from the question, and we got back to work.

For the next half hour, we worked seamlessly together. Charli filled boxes, with a sleeping baby on her chest, Grandma shifted her attention to the gravy, claiming she was the only one who could get it just right, and I assembled the roasted vegetables. It was noisy, busy, and warm, and for once, it didn't feel like I was trying to keep up with the crazy pace of the rest of the world.

"This is really nice," I said under my breath, mostly to myself.

"What is?" Charli glanced over.

"Being here," I admitted. "Cooking with Grandma. This town. It feels…good."

My old friend gave me a tender smile. "That's because you fit here, Harper. Some things don't change."

Her words stayed with me as we worked. By the time all the dinners were packed and stacked on the counter, I was both exhausted and strangely full, like my chest couldn't hold everything pressing against it.

Or more specifically, the swirl of emotions and conflicting feelings I'd been holding in for far too long.

"Excellent work, everyone." Grandma wiped her hands on her apron. "This might have been our highest number of Christmas dinners yet. We could never have done it without all of your help." Her eyes locked on mine. "*All* of you."

Before I could say anything, a knock sounded at the back door, followed by a rush of cold air.

"Sorry to interrupt." Grayson's deep voice carried into the kitchen. "But I'm here to collect my caroling partner."

My heart tripped in my chest, and I glanced up at the clock over the stove. I'd completely lost track of time

"Did you finish delivering all the presents already, Santa?" Charli asked.

"Hey." He turned to her, as if he'd only just noticed that she was there. "I did. My Santa duties are all finished." He turned back to me. "I'm ready for some caroling. Am I early?"

"No," I said quickly. "Sorry, Gray. I didn't—"

"Go on." Grandma waved me toward the door. "We're all done here. Kevin can close down the kitchen on his own."

"But it's Christmas Eve." I reached for Grandma and held her hands. "Do you want to come with us?"

She laughed. "Oh, sweetheart. No one needs to hear my singing voice. Tilley's going to pick me up to take me to the senior center. I'll see you back home later."

"You're sure?"

"Positive." She gave me a look that brooked no argument. "Besides, I think you've earned a little fun."

Charli's grin was all too knowing. "Go." She winked.

I untied my apron, suddenly hyperaware of the flour on my sweater and the heat still clinging to my cheeks. As I stepped toward the door, Grayson's gaze met mine, warm and steady, reminding me of the way he'd looked at me lying on the rug in front of the fire the night before, and just like that, my pulse was racing all over again.

Grayson

THE LAST VERSE of "We Wish You a Merry Christmas" finally trailed off. The last song in the songbook, I closed it and wrapped my arm around Harper. She snuggled into my side automatically.

"All done?" She looked up at me with a hopeful grin.

"I mean, we could start at the beginning again if you want? Maybe there are some houses over—"

"No!" She grabbed my cheek and turned me back toward her.

I laughed and kissed her. It was getting easier and easier to believe that what we were doing was real. Probably because it felt real. *Very* real.

She melted in my arms, and I would have happily kissed her right there in the middle of the snow-dusted street all night if there hadn't been a smack on my shoulder.

"Okay, you two. Enough already." Brody laughed. "The time for festive cheer is over; you can go get a room."

"Didn't they do that last night?" Lauren appeared over his shoulder and laughed.

Harper pulled out of my arms and slapped the carol book against Brody's chest. "What? Are we in high school again, you guys?"

"I mean, it kind of feels like it, seeing the two of you back together."

"Very funny." I shot Brody a look and reached for Harper's hand, tugging her away from my big brother before he could say anything stupid. Well, even more stupid. "We're out of here."

"Okay, okay." Brody didn't bother to hide his laughter. "See you tomorrow, guys." He looped his arm casually over Lauren's shoulder and steered her in the opposite direction.

Watching them, I couldn't help but think of how easy it could be with the right person. The person who felt like home. Of course, Brody and Lauren continued to insist there was nothing romantic between them, but they didn't see themselves the way we did.

Was that how others saw Harper and me?

When Harper squeezed my hand, bringing me back into the moment, all thoughts of my brother and Lauren vanished, replaced by the one woman who already *did* feel like home for me.

We walked together under the streetlights until we arrived at the back door of the restaurant and her apartment. "Come up," she said. "I want you to see the tree."

The ring weighed heavily in my pocket. I wanted to give it to her. More than anything, I wanted to give it to her and see her reaction. But the words weren't there yet. It hadn't felt right. Not yet.

"I'd love that."

Upstairs, the tree cast the cozy living room in a warm glow. Harper shrugged off her coat and boots. "I'll make us an eggnog."

I shed my own parka and boots by the door and wandered to the tree, inspecting the delicate ornaments when she returned with two glasses.

"The tree looks beautiful, Harper. Willa must love it."

"She does." Even in the dim light, Harper's smile was bright. "I can't thank you enough, Grayson. And not just for the tree. For…" A tear slipped down her cheek, but she wiped it away quickly.

"You don't need to thank me for anything." I led her to the couch. "You know I'd do anything for you, Harper. And for Willa. You don't need to—"

"I know." She stopped me. "But this…you…you've gone above and beyond."

I slipped my arm around her shoulders and pulled her close. "And I've enjoyed every second."

She chuckled and shook her head. "It has been fun."

And then the laughter disappeared, as she tilted her head toward mine.

My hand cupped her cheek, leaning in close.

"Stay," Harper whispered. "Stay tonight."

My chest tightened. I wanted to. More than anything, I wanted to spend another night with Harper. But the sound of the door downstairs and the creaking on the stairs made us both jerk upright.

Willa bustled in, looking more spry than I'd seen her in weeks. Her cheeks were red from the cold, her scarf half undone, as she hummed a carol.

"Don't mind me, you two." She winked in our direction and set her purse on the table. "Pretend I'm not here."

Harper laughed. "How was your night, Grandma? You look like you had fun."

"I'll tell you," Willa started. "The senior center is a lot more fun than you might expect."

"Oh, yeah?" I sat up.

"Absolutely, Grayson." Willa turned to me, the smile brightening her face. "Those ladies know how to have a good time. And the homemade Irish cream that Tilley brought was delicious."

Harper burst out laughing. "Oh, I see. All the *fun* at the senior center is booze fueled."

"Harper Bennett." Willa put her hands on her hips and pretended to look offended. "I'll have you know that there's nothing wrong with having a few festive drinks to celebrate the occasion."

"Oh, Grandma." Harper put her arms around her grandma in a big hug. "You know I'm teasing."

"The real question is, did you bring any of that Irish cream home with you?"

"You know I did, Grayson." Willa winked over Harper's shoulder in my direction. "Are you staying?"

Again, I felt the flash of need, but it didn't feel right. Not yet.

"I want to," I said honestly. "But I think I should probably get home. I promised Quinn I'd make the cinnamon buns for brunch, and I need to get them ready tonight or they won't be raised enough." It wasn't a lie. Traditionally, I had been in charge of the overnight cinnamon buns for our family Christmas brunch. Which was why I'd prepared them before heading out earlier. "But I'll see you both tomorrow afternoon for dinner."

I kissed Willa on the cheek. She gripped my arms and looked me in the eye. "Merry Christmas, Grayson."

"Merry Christmas, Willa."

I slipped away, with Harper following me to the back door. "You're sure you don't want to stay?"

Nothing sounded better than spending the night in a single bed, the love of my life in my arms. Except maybe knowing that it was finally real.

Finally forever.

My hand slipped into my pocket, my fingers wrapping around the ring box.

For forever, I would wait.

"You know I want to." I released the box and pulled her close once more, giving her a sweet, slow kiss. "But it's Christmas. Enjoy it. I'll see you tomorrow."

"Merry Christmas, Grayson."

"Merry Christmas, Harper." I let myself hold her eyes for another moment before I saw myself out the back door and into the night.

Chapter 17

CHRISTMAS DAY

Harper

The scent of coffee and cinnamon filled the air in the apartment, wrapping around me like the warm blanket Grandma had just unwrapped. "It's lovely, sweetheart." She ran her hand over the soft wool. "So cozy and warm. You spoil me."

"The winters are so cold here, you deserve a cozy new blanket. But I hardly think I spoil you."

"I told you not to get me anything, Harper." She pursed her lips in mock disapproval. "I told you that I already got everything I wanted for Christmas this year, having you home." She waved her hand toward the tree. "And this gorgeous tree. I can't think of anything else I could ask for."

I knew exactly what she could, and likely would, ask for. Having me stay in Trickle Creek would be the very best Christmas gift I could give Grandma. We both knew it. What she didn't know was that I'd already made the decision.

I'd woken before dawn to sit by the tree. Enjoying my

coffee in the quiet glow of its lights just like I had when I was a girl and would wake up to see if Santa had visited. Maybe it was the stillness of the morning that had given me clarity, or maybe it was Grayson, or seeing Charli again and holding her baby. Maybe it had been being with Grandma in the restaurant, or more likely, it was a combination of everything that had happened in the last few weeks that had made it easy to see it. But for the first time in as long as I could remember, I yearned for something new.

With confidence, I finally replied to Captain Howard:

> Merry Christmas, Captain. I'm sorry for the late notice, but I'm not going to be able to accept the position this time. Thank you for the opportunity.

I wasn't sure yet exactly what it was going to look like, but I felt in my gut it was time for something new. Maybe something permanent. Something that could include staying a little closer to home.

Before I could attempt to tell Grandma about everything I'd been thinking of, she thrust another package into my hands.

"Grandma. You've already given me so much." I gestured to the small pile of gifts I'd already unwrapped. A homemade scarf with matching mittens and a knit cap, a festive tea blend from Lauren's store, and the new paperback from Plot Twist I'd been wanting to read. "Besides, I thought we said no presents."

In response, she wrapped her new blanket tight around her shoulders. "I'm not giving back my blanket."

I laughed. "Fair enough."

"Besides, this gift is different." She gestured with her chin. "Open it."

Obediently, I tugged the ribbon and pulled back the paper

to reveal a small wooden box, corners worn with age, the lid scuffed from use. "Oh!" My hand flew to my mouth as I stared at the old recipe box that had sat on her counter my entire life.

As a child, I'd spend hours flipping through the cards, reading her handwritten recipes, all with specific notes scrawled along the edges. More recently, I'd pulled out the restaurant favorites to show Kevin.

"This is your—"

"It's *yours* now." Her smile was soft. "Every sauce, every pie crust, soup and salad dressing. It's time you had it, sweetheart. And hopefully, add to it."

My heart squeezed. Tears pooled in the corners of my eyes. "This is...thank you." I put the box down and crossed the couch to hug her. "I love you, Grandma."

"Oh, sweetheart. I love you, too."

When I sat back, a tear slipped down my cheek. "I don't know what to say."

Her hand covered mine. "Say that you'll add your own special recipes to the box," she said firmly. "And when the time is right, I hope you'll pass it to someone else."

I swallowed hard and nodded. "Of course, Grandma."

"Good." Her smile was warm as she sat back in her seat. "That's the only gift I need this Christmas."

I blew out a breath and, with the wooden box still on my lap, I reached over and took her hands in mine. "There's something I want to tell you."

She blinked slowly. "I think I know what this is about."

"Wait." I examined her. "You do?"

She nodded. "I notice more than you think, Harper."

"So, you already know that I've decided to stay?"

Her mouth dropped open, telling me that she didn't know that at all. "You're..."

I nodded, unable to stop the smile from stretching over my face. "I'm staying in Trickle Creek," I said. "I told Captain

Howard I couldn't take the job after all. I'm ready for a change."

Tears pooled in her eyes. "You're staying? Really?"

"I don't know exactly what it looks like yet," I said. "But I'm going to stay."

"Oh, Harper." Grandma pressed a hand to her mouth in an effort to stifle the sob. "This really is the best present I could ask for."

I pulled her into another hug. When we pulled apart, I handed her a tissue to wipe her tears before taking one for myself. "Don't say anything yet, okay? Grayson doesn't know."

"You didn't tell him?"

I shook my head. "I wanted you to be the first to know. And…well, I'm not staying *for* Grayson, Grandma. I'm staying because…" I closed my eyes for a second and blew out a breath. "I'm staying for me," I said when I opened them again. "This is what I want. It feels right."

She pressed her lips together, inhaled deeply, and nodded. "It *does* feel right. And I promise I won't say anything." She mimed the act of zipping her lips and locking them.

She looked so silly, I shook my head, laughing, before I remembered that earlier she'd thought she knew what I was going to tell her. "What did you think I was going to say? Earlier?"

"It doesn't matter." Grandma shrugged innocently. "The only thing that matters is that you're staying. You've given me the best Christmas I can remember."

Her words reminded me of the lie I'd been telling her and the reason why. The smile fell from my face. I dropped my head and looked at the recipe box still in my lap.

I let my hand slide back and forth on the top of the worn wood. "Grandma?" I said after a moment. "I need to know. How bad is it?"

She gave a little laugh, but it was too light. "What, dear?"

I gave her a look, and her smile faltered. "We're not doing this today, Harper."

"Grandma, I—"

She reached out and patted my hand, her voice gentle. "It's Christmas, Harper. We can talk about this later."

I sighed. "You've been saying that since I got here, Grandma. I need to know."

"And you will, sweetheart. Just not today. Today isn't about that. Today is about joy and being together. We have so much to celebrate—even if I'm not allowed to mention it yet," she added quickly. "Besides, we have a very big family dinner to get ready for, don't we?"

The smile returned to her face, and I couldn't bring myself to push any harder. She was right; there'd be time to discuss the details later.

Especially because I had a feeling I wasn't going to like what I heard.

Grayson

BRODY'S KITCHEN was in chaos, which meant it was just like every other holiday I could remember. Ethan stood at the counter, mashing potatoes with a precision and dedication to detail that made Delaney laugh as she pointed out all the nonexistent lumps.

Reid carved the turkey and threatened to stab Preston if he tried one more time to sneak a piece off the tray, and Brody piled fresh buns on a platter.

With nothing left for me to do, I poured myself a beer and leaned back against the counter.

"What do you think of the new brew?" Ethan lifted his head from the pot of potatoes long enough to notice me.

I took a sip and then another. "Honestly?"

He nodded.

"It tastes like the others." I laughed at his resulting scowl, but it was true. "Beer is beer, brother. I can't tell all the minute details like you. But I do know when I like one. And I like this one."

"Good enough." Ethan shook his head and resumed his mashing.

I waited a few minutes, enjoying being around the hustle and bustle of the day, before I raised my voice enough to be heard over the chatter. "So I told Ollie I wanted to buy the store."

The room went quiet for half a beat before Brody said, "It's about time, brother."

"No shit." Ethan grinned.

"You deserve it, Gray." Reid nodded. "That store should have been yours years ago."

"Well, it's not mine yet." I resisted the urge to glance at my phone and my, as of yet, still unanswered text message. "But I have a plan and hopefully I can get the loan I need to make it happen." I left out the part where Ollie hadn't actually responded to me yet. "If all goes to plan, it'll officially be Lyons Hardware in the new year."

"Hell yeah." Preston did a fist pump before taking the opportunity of the distraction to snag some turkey off Reid's platter.

"So I guess you're really here to stay then," Ethan said. "No bailing to travel the world?"

I shook my head and looked between my brothers. "Why would I do that?"

It was Reid who answered. "What about Harper? Is she staying too, then?"

The question hit me harder than I cared to admit.

"I'm not going to lie, man." Brody wiped his hands on a towel. "It's getting pretty hard to see where the fake stuff ends and the real stuff begins." He eyed me. "From where I stand, it all looks pretty damn real."

"He's not wrong," Ethan joined in. "What's going on there?"

Reid didn't say anything. He didn't have to.

I shook my head and looked into my beer. I didn't know how to answer. The truth was, I wanted it all: Harper, the store, the life in Trickle Creek that I'd always dreamed of. The one I'd been pretending to have all month.

But wanting it and knowing how to make it happen were two very different things. My hand drifted to my pocket, brushing up against the small box I'd been carrying around all day. I hadn't said anything to my brothers about it. Especially considering I didn't know what I was going to say to Harper when I gave it to her. Or how she would react.

Before I could answer, the doorbell rang. Moments later, I heard Quinn yell, "Merry Christmas," from the other room.

I put my half-finished beer on the counter and clapped my hands together. "Time for dinner."

Grayson

JUST LIKE EVERY family dinner we had, it was a blur of activity. Only this one was amplified with Christmas cheer. Plates clattered; voices overlapped as dishes were passed back and forth across the table that was made bigger than ever with the addition of Delaney and Avery to the family...along with Harper and Willa, of course.

I couldn't help but hope it was a permanent addition. They both looked like they belonged there. As far as I was concerned, they did. They always had.

And hopefully they always would.

"Harper, tell me about the boat." Quinn had strategically positioned herself right next to Harper at the table and had been peppering her with questions about yacht life since they'd sat down. "How many rooms does it have? Is there a pool?"

Harper laughed as she scooped some mashed potatoes onto her plate. "It depends on the boat," she answered. "But there's usually one big stateroom where the primary guests stay and then two or three other rooms for their guests."

"Wow."

"And of course, there's the staff quarters," Harper continued. "But they're much smaller, and I usually have to share a room with bunks."

"You get to sleep in bunk beds?" Quinn's face lit up. "That's so cool."

Everyone laughed.

"That's the part you think is cool?" Ethan shook his head. "We can get you bunk beds if it'll mean you'll clean your room."

Quinn shot her dad a look and turned back to Harper with more questions.

I only half listened as Harper explained the staff quarters to my niece. I couldn't help but compare the cramped living quarters on a boat to my house a few streets over and the king-sized bed we could share. Maybe I couldn't compete with the exotic locations, but there were other ways I could compensate.

My hand slid to her thigh under the table, and I squeezed, just a little, before once more tuning into the conversation.

"What's the most outrageous thing you ever had to cook for a guest?" Avery asked. "I'm always so curious about guest requests."

"I'm sure they're a little different than the types of requests you get at the inn," Harper said. "And to be honest, they're not actually that outrageous. Most of the time, our guests are pretty basic. They like good food with delicious ingredients."

"Both of which I'm sure you deliver," Ethan said.

She blushed a little. "I do my best. But to be honest, as much as I enjoy challenging myself and creating new and innovative dishes, my favorite things to cook are actually the simple things. Fresh-baked sourdough, or Grandma's French onion soup." She smiled across the table at Willa. "The dishes that remind me of someone I love, or a place I love, are always my favorite and you know what, the guests always love them, too."

"Of course they do," Willa said proudly. "When you cook from your heart, it always shines through."

"You taught me that, Grandma." She held her grandma's eye for a beat before lifting her gaze. When her eyes locked on mine, it felt as if she were speaking directly to me. "Food is about connection. Not just fancy techniques."

I swallowed hard, shifting in my seat.

Brody cleared his throat. "That's what I keep trying to tell this family, Harper. They groan about regular family dinners, but it's about more than the food."

"We love them," I said, not taking my eyes off Harper. "Even if some of us don't love doing the cooking part."

She smiled softly at me. "Hey, not everyone was made to be a chef. Being able to sit, drink wine, and keep the chef company while she cooks is also a very important job."

"And that's why we work so well together." The words slipped from my mouth without even thinking. But I wouldn't have taken them back even if I could, because it was true.

We did work well together.

We always had.

The conversation shifted to other topics—memories of Christmases past, Quinn lobbying for a puppy, Preston complaining about the potential development of his favorite trail system, and everyone talking over one another as the dishes were passed around again for second and third helpings.

And the whole time, the only thing I could think of was how perfect it all was and how I never wanted it to end.

This. Harper. My family.

All of us together.

For the first time, it felt like it was all within reach.

Chapter 18

Harper

It had been way too long since there'd been a Christmas where I wasn't the one in the kitchen cooking for charter guests or high-profile clients instead of family and loved ones. Even longer since I'd had a holiday that I actually got to spend with those loved ones.

I liked it.

A lot.

With dinner over and the dishes cleaned up, the chaos of the feeding frenzy had shifted to a new type of craziness. This time centered around the Lyons's traditional Christmas game of Pictionary. In the living room, Preston and Reid were arguing over a drawing that could have either been a horse or a fireman, and Quinn loudly challenged her dad's addition skills when it came to the score while everyone else sat back, laughed, and shook their heads.

I'd settled Grandma into a chair in the corner with her new blanket when she insisted she wanted to stay and enjoy all the games, even though she looked like she might fall asleep at any moment.

I almost got sucked into the drawing debate when Grayson caught my eye from the hallway and gestured for me to follow him out to the porch.

Outside, the cool air was a welcome contrast to the heat of the house. He wrapped a heavy fleece blanket around my shoulders and pulled me in for a quick hug.

"This was nice," I said against his chest. I breathed deep and settled into his arms. "*Is* nice. Your family hasn't changed a bit."

He pulled back and raised an eyebrow until I laughed.

"Okay, obviously, some things have changed. Quinn is an excellent addition."

"She is."

"And Avery and Delaney are amazing, too."

"They really are," Grayson agreed. "I'm actually surprised Lauren isn't here, but I can't keep up with whatever's happening with those two."

"Your mom doesn't come up for the holidays anymore?"

Grayson shook his head. "She doesn't come back to Trickle Creek for much these days." His voice held a thread of disappointment. "But she's happy down south," he continued. "She has a full life, and her arthritis is so much better in the heat. Hopefully she'll come up this summer when Delaney and Ethan's baby is due."

"That would be nice." I let myself get pulled back into his arms. "Being with family is so important." It was something I was feeling more and more.

Grayson turned me in his arms, so I was pressed up against his back and could look out onto the snow-covered yard. The soft glow of the Christmas lights strung above the porch cast a colorful display of light onto the snowflakes that fell lazily from the sky. I leaned my head back against his chest with a contented sigh.

"This is the best Christmas I've had in a very long time," I confessed after a moment.

"Really? It beats out a sunny, beach holiday?"

"In every single way."

Behind me, Grayson shifted, his arm moving to his pocket. I turned to see him produce a box from his pocket. My heart leapt into my throat in a moment of panic.

"Grayson, what—"

"Don't worry." He laughed. "It's not like that. Just a little Christmas gift."

Some of the panic receded. "But I didn't get you anything. I didn't even think about—"

"Harper." He stopped me with a shake of his head before lifting the lid of the box to reveal a simple silver ring.

I knew that ring.

There was nothing flashy about it. A simple stone in a silver band with a deep-purple amethyst.

I remembered the night he gave it to me. We were seventeen, full of love and hope. Grayson had promised me forever that night, and I'd promised it right back with my whole heart.

Just as clearly, I remembered pulling the ring off my finger and throwing it at him the night we broke up, hot tears blurring my vision, my heart shattering into a million pieces. I remembered the ring bouncing on the gym floor before skittering away, a painful symbol of everything I'd just lost.

"You kept it," I whispered.

"I did." His voice was low and rough. "Of course I did."

My throat tightened, my heart stumbling over itself. These last few weeks with him had been so nice, but we'd never talked about the elephant in the room. We'd never addressed the fact that he'd broken my heart. "But, why?" I tore my gaze away from the ring to look him in the eye. "Why would you keep it after…after that?"

He blew out a slow breath, his eyes never leaving mine. "Because when I told you I didn't love you, I lied."

My heart stuttered.

"I knew that if I didn't let you go—no, push you away, you would have stayed in Trickle Creek."

"I wouldn't have—"

"You would have." He cut me off. "We both know that's true."

I closed my mouth and nodded. He was right.

"The truth is, Harper, I loved you too much to let you stay for me. You deserved to chase your dreams and live the life you were meant to live. And I knew, even then, that wasn't in a small town with a small-town boy."

My heart broke all over again. Deep down, I think I always knew why Grayson had done what he'd done. Maybe selfishly, I didn't want to face it because by not admitting the truth to myself, it was easier to let myself leave. Because as much as I loved him, and I did, going to culinary school in Paris was my dream, too.

"And it worked." He shrugged. "You left. And the things you've accomplished…" He shook his head, his eyes bright with pride. "I wouldn't change what I did. But I couldn't let go of this." His eyes dropped to the ring again, and mine followed. "This has always been yours."

The tears pricked at my eyes before I could stop them. My hand trembled as he lifted the ring from the box and pressed it into my palm. It felt heavier than a thin silver band should, like all the years between us were weighing down on us.

"Grayson…" My voice broke, and I had to clear my throat. "These last few weeks…this Christmas…being with you, it's been…" I shook my head and laughed a little at my inability to find the words to tell him my news. "It's been the best month…

can you believe it's only been a month?" I shook my head in disbelief before continuing. "But it's been the best I can remember in a very long time."

His jaw tightened at my confession. "Harper, I—"

"There you two are." We both jumped back to see Grandma in the doorway, already bundled in her coat. "I think I'm ready to head home."

Grayson straightened and tucked the ring box into his pocket before she could see. "I'll grab my keys." His voice was steady, but I caught the flicker of something in his eyes before he turned away.

I closed my fingers around the ring, my chest aching with everything left unsaid.

"I'll go say goodbye." Grandma went back inside, leaving me alone on the porch.

I opened my hand and looked down at the ring still resting in my palm. My chest squeezed, but it was no longer uncomfortable.

My heart thudded as I turned it over once, twice, and then slid it onto my finger. It fit perfectly, as if it had never been gone.

Chapter 19

Grayson

I carried the empty pie plates and containers of leftover turkey dinner Brody had packed up for Willa, up the stairs and set everything in the kitchen while Harper helped her grandmother off with her coat. My eyes were pulled to the Christmas tree in the corner of the warm apartment.

It really was the perfect tree.

"Grayson." Willa clasped my hands. "Thank you for everything. It was a lovely day."

I pulled her in for a little hug and pressed a kiss to her cheek. "Thank you for bringing the pies, Willa. I'm not sure how we all found room, but they were absolutely delicious as usual."

She waved her hand in dismissal. "Everything was absolutely scrumptious. I very much appreciate the invite. Now, don't disappear on my account. There's more of that homemade Irish cream in the fridge; you must try it."

"I don't think I could say no to that," I told her.

"Good." She gave me an over-the-top wink before turning to Harper. "It was the perfect day, dear. Merry Christmas."

"Merry Christmas, Grandma. Sleep well."

We waited until Willa disappeared into her room, the door clicking softly behind her.

Harper shook her head with a little smile. "You really want some Irish cream?"

"You know I do." I pretended to be shocked. All I really wanted was Harper. It wasn't a secret anymore.

Harper disappeared into the kitchen for a few minutes before returning with two glasses. The sweet scent of the cream mixed with the whiskey reached my nose as she handed me a glass.

"To Christmas."

"To Christmas," I echoed, my eyes lingering on her as we clinked our glasses together.

We settled on the couch, the tree lights reflecting in her hair and our glasses on the table in front of us.

She curled her legs under her and pulled her hair back from her head, using an elastic that seemed to come out of nowhere to tie it back in a thick ponytail. It was then that I saw it.

The ring.

The amethyst caught the light, making it sparkle much brighter than it was. Or maybe it was the fact that it was finally back on Harper's hand where it belonged that made it shine?

I caught her hand in mine and held it for a moment, unsure what to say. Unsure what it meant. I bent my head and slowly pressed a kiss to her finger. "It looks good."

She smiled a little and opened and closed her fingers, taking a moment to look at it. "It's been a while," she said. "I can't believe it still fits."

"Like you never took it off."

"But I did." Her smile dipped as she looked up at me. "I

can't believe you…" The words faded away, and her gaze dropped.

I knew what she was thinking about. It was the same moment I replayed in my mind so many times over the years. The second my eighteen-year-old mouth had uttered the words that broke both of our hearts. I hadn't thought I was capable of it. But my love for her was strong enough to do the unthinkable.

"You know why I did it." It wasn't a question. I wrapped my fingers around her hand, unwilling to let her pull away again. "A part of you always knew." Again, it wasn't a question, but she nodded, confirming what I already knew.

She was quiet for a moment. "Not at first, of course." Her voice was soft. "I was just so hurt after that night. I needed to get as far away from here and you as I could. I begged Grandma to let me leave early. I couldn't face being here and seeing you…"

My heart clenched.

"For the first few weeks after I got to Paris, all I did was cry, and then I got mad," she said. "I was so mad at you, Grayson. I couldn't understand why you would throw us away so easily."

It had been anything but easy, but I kept my mouth shut and let her finish.

"Once classes started and I lost myself in the lessons, the anger faded. I started feeling like myself again and then, more like myself than I ever had in my life. I went to cook and create, and at that school I discovered that part of myself."

It hurt to hear that she'd found herself without me. But wasn't that what I'd always wanted for her?

"It was only then that I really allowed myself to think about why you'd done it," she continued. "I didn't let myself think about it too much because it still hurt." When she looked up at me, I could see that pain reflected in her eyes. "But yes, part of me always knew that you'd done it for me. So I'd go."

Maybe I should have been glad to hear her admission. Knowing that she hadn't spent the last fifteen years hating me for what I'd done to her—to us. Instead, it made me sad.

I lifted her hand and threaded my fingers through hers. "I'm sorry," I said after a moment. "The last thing I ever wanted to do was hurt you." I swallowed hard. "But I'd do it again if it meant you would have the incredible career you've had."

Before she could say anything or refute what I'd just admitted, I cupped her face in both my hands, looked deep into the eyes I'd memorized for my entire life, and kissed her.

When I finally pulled back, just enough to breathe, I whispered against her lips, "Harper, I don't think I can pretend anymore."

Her answer was a kiss of her own, fiercer this time as she pulled me down on top of her against the cushions.

Harper

THE GLOW-IN-THE-DARK STARS on the ceiling of my childhood bedroom blurred overhead as Grayson's mouth moved over my body.

We'd been here before, in my single bed with stuffed animals on the shelf above us. Trying to be as quiet as we could while we fumbled our way through the feelings we couldn't quite make sense of.

This was different. And somehow it was different from our night in the lodge, too. It was…more.

So. Much. More.

The knowledge of that both scared me and urged me forward.

The mattress dipped beneath his weight, his mouth hot on mine, and all at once, I needed more.

I tugged his shirt over his head, my palms skimming the hard planes of his chest, pulling him back up to me so I could once more feel his lips on mine.

I broke the kiss long enough to breathe, my forehead pressed against his. "I was so mad at you," I confessed. "For so long. Maybe even still. It wasn't your call to end us, Grayson."

He stilled, his breath catching. His thumb brushed my cheek, tender even as his body trembled above mine. "I know," he said. "I'm sorry, Harper. But I meant it when I said I'd do it again. I'd endure that a thousand times over if letting you go meant you would chase your dreams."

A lump rose in my throat. "It did," I said softly. "But it didn't stop me from wanting you."

Whatever control he had left snapped. His mouth crashed back to mine, hungry and desperate, his hands sliding under my sweater, tugging it up and off me until I was bare to him. The heat of his skin against mine made me arch into him. My need for him overwhelmed me.

"I never stopped wanting you," Grayson breathed. His mouth closed over my nipple; a low, primal moan slipped from my throat. "Never stopped wanting *this*."

His hands skimmed lower, down my body, while his mouth sucked and teased, driving me crazy. When his fingers slipped between my thighs, I cried out, quickly muffling the sound with the pillow. His fingers stroked slowly, insistently, until my hips lifted from the bed.

"God, Harper," he groaned against my skin. "You're so damn perfect, muffin."

My heart caught, and I stilled at the use of the nickname he'd coined when we were kids. He was the only one I'd ever let use it. What had started as a joke had quickly morphed into an intimate pet name. Hearing it now did something to me.

"Gray."

He was there in a flash. His mouth hovered over mine, his

hand still between my legs, still slowly stroking, building the fire inside me as he waited to see what I'd say next. But the words wouldn't come. I opened and closed my mouth, unable to say what I wanted to. What I *needed* to.

Instead, I reached up, wrapped my hand behind his neck, and, looking into his eyes, whispered, "I need you."

He let out a low growl that let me know he felt the same. His mouth once more collided with mine, as he slipped a finger between my folds at the same time that his thumb found my clit. He pressed with just enough pressure for me to fall apart completely.

I clutched at his shoulders, breathless. Above me, the stars spun in wild constellations as the waves of my climax crashed through me.

And when he slid into me, slow and deep, filling me completely, I buried my face in his neck as I moaned his name, every part of me sparking to life.

We moved together. Not rushed, not frantic. But steady and sure, as if we had all the time in the world. Every thrust, every kiss, each whispered word carried the weight of all the time we'd lost, and everything we'd found again.

The fire that had always been there between us as teenagers flared back to life in an undeniable blaze, tempered only by the years we'd spent apart, and the ache of knowing what it felt like to lose each other.

And when I shuddered around him again, his name once more on my lips, I knew with terrifying certainty that this wasn't just sex. It was love.

It always had been.

Only now, I was home.

Grayson

HARPER WAS CURLED half on top of me in her tiny childhood bed, her chest pressed to my chest, her breath evening out with each passing second. Her hair had slipped from her ponytail, lying in a dark mass of tangles over her back.

My arm wrapped around her waist, holding her close as if she might slip away if I let go.

"You're quiet," she murmured, her voice thick with sleep.

"Just thinking about how damn lucky I am right now, muffin," I whispered, using the pet name I'd given her in high school after she baked me a batch of lemon poppy seed muffins for my birthday.

"It's been a long time since you've called me that."

I stroked her hair slowly. "Is that okay?"

She nodded against my chest, not lifting her head. "Very okay."

My smile took over my face as her body relaxed against mine, a soft hum of contentment slipping from her lips. She was asleep in moments, but I refused to close my eyes.

It had been the perfect Christmas, and I wasn't ready for it to end. I would happily freeze time to keep Harper asleep in my arms forever.

The buzz on the nightstand broke the silence. I looked over to see her cell phone light up, the screen glowing bright in the dark room. I glanced down, meaning to ignore it, until I saw the name.

Captain Howard.

My chest tightened.

The preview line glared back at me:

> Good news. The charter is starting early.
> Anchors up on New Year's Eve. Having you
> aboard...

The words might as well have been a knife to my heart. I

forced myself to look away as the light from her phone faded to black again. I focused on Harper instead. Her lips parted slightly, her hand still resting over my heart. She looked like she belonged there.

But the message I'd just seen echoed in my head.

She hadn't promised me anything. We'd talked about the past, but not the future. This whole thing…*us*…it had always been temporary. It was for Willa. For Christmas only.

Of course she was still going to leave. Her life was out there. On boats, in exotic locations. Not in a small town in the middle of the Canadian Rockies. She was always destined for more than the small-town life I offered.

Why would I think that had changed?

The old wound cracked open, the same pain I'd felt all those years ago tearing through me again. Only this time it was worse, because I knew damn well what it felt like to let her go. To lose her.

And I didn't have a clue how I would survive it a second time.

Chapter 20

Grayson

I woke before the sun, Harper still tangled in the sheets, half on top of me. For a long moment, I watched her sleep, memorizing the way her chest rose and fell with each gentle breath, the peaceful look on her face.

Trying not to wake her, I slipped quietly out of the bed and padded barefoot into the kitchen to start a pot of coffee. A big part of me wanted to grab my things and take off into the cold morning before she could wake up and break my heart all over.

I'd lain awake for hours after seeing the message from her captain, trying to decide what to do, and ultimately, I'd decided that we weren't kids anymore. I'd made the assumption once before that there wasn't room enough in her life for me and for following her dreams. I wasn't going to make that mistake again. No more assumptions.

This time around, I was going to talk to Harper like the adults we were, and together we'd figure things out. And they had to work out because the alternative was no longer an option.

The familiar routine of measuring the coffee grounds calmed me. At least I still had the store, I told myself. I was confident in my business plan. Once I finally had a chance to discuss it with Ollie, he'd think so, too.

I needed to focus on the things I could control. And at least for the moment, that was the store. It had been the one constant thing in my life for so long, the thing I'd been successful at when everything else felt like it was falling apart; I had the hardware store to throw myself into. And that's exactly what I'd done. There was a reason the store had become so much more successful in the last few years after Ollie had stepped back. I knew he saw it, too.

And once it was mine officially, then I would really have—

My phone vibrated in my pocket, pulling my attention.

Right on cue. Relief washed over me when I saw Ollie's name on the screen.

I took a breath and pressed the button to accept the call. "Merry Christmas, Ollie." I tried to sound steadier than I felt.

"Grayson. I'm sorry I didn't return your message sooner. You know how I feel about text messages."

I shook my head with a small smile.

"And with the holidays and everything, it's been a bit busy around here for the last few days."

"I can imagine," I said. "I'm sure those grandchildren of yours are a lot of fun during the holidays."

"And loud," he said gruffly, but I could hear the smile in his voice. "It's taken me this long to find a quiet second to return your call."

I swallowed hard and leaned back against the counter. "Well, I'm glad you did, Ollie. I've been wanting to talk to you about your plans for the store and throw my hat in the ring to—"

"About that." He cut me off. "I wanted to give you a heads-up about what's going on."

It was about time, although I didn't bother saying that.

"Everything's happened quite quickly," Ollie went on. "I wasn't even thinking about selling, to be honest. I mean, things seemed to be running pretty well on their own, and I haven't felt a need to step inside the store in months. It all seemed pretty good, ya know?"

I did know. There was a reason things were running so well. I knew he didn't intentionally miss the fact that I was the one who kept things ticking along so smoothly, but still, it stung.

"But when opportunity knocks, you don't ignore it, ya know what I'm saying?"

"Not really, Ollie," I said honestly. "Did someone approach you?" A sliver of doubt started to creep in as I worked to decipher exactly what Ollie was telling me.

"Oh yeah, I guess I left that part out."

"You did." I tried not to sound frustrated. "What was the opportunity?"

"Homeworks," he said simply.

And with one word, I felt my dreams start to slip away. I still stood in the kitchen, but I could no longer feel my feet. Blackness crept in around the edges of my vision.

Unaware, Ollie kept talking. "You know the franchise, right? It's pretty big, and they saw potential in my little store."

Of course they did.

"When I showed them those numbers you ran for me a few weeks ago, that pretty much clinched it. They were impressed that a little, small-town, independent store like ours could be pulling those kinds of numbers without corporate backing. They made me an offer a few days ago."

And just like that, the bottom fell out of whatever hope I had left. "They..." I cleared my throat. "They made you an offer?"

"Sure did. A damn good one, too."

Right. I would never be able to compete with an offer from a major franchise. Sure, I had a business plan and a savings account to take to the bank for a loan. But there was no chance in hell my offer could come anywhere close to what they could do.

It was over.

"Grayson? You still there?"

I blinked and tried to focus. "Yeah," I said, not recognizing my voice. "I'm still here. What were you saying?"

"I was just saying that when I got your message the other night, I was surprised. I didn't even realize you were interested in the store."

"I tried to mention it the other day," I said. "When you told me you'd decided to sell. Of course, I had no idea Homeworks was interested."

"You did? I really am sorry, Grayson. I didn't even—"

"You didn't even suspect that I might want to talk about it?" I scrubbed my hand over my face, trying in vain to hang on to some level of composure before it all crumbled away. "Really? After all these—" I stopped myself. There was no point burning a bridge because I was upset. Instead, I swallowed hard. "Yeah. I was… No, I *am* interested, Ollie. That store's been a big part of my life and…a franchise? Really?"

"I'm sorry, Grayson. I didn't realize you were interested in buying. All these years, you never said anything."

I'd assumed he knew. All the extra hours I'd put in. The unpaid time on weekends and holidays. The research into new products and services that we'd brought in. But I'd never *said* anything. That was on me.

"I wish you'd said something," Ollie continued. "They've made a strong offer, and if I'm being honest…well…I'm getting older, and the security this can give me…well, it matters."

"Of course it does," I managed.

There was a beat of silence on the other end before he spoke again. "I'm sorry, Grayson. I really didn't know. I didn't even think…but well, maybe they'll keep you on as a manager or something."

He kept talking, something about how nothing was finalized yet, how maybe we could sit down after the holidays and figure things out. But the words barely registered.

"Yeah. Maybe." The sound of the bedroom door told me Harper was awake. "Listen, Ollie, I've got to go. Happy holidays."

I hung up before I had to hear any more. I'd already heard enough. The life I'd let myself imagine for even the slightest moment—my name on the hardware store sign, Harper in my arms, building a life together—it all shattered with a brief phone call.

It was over.

I'd just dropped the phone on the counter when Harper walked into the kitchen. She'd pulled an oversized sweatshirt and shorts on, but her dark hair was still loose in half-tangled, very sexy waves that cascaded over her shoulders.

"Hey there." She cocked a hip and leaned against the doorjamb, looking so damn kissable that it took all my restraint not to close the distance between us.

"Sorry if I woke you. Coffee?"

"I'd rather have you back in bed with me."

Her words were like a knife to my heart. I wanted to be back in her bed, too. Before I'd seen the text from her captain, before the phone call with Ollie. Before I'd learned that I was about to lose everything.

Again.

How could I ask her to stay or even discuss the alternatives with me when I no longer had anything to offer her? She deserved so much more than a small-town life with a man who'd just let the biggest opportunity of his life slip away because, once again, he hadn't *said* anything.

I turned away, busying myself with the coffee so she couldn't see my face and the pain that was no doubt written all over it.

I was losing everything.

And this time, I wasn't sure how I'd be able to survive it, but I sure as hell wasn't going to take her down with me.

Harper

SOMETHING WAS WRONG.

I'd felt it the moment I'd woken up to a cold bed. He was gone. My heart sank, but only until I heard his voice in the kitchen and the warm, rich scent of fresh coffee hit me.

I took a moment to lie in bed, remembering the night before, spinning the silver ring on my finger, letting myself bask in the type of happiness that had eluded me for so many years before joining Grayson in the kitchen.

"Hey there." I leaned against the doorway, waiting for him to look up. The second he did, I saw it. Something *was* wrong.

"Sorry if I woke you. Coffee?"

I shook my head and tried to keep my voice light despite the fear creeping up my spine. "I'd rather have you back in bed with me."

He squeezed his eyes shut and turned away, confirming what I already knew.

"Gray?" I closed the distance between us and reached out, fingers brushing his arm. He flinched, just a little, but I saw it. I felt it. "What's going on?"

"You should probably start packing, huh?" His voice was flat. He didn't turn around.

My stomach dropped, the icy fear crawling over my scalp. "What are you talking about?"

"The holidays are over." Still, he didn't turn.

"That doesn't—"

"I saw the message." He finally looked at me, and the distance in his eyes made my chest ache.

"Message? I haven't seen my phone—"

"Congratulations. I guess you're heading for the Med."

What?

It took me a second to process, and then the heat rushed to my cheeks as I realized what might have happened. "Oh no. I haven't—"

He gave a sharp shrug, already retreating. "You know what? It doesn't matter." He shook his head, and my heart cracked at the coldness of his expression. "You don't owe me an explanation, do you?"

"It's not—"

"This is what you want." He cut me off. "It always has been."

I stared at him, my chest tightening. "Grayson. That's not at all—"

"Don't." His voice cracked slightly before he cleared his throat. He looked away, back to the counter. "Don't make this any harder."

"Make *what* any harder?"

The silence stretched between us, sharp and jagged. I wanted to reach him, to shake him, make him see the truth. But he'd already pulled away from me. He'd retreated behind the walls I was so sure we'd broken down.

Before I could find the words to get through to him, to tell him the truth, that I'd turned down the job and I was going to stay in Trickle Creek, Grandma's door creaked open and she joined us in the little kitchen.

"Morning, you two," Grandma said, a huge grin on her

face. "It's nice to see you here this morning, Grayson. The coffee smells delicious."

To his credit, Grayson straightened instantly, his expression smoothing into something unreadable and exceedingly polite. "Good morning, Willa." He pressed a quick kiss to her cheek. "I was actually just heading out. There's something I need to take care of." He grabbed his coat from the hook by the door before I could stop him. "I'll see you later."

And just like that, he was gone, and I was left wondering what the hell had just happened.

I reached for the counter to steady myself, my heart pounding while Grandma stared at me, questions in her eyes that I couldn't answer.

I closed my hand into a fist, feeling the thin metal of the ring press into my finger while doubt gnawed at me. Had I been wrong about Grayson? About staying? About everything?

Chapter 21

Harper

The card blurred in front of me, Grandma's neat handwriting swimming across the faded old index card. I'd been staring at all the cards for over half an hour, trying to decide what dish I wanted to tackle first. Which ones I might want to make my own, and those that needed to be preserved because they were already perfect.

I'd made a few little piles, but nothing stuck. I'd shuffled and reshuffled most of the cards more times than I could count. I couldn't focus on anything. My thoughts wouldn't settle.

I'd gone over and over things with Grayson the morning after Christmas, and I still couldn't make sense of any of it. Yes, I understood what he *thought* he knew. After he left, I saw the text from Captain Howard.

> Good news. The charter is starting early. Anchors up on New Year's Eve. Having you aboard would make this season complete. Let me know if you change your mind.

It didn't take much to figure out that Grayson had seen part of the text and had assumed the worst.

What I couldn't figure out was why he wouldn't have talked to me about it. Why had he been so cold and distant toward me, and why, after everything, would he assume that I could just leave without looking back?

With a frustrated sigh, I set the box aside and rubbed my temples.

In the days since Christmas, Trickle Creek had experienced a cold snap, and there hadn't been much in the way of foot traffic in the plaza or shoppers milling about. Everyone was hunkered down at home or in their rental accommodations with cups of hot chocolate and roaring fires to keep them warm.

Which was why a flash of movement outside the frosted window caught my attention.

Grayson.

He was bundled up in a parka with a knit toque, his broad shoulders bent beneath the weight of a stack of folding chairs, his breath visible in the icy air. I watched while he dropped the chairs near the gazebo and the half-assembled stage that was being built for the New Year's celebration.

He turned to pick up another load, his jaw tight, the scowl noticeable even from a distance. I didn't miss the way he avoided looking at the restaurant.

Enough was enough.

I shoved back from the table, grabbed my coat off the rack by the door, and stepped out into the cold. "Grayson!"

He froze for half a second, then kept moving. He'd been avoiding me for days. Leaving my texts unread, my calls unanswered. I'd had more than enough.

My breath puffed out sharply in front of me as I marched across the icy plaza. "Don't you dare ignore me, Grayson

Lyons." I planted myself in his path, giving him no option but to stop or bump into me.

"What do you want, Harper?"

His expression was unreadable, guarded in a way that sent a chill through me, in a way that not even the subzero temperatures outside could.

"I'm busy."

"That's bullshit and you know it." I swallowed hard, trying to steady my voice. "You've been avoiding me. Pretending nothing's wrong. You owe me more than that."

His laugh was short and sharp, nothing like the warm sound I loved. "I don't owe you anything."

The words cut deep. "What the hell is that supposed to mean?"

"You know what it means."

"No." I wrapped my coat tighter around me and crossed my arms. "I don't."

"You already know I saw the message," he said. "The captain. Anchors up, Harper." He held up his hands in a mockery of air quotes and sneered. "Congratulations. You got everything you always wanted."

I didn't know this version of Grayson. This cold, closed-off version. And I didn't like it.

"You didn't even let me—"

"Explain?" He cut me off with a sharp shake of his head. "Don't bother. You've always wanted more than this. I can't believe I thought that this time I might actually be enough for you. But you know what? I'm done standing here like a fool waiting for you to figure it out, Harper. I'm done."

His words hit me like a slap, stealing my breath and my words.

"Leave." He waved a gloved hand, dismissing me when I didn't speak. "You always do."

The plaza spun around me. "You're such an ass," I said finally.

"Whatever." His voice was flat. Final. "Like I said, I'm done."

I stared at him. The man I'd loved my entire life. Even when I tried not to, there was always only Grayson. Looking at him, I saw the same walls he'd put up all those years ago, felt the same ache. History was repeating itself in the cruelest way. Only worse, because I'd let myself believe that this time it might be different. My throat burned. "If you're so sure that I was just going to leave like that, then you don't know me as well as you think you do."

"I guess not."

"Screw you, Grayson."

My hand trembled as I yanked the ring from my finger. Again. With tears stinging my eyes and freezing on my cheeks, I hurled it at his chest. Again.

"Keep it this time."

Grayson didn't even move his hands to try to catch it. I watched as it bounced off his chest and hit the snow at his feet.

I looked up at his cold stare one last time. My chin trembled, but I wouldn't give him the satisfaction of seeing me cry.

I spun on my heel and, boots crunching hard in the snow, stormed back across the plaza to the warmth of the restaurant.

I didn't turn around. What was the point?

Grayson

THE WIND CUT through my coat as I hauled another board toward the half-built stage. My fingers were stiff inside my gloves and my breath came in harsh puffs of icy air, but it didn't matter. I welcomed the sting of the cold, the distraction of the repetitive work, anything to drown out Harper's voice in my head and the look in her eyes when she threw the ring back at me.

I squeezed my eyes shut for a moment before shaking it off again. It wasn't worth it. The heartache, the drama…I couldn't do it again. Not when she was so clearly not in it with me. And she wasn't. Not if she could leave so easily, without so much as a word to me about it.

No.

Not again. Harper wasn't my future. She never was, and it was long past time I realized that and moved the fuck on.

"Hey."

I jerked my head up to see Quinn standing over me, bundled in a purple coat with a matching purple knitted toque with a sparkly pom-pom that was nearly as big as her head attached to the top.

"Hey, kiddo. What are you doing out here? It's freezing."

She shrugged. "I saw you and…well…here." She thrust out a mittened hand. "I think this belongs to you."

The ring.

The sight of it hit me square in the chest.

After Harper had thrown it, I'd let it bounce into the snow, unwilling to go in search of it a second time. I may be a slow learner, but I did learn. Eventually.

"That's not mine." I turned away from my niece and picked up the hammer again.

"Yes, it is," she said with the confidence only a thirteen-year-old could have. "Or it's Harper's, but either way—"

"Quinn," I snapped. "Not now. I'm busy."

She didn't move. "You don't have to bite my head off, Uncle Gray. I was just trying to help. I thought you might want it before some kid finds it and thinks they struck gold." She thrust her hand in front of my face.

"Quinn," I growled, and swatted her hand away. "Drop it, okay?"

The moment the words came out of my mouth, I regretted them. I rocked back on my heels and looked at my niece.

Her eyes were narrowed into slits, her lips pressed tight. "You don't have to be such a jerk, Uncle Gray. I was just trying to help. Because I saw you and Harper, and it looked important." She set the ring on a folding chair with exaggerated care. "Next time I'll let the random kids fight over it."

Before I could apologize, she spun around and took off, running toward the brewery.

"Quinn," I called after her, but it was too late. "Fuck."

I shook my head and made a note to take my niece a hot chocolate with extra marshmallows from the Bean Bag when I was finished. She was right; I didn't have to be such a jerk. Not to her.

I clapped my hands together in an effort to bring back some feeling and continued with my work. The only way the stage was going to be ready for the plaza New Year's celebration was if I did it. Just like everything else around town that fell on my shoulders. It didn't seem to matter whether I wanted to do it or not; somehow, I was always volunteered for whatever task Tilley could think up.

I didn't usually mind, and it was true that I needed the distraction from the fact that my life had just totally blown up; still, it pissed me off, just like everything else had since I'd walked out of Harper's apartment on Boxing Day.

I swung the hammer, harder than necessary, and missed the nail I'd been aiming for, cursing as I lined it up again.

"Is that making you feel better?" Ethan's voice came from behind me. "Or was it being an asshole to my daughter that helped?"

Fuck.

I lowered the hammer and turned around to see my brother, arms crossed over his chest, glaring at me. Before I could speak, he continued.

"Whatever the hell is going on with you, Quinn didn't deserve that. You don't get to take your shit out on my kid just because you can't seem to figure your life out."

Heat rushed up my neck—part shame, part anger. Before I could get a word out, Reid appeared next to Ethan.

"Why don't you let me take this one?" He clapped our brother on the shoulder. "I've got this." My twin turned back to me, his expression like steel.

Ethan muttered something under his breath and stalked away, leaving me with Reid.

I shook my head and moved to turn back to my work. "Look, I know Quinn didn't deserve that. I was an asshole, and I'm going to make it up to her. I just—"

"What the hell is going on?" Reid interrupted me. "You're not usually such a dick. That's my job. And Quinn said she saw you and Harper fighting. Something about a ring."

"I don't want to talk about it."

Reid shook his head with a humorless laugh. "I knew it."

"Here it comes," I said flatly.

"You're damn right, here it comes," Reid shot back. "You knew this was going to happen the second you let her back into your life. The second you agreed to pretend to be something with her, that you never quit being in your mind."

His words hit way too close to home.

"I'm not doing this with you right now, Reid."

"The fuck you aren't." He grabbed my shoulder, spinning me around as I tried to turn away. "Let me guess, you forgot the whole thing was only for show and now she's going back—"

"Yes!" I yelled. "Happy now? I let myself fall in love with her again…or maybe I never quit…" I shook my head for a moment before looking at my brother again. "And yes, she's leaving again. She took a job and sets sail on New Year's Eve. Fool me twice and all that shit."

I dropped the hammer on the half-built stage and blew out a breath, out of steam after my outburst.

"And you're just going to let her go?" Reid said simply. "Without a fight? Just like last time, huh? How'd that work out for you?"

Frustration and rage bubbled up inside me. They weren't feelings I was used to, especially aimed at my twin brother, but I'd had just about enough of the interrogation. Nothing was going to change this. Not this time.

"It's not the same thing, Reid."

"You're right." He nodded smugly. "You're not kids anymore. Now you have something to offer her. A life. Stability. A future."

"Wrong," I snapped, the words burning out of me before I could stop them. "I don't have a damn thing to offer her. Ollie's selling the store to a fucking franchise. It's gone. Every single thing I worked for, everything I planned, everything I thought I could have—it's over. So yeah, I don't have a single fucking thing to offer her. Why shouldn't she leave?"

The silence that followed my outburst filled the cold air around us. Reid stared at me, his mouth pressed into a line as he assessed me.

"You're an idiot," he said finally.

"You're right," I agreed. "I was an idiot to believe that this town, that I…could ever be enough for her."

"No," Reid said pointedly. "You're an idiot because it's not about any of that. None of that stuff matters."

I moved to speak, but he stopped me. "You love her," Reid continued. "And she loves you. *That's* all that matters. And you're still going to throw it away because you're too damn stubborn to believe that's enough. That *you're* enough?"

"Get out of my face," I growled.

He held my gaze for a long moment, then shook his head. "Fine. But you know as well as I do that if you let yourself make the same mistake twice, you'll regret it for the rest of your life." He turned and walked off, leaving me alone with my thoughts.

As soon as he was out of sight, all the fight drained out of me. I sank down on the edge of the stage, my breath fogging the air. My eyes landed on the ring, still sitting on the chair where Quinn had left it.

For a long moment, I stared at it. My gut twisted with guilt and regret as I contemplated what to do with it. I should leave it for someone else to find. Or throw it as far as I could to get it out of my sight.

Ultimately, I pulled my glove off, reached out, and closed my fingers around the cold metal.

Harper was gone. The store was gone.

Some things weren't meant to last.

It was time I accepted that.

Chapter 22

Harper

The kitchen smelled like roasted garlic and simmering stock, the kind of warm, comforting scent that never failed to anchor me. Kevin was at the stove, coaxing sauce through a sieve with careful precision, while I finished plating the risotto we'd been experimenting with together.

"This is really good, Kevin." I lifted the spoon to my lips for another taste. "You've really got something here."

"You mean *we* have something here." He joined me at the counter and picked up a spoon of his own. "This was a joint effort, and you know it." He took a bite. "But damn, you're right. It's spot-on."

We each allowed ourselves another bite before Kevin took the plate out to the dining room for Erin to try. "You know," he said when he returned, "I did enjoy the collaboration with you today, but I want to make sure you don't think I *need* the interference." He wiped his hands on the towel tied to his apron. "Are you happy with what I'm doing here so far, Harper?"

"Oh, yes." I set my knife down and looked up at him. "I'm sorry if I gave you any other impression, Kevin. You've been great. The way you've jumped in and handled things has been amazing. And you are really talented." I stopped myself just short of gushing, aware that I didn't want to overdo the praise. Truthfully, he was doing a fantastic job, but I was self-aware enough to see how he might feel a bit micromanaged in the last few days.

"That's good to hear." He nodded and smiled at me. "I just wanted to be sure."

"I know I've been around the kitchen a little more in the last few days, but I promise, it has nothing to do with the job you've been doing. And everything to do with…" I stopped myself from oversharing. I didn't expect that my fight with Grayson was a secret, especially considering we'd had it in pretty as much as public a place as possible. But secret or not, I didn't feel like rehashing anything with Kevin.

Or anyone.

"I've just had a few things to work out," I said instead, letting him fill in the blanks. "And I don't know about you, but the kitchen has always been a soothing place for me."

"I get that." He nodded. "A good kitchen will have that effect, and this is a very good kitchen."

He was right about that. It was a *very* good kitchen. I'd spent the last few days immersing myself in the routine of chopping, stirring, and creating, and it *was* making me feel better. At least until I left my apron behind and returned to the real world. As soon as I stepped beyond the swinging doors, reality—and the pain of everything that came with it—rushed back.

"Truthfully, Kevin, I've actually decided that I'll be staying in town a little bit longer." I spoke the words in a rush before I could change my mind. "I don't want you to think that means there won't be a job here for you. Quite the opposite, really.

But I know I told you that I'd be leaving and you'd have free run of things here."

"It's fine." He laughed and held up his hand. "In fact, I think it's great that you're staying."

"You do?" I tilted my head and examined him closely, but there was no sign of insincerity.

"Really. You being here lifts everyone," he said. "I've really noticed it. The staff, the customers…Willa. You bring a good vibe, Harper. I think it's great if you're staying longer."

I swallowed hard, trying to absorb his easy acceptance when I still hadn't fully reconciled it for myself. "We'll see how it goes."

"You are going to stay?"

I turned to see that Grandma had slipped into the kitchen behind me. Her scarf in her hands, her purse hanging off her arm, she watched me in that quiet, knowing way of hers. The way that always made me feel like she could read every thought I was trying to hide.

"I told you that at Christmas, Grandma." I walked to her and led her to the chair in the corner by the prep table. "Don't tell me you forgot?" Alarm bells sounded in my brain. Was she starting to forget on top of everything else?

"I remember." She swatted me away and set her purse on the table. "I just wasn't sure if you'd changed your mind after everything that happened."

I tipped my head and examined her.

"Don't stay because you think you owe me something, Harper," she continued. "Stay for yourself, if you stay at all."

"Why wouldn't I stay?"

"I think I'm going to go see how Erin liked that risotto," I heard Kevin say from behind me before slipping out the door, leaving Grandma and me alone.

"Why wouldn't I stay, Grandma?" I asked her again. My

chest tightened around the knot that never seemed to fully go away these days.

Her gaze softened. "I saw the fight in the plaza, Harper. Everyone did. Or they heard about it."

Heat rose to my cheeks, shame mingling with grief. Of course she'd seen it. I wasn't surprised. Not really. Only that she hadn't said anything until now. She'd let me sit with sadness for the last few days while I tried to work it out for myself. "I'm sorry, Grandma. I didn't mean for that—"

"Nonsense." She waved away my apology. "Don't worry about what people saw. It doesn't matter. What matters is—"

"No." I stopped her. "I'm sorry because I lied to you." I blew out a heavy breath. It was long past time I confessed the truth. "Grayson and me. It was never real. I convinced him to pretend that we were back together for the holidays. I knew how happy it would make you if you thought that I was...well, it doesn't matter. It was a stupid idea and I never should have lied to you like that." I looked into her eyes, but they gave nothing away.

After a moment, she frowned, disappointment threading through the lines of her face. "Why would you do that, Harper?"

"You said you were sick and..."

"And you wanted me to have one last happy Christmas before I kicked the bucket."

It wasn't a question; still, I nodded. "I guess I just didn't want you to worry about me."

She dropped her gaze for a moment. "No," she said finally. "I don't believe that." Before I could open my mouth to object, she continued. "I don't believe you'd put yourself and him through such an elaborate lie if there wasn't at least a part of you that wanted it to be more."

Her words pierced straight through me.

"Besides," she said. "You're not a good liar. You never were."

The lift in her voice stopped me. "Excuse me?"

"And as far as acting goes, Harper..." She clucked her tongue. "It's not your strength."

My mouth fell open. "So, what you're saying is that you *knew* we were pretending the whole time?"

"I didn't say that," she said matter-of-factly. "But I'm also not saying that."

I blinked, trying to make sense of what she *was* saying. But she continued before I could follow up.

"What I'm saying is that I don't think you've been acting at all." She reached across the table and took my hand in hers. "Not about how you feel about him."

I shook my head, fighting the sting in my eyes. Her simple assessment was so accurate, it threatened to undo me. "It doesn't matter now anyway," I said quickly. "Whatever it was, it's over. I...he..." I waved my hand in the air. "I'm staying, though," I added. "That's what matters now. So, don't worry. I'll find a way to be happy here. In the kitchen, without..."

"Harper." Grandma squeezed my hand. "This isn't your burden to carry," she said softly. "You know I want you to stay, if that's what *you* want. You can make this place your own, whatever you want that to look like. But if it's not what you want, we'll let it go. Life is too short to be spent chasing the wrong dream."

My throat tightened. I wanted to tell her that I'd already learned that, but the words stuck in my throat. Instead, I nodded and muttered, "Thank you, Grandma."

She gave me one more smile and pushed up from her seat, adjusting the scarf around her neck and hooking her purse over her arm again.

"Are you going out?"

"Don't you worry about me," she said. "I have a few errands to do this afternoon."

"Let me grab my coat. I'll—"

"No, no." She waved me off. "I've already got someone lined up to take me. I know you have other things to worry about."

"Let me guess." I forced a smile of my own. "Tilley?"

"Try not to work too hard." Grandma ignored my question. "I'll see you later, dear."

And then she was gone, leaving me in the warm kitchen with the weight of her words echoing in my head.

I'd been so focused on helping Grandma keep what she had that I'd never considered the possibility of turning Willa's Whisk into something new. Something *mine*.

But as I looked around the familiar kitchen, for the first time, I saw it in a different light. One that sent a spark of excitement through me.

Grayson

I NEVER SHOULD HAVE AGREED to this.

Of all the things I could be doing with my time, playing chauffeur to Harper's grandma was not exactly at the top of my list. Not when every second in Willa's company reminded me sharply of her granddaughter.

But the truth was, I never could say no to Willa Bennett.

Or anyone in this town, really.

I held open the passenger door as she settled into the seat.

"Such a gentleman," Willa said with a grin.

I certainly didn't feel like a gentleman as I closed the door gently and moved around to the driver's seat.

"Your vehicle is always so clean," Willa commented as soon

as I pulled out of the parking spot. "You know, I'd say that you really are Trickle Creek's best Uber driver, Grayson."

Despite myself, I smiled and shook my head. "I'm pretty sure Uber drivers get paid, Willa."

We both knew I wasn't about to accept any payment from her, or anyone else. Of course, if the new owners of the hardware store brought in their own management, I'd be without a job, and maybe driving the elderly around town would soon become more than just a volunteer activity.

"No need to frown, Grayson," Willa said, easily detecting the shift in my mood. "I'll be sure to give you a generous tip or recommend another thank-you gift from the festival committee."

The playful tone in her voice caught me by surprise. I whipped my head around and narrowed my eyes in question. "What are you talking about? Did you have something to do with the gift certificate for the lodge, Willa?"

She shrugged innocently, but there was nothing innocent about the sly little smile on her lips.

"Willa."

"Grayson." She pressed her lips together and spoke firmly. "There's nothing wrong with giving a valuable volunteer a generous thank-you gift," she said. "Besides, I thought maybe the two of you could use a little alone time during such a busy season."

My heart squeezed and immediately steeled. "You didn't have to do that, Willa," I said through gritted teeth.

"I know." She turned to face out the windshield again. "You know, you've always been the dependable one, Grayson. Always the first to show up. To fix things. To volunteer whenever anyone needed a helping hand."

I shrugged, my hands tightening on the wheel. "Someone has to."

"Sure." Her voice was warmer now, but sharper too. "But when does somebody show up for you?"

The shift in conversation took me off guard. I glanced over at her. "Pardon me?"

"I mean it," Willa continued, as if I hadn't questioned her. "When do you get to let yourself want something?"

My chest clenched. I didn't have an answer, not one I could share with her, anyway. I couldn't tell Harper's grandmother that I *had* allowed myself to want something. Some*one*. And it had just left me with a broken heart. So what was the point?

But I couldn't say any of that, especially considering she must know that Harper and I had *broken up* or had a fight or whatever it was we were supposed to call it.

Instead, I said nothing, staring at the road, gripping the wheel harder as I navigated the streets through town.

The silence stretched between us until I pulled up at the front of the library. Willa gathered her purse, but hesitated before she opened the door. I was about to hop out and open the door for her, but she stopped me with a gentle touch on my arm.

"You know, Grayson, you deserve more than just being the man who makes everyone else's life easier," she said softly. "I hope you realize that before it's too late."

And then she was gone, walking carefully toward the entrance, leaving me alone with my thoughts while she browsed the shelves.

I leaned back against the seat, staring through the windshield without really seeing the snowy street in front of me.

She wasn't wrong. Not entirely. But she wasn't right either.

I *had* let myself want for something.

Harper.

It was always Harper. It had always been Harper I wanted. But where had that gotten me?

It always ended the same way. With her walking away and leaving me alone, wanting.

And the store. I'd wanted that, too.

I blew out a rough breath, shaking my head.

Wanting had already cost me too much.

And now, there wasn't anything left to lose.

Chapter 23

Harper

The lunch rush had slowed to a lull, the dining room quiet except for the soft clink of cutlery from the last table of regulars in the corner. It was only our third day of offering lunch again, and already it seemed to be a hit with the locals who, as it turned out, had missed it.

I was stacking menus when the door swung open and Charli breezed in, her cheeks flushed from the cold. My friend looked different, and it took me a minute to realize it was because her baby wasn't strapped to her chest. Instead, she had a giant tote bag slung over her arm.

"Hey." She greeted me with a wave, crossing the dining room to give me a big hug. "How are you?"

I tilted my head in question, but the look on her face told me that she'd already heard the news. Not that I was surprised; the whole town had likely heard. Maybe even people in the town over.

"No Poppy today?" I ignored her question.

"She's hanging out with her Auntie Kat today. I'm doing

inventory at the store," Charli said. "This is a super slow time for me. All the Christmas arrangements are done, and I have a few weeks before the Valentine's Day rush, so it's a good time to take stock. So I thought I'd treat myself to a little takeout lunch order."

Charli's shop, Alpenglow, offered up a combination of fresh flower arrangements and everlasting dried pieces, too. But the window box and shop displays she'd done for almost every store in the plaza had been the real success, and the reason all our businesses looked so good year-round. She worked hard, especially now that she had a baby.

"I think lunch is the least you deserve," I told her. "Please tell me you ordered a piece of Grandma's apple pie for dessert?" When she shrugged, I shook my head. "I'll pop one in for you. Let me go grab it from the kitchen."

"Harper, wait." She stopped me. "You didn't answer my question."

"What was that?" I turned.

"How are you?" she asked again. "I heard. About the plaza, the other day."

My stomach dropped, but I nodded. "Good news travels fast."

Charli tilted her head. "I think it was pretty hard not to notice," she said. "From what Kat told me, there was yelling, and you threw a ring at him."

Wow. I was going to need to remember that there were eyes everywhere in Trickle Creek. I shook my head and blew out a breath.

"She said it looked like more than a little spat," Charli continued. "I just wanted to check to see...well..."

"I'm fine," I lied. I did my best to put a bright smile on my face, calling on my years of customer service. "Why wouldn't I be?"

Charli pressed her lips into a thin line and stepped toward

me. "Harper. I know we haven't seen each other much, or at all, in the last few years, but we're friends. You can talk to me. It's okay."

I exhaled slowly, and the all too familiar feel of tears burned in my eyes. When was the last time I'd had a friend to confide in? A *good* friend? Living and working on charter boats didn't really lend itself to making long-lasting friendships. It was such a transient career that as soon as you built any kind of relationship with someone, it was time to move on. I'd made a few friends, but none that I would feel comfortable talking to about relationship issues. None as close a friend as I'd been with Charli once upon a time.

"Can I tell you something?"

She nodded. "You know you can."

I led us both to an empty table at the far end of the dining room. She shrugged out of her coat and dropped her tote bag on the floor. "The thing with Grayson," I started as soon as we were settled. "It wasn't real."

She screwed up her nose. "What do you mean, it wasn't real? The fight?"

"No." I shook my head, suddenly feeling awful for lying to everyone. And for having such a stupid idea in the first place. "Oddly enough, *that* was real. In a weird way. Because the thing is, the rest of it, the whole," I used air quotes, "*relationship*. It wasn't real. I asked Grayson to pretend that we were back together again for the holiday. For Grandma."

Charli shook her head slowly, clearly trying to make sense of what I was saying. I couldn't blame her. Hearing it out loud made it sound even more ridiculous than it already was. "So, you're telling me that you weren't really dating all this time?"

I shrugged and nodded at the same time. "Grandma told me she was sick, and then once I got home, and she saw me talking to Grayson again, and she was so happy, I don't know…I just kind of panicked, I guess. It's dumb, I know. But I wanted her to have a really happy holiday in case it was her last… Well, I just wanted it to be a good one."

Charli nodded slowly. "So, you're trying to tell me that it was all fake?"

I nodded again.

She inhaled slowly through her nose and sat back in her chair, leveling her gaze on me. After a moment, she said, "Bullshit."

I sat back, stunned. "Excuse me?"

"Bullshit," she said again. "You're forgetting that I saw the two of you together on multiple occasions, and more than that, I knew you both back in the day. And I saw the way you were then, too."

"Uh, huh. But—"

"You weren't faking it," she said matter-of-factly. "There's no way that was fake."

"It was." It hurt more than I cared to admit, but it was the truth. The only reason Grayson agreed to be my fake boyfriend was for Grandma. "He was just doing me a favor."

"Because Grayson Lyons would do anything for you."

It wasn't a question. Still, I nodded.

"Because he's in love with you," Charli said. "He always has been, Harper. And he always will be. You know that."

I opened my mouth to deny it, but closed it again. There was a time, not too long ago, when I might have agreed with her. But she hadn't heard the awful things he'd said to me, or the cold look in his eyes when he'd said them. That wasn't love.

"Nothing about what I witnessed for the last few weeks was fake." Charli shook her head. "I don't buy it."

I blinked at her. "Why not?"

"Because," she leaned in, "neither of you are a good enough actor to fake the way you both looked at each other. Especially when you didn't think anyone was watching." Her voice was steady, her gaze locked on mine. "I know you two," she continued. "But even if I didn't, I would have been able to see the love radiating from both of you. Besides," she sat back and crossed her arms over her chest, "from the way I hear it, the fight in the middle of the plaza was pretty passionate, and I don't think you can have that kind of passion without love."

Her words struck me in the chest.

"Look, Harper." Her tone softened. "I don't know what the fight was about, or why you seem to think that what is, and always has been, love between the two of you isn't all of a sudden. But what I do know is that life doesn't always give us a second chance, and when it does, you need to grab onto it with both hands. Because if you don't, you could be missing out on the best thing to ever happen to you. Trust me."

Not long ago, Charli and Symon had their own second chance, and it had led to them being happily married, with the cutest baby ever. She knew what she was talking about.

But I wasn't Charli.

It wasn't the same.

"I don't want to overstep any more than I already have," Charli said. "But something tells me that what the two of you have is probably worth another try. I know Grayson has a lot going on right now, with the store being sold and all."

"He was going to make Ollie an offer," I told her. "Of course, I haven't heard how—

"Oh." Charli's face fell. "I thought maybe you knew," she said. "You know how news travels in this town."

"Knew what?" Worry knotted low in my gut.

"Ollie decided to sell the hardware store to a franchise," she said simply. "Word on the street is that Gray's pretty upset about it. You didn't know?"

I shook my head, stunned. "No." My heart hurt for Grayson. He'd put so much of his life into the store; it was so much a part of him. "He must be—"

"Devastated?" she finished for me. "Not himself?"

I nodded.

Charli's smile was warm as she gathered her coat and tote bag. "I should probably grab my lunch and get going," she said. "But whatever you decide to do, Harper, I hope you remember that you guys aren't kids anymore. Don't let history repeat itself when it doesn't have to. You can tell him how you feel this time. Don't let him push you away."

Grayson

AFTER THE LIBRARY, Willa had a few more stops she wanted me to make. Dutifully, I drove her to the grocery store, waited by the curb while she picked up a few items, and then made the short drive across town to the senior center.

The car was quiet except for the crunch of the tires on the snow and the gentle hum of the radio. Willa sat beside me, her shopping bag tucked neatly at her feet, her gloved hands folded in her lap.

We hadn't spoken much since the library, so it took me off guard when she spoke up. "I see the way you look at her."

My hands tightened on the steering wheel. "It doesn't matter," I muttered. "It wasn't real."

I wasn't sure whether she knew the truth or not, and despite the hurt I was feeling, I felt guilty for the lie we'd told Willa. And the bigger lie I'd been telling myself the entire time. Because it had been real for me. Every single second.

"Yes," Willa said simply. "It was. And before you try to tell me about the stupid arrangement the two of you had to fool me, let me be the one to tell you that I know about it. And I also know that whatever you're trying to convince yourself of, it was real. It *is* real."

I sucked in a breath. It shouldn't surprise me that Willa knew the truth. Harper would have told her after…well, after our very real fight in the plaza. That was, if she hadn't figured it out already. Not much got past Willa. "Real or not, it still doesn't matter," I said after a moment. "She's leaving."

"Would that make a difference?"

Her question took me off guard.

"That's not a fair question."

"It sure is." Willa's voice was firm. "Would it make a difference in how you felt about my granddaughter if she were staying?"

I inhaled slowly. I couldn't even let myself entertain the thought. I'd already gone over it a thousand ways. In all outcomes, I got hurt.

Again.

"It doesn't matter, Willa. Because she's leaving."

"No." Her voice was calm but sure. "She's not."

I turned my head, certain I'd misheard her. "What?"

"She's not leaving," Willa said. "She turned down the job."

My foot slipped off the gas pedal. It took me a second, but I refocused, sure I hadn't heard Willa properly. "She turned down the job?"

Next to me, she nodded. "The yacht. The head chef's job. The Mediterranean. All of it."

For a moment, I forgot how to breathe. My chest was so tight, it hurt. "But…I thought…I mean, I saw…" I shook my head clear.

"Whatever you think you know, Grayson," Willa tilted her head and gave me the side eye, "there's never a time when it's not worth having the conversation instead of assuming."

Willa's words sank deep, bumping up against all the things I hadn't asked Harper. All the things I'd been too afraid to hear, so I stayed quiet.

My mind worked overtime to make sense of what Willa was saying. Finally, I said, "So she decided she couldn't leave you again. I know she's been so worried about you and—"

"Grayson." Willa's voice was firm. "I think you know me well enough to know I would never let my granddaughter make such a major life decision because of *me*. And I think you know Harper well enough to know that as much as she might worry about me, that is not why she made this choice."

Was it for me?

I knew instinctively that even if I played a role in Harper's decision, there was more to it than that.

Unable to focus on the road, I pulled over and put the car in park, resting my hands on the steering wheel.

"Look at me."

I turned to see Willa's smile curving gently, but knowing.

"She's not staying for me. And she's not staying for you. I think you already know that."

I nodded.

"I'm sure both of us had something to do with her decision," Willa continued. "This is about her. And what she wants." Her eyes softened as she watched me. "But that doesn't mean you can't be part of that."

I swallowed hard and turned my gaze back to the dashboard.

"I've said it before, Grayson. You've spent far too long making sure that everyone around you has what they need. It's okay to want something for yourself." Her tone was maternal, but firm. "It's okay to choose yourself *and* her."

I didn't hesitate. "I do choose her, Willa. I always have."

She gave me a look that told me she didn't believe me. "Have you ever told her that?"

"Of course I—no." The realization hit me hard.

Over and over, I'd wanted Harper. I'd *chosen* her. But when my back was up against the wall, every single time, I pushed her away before she could do it first because I was a fool, thinking that it would hurt less that way.

And I'd done it again. Instead of fighting for her and telling her exactly how I felt, once more, I'd pushed her away.

I dropped my head and swallowed hard.

I'd been such an idiot.

And this time it might have cost me everything.

She didn't rush me, but when I finally looked up, Willa was watching me carefully. "It's not too late, Grayson. If you truly do choose her, I think it's long past time you tell her that, don't you?"

Chapter 24

NEW YEAR'S EVE

Harper

The kitchen had been a blur of activity for the last few days. When Kevin came to me with the idea of creating a New Year's feast, I'd been hesitant at first. But only because of the short timeline. Could I pull together impressive dishes in only a few days? Even with Kevin's talented help, it would be tough. And if we could do it, could we sell the tickets to make it worthwhile?

It turned out that the answer to both questions was—yes.

I'd pushed myself harder than I had in a long time, coming up with just the right dishes that would be accessible to locals and tourists alike, but still impress. Kevin was an incredible help, and it turned out we made an amazing team.

Once word got out, every plate and every table was sold out within hours. And after long days and even longer nights, every customer walked away raving about the food and stuffed full.

For the first time, I didn't feel like I was borrowing Grandma's dream. I was building my own.

And it felt good.

Really good.

But with dinner service over, and our customers all heading out into the cold night to join in the New Year's Eve celebrations in the plaza, my stomach was once more in knots. I'd managed to focus on the feast and making sure every detail turned out perfectly, but that didn't mean that thoughts of Grayson still didn't sneak into the quiet moments.

And even the loud ones.

The truth was, thoughts of Grayson were never far away, and that wasn't likely to change anytime soon. Which meant I needed to find him and talk to him, no matter what the outcome was.

I left Kevin and our part-time staff to handle the cleanup and stepped out into the bustle of the plaza.

Our fight, and his words, still hurt. Every time I closed my eyes, I could see the look on his face and how closed-off he was before hearing anything I had to say. If he didn't want me, I knew it would sting. But I'd survive.

And the one thing I knew for sure: I couldn't let another year roll over without saying exactly what I should have said years ago.

The plaza was alive with music and laughter. People were everywhere: gathered around the fire pits, surrounding the vendor stalls, or dancing in front of the stage to the live band. I had to admit, Trickle Creek really did know how to throw a party.

I scanned the crowd as best I could, standing on my tiptoes in an effort to see above the throngs of people. I spotted a handful of people I recognized, including Reid, Avery, Brody, and Lauren, gathered in front of Ethan's beer booth. Grayson had to be around somewhere.

He'd been in charge of building the stage, and there was no doubt in my mind that Tilley had him doing all kinds of other things, too. He was always around, fixing something or helping in some way. Of course he'd be there. But every time I caught a glimpse of him, it turned out to be someone else.

I'd worked my way all the way to the edge of the stage, and there was still no sign of him.

"Harper!"

I turned to see Tilley bustling toward me, her clipboard clutched tight to her chest, and sparkly gold star earrings swinging.

"I've been looking for Grayson everywhere," she said. "It's almost midnight, and I need someone to make the announcements before the countdown."

My heart twisted. "Sorry, Tilley. I'm looking for him, too."

"Well, as soon as you—"

"No." I stopped her, the words tumbling out before I could second-guess them. "Grayson's done enough for you. I need him more than you tonight."

The older woman's brows shot up, surprise flicking across her face. Then, just as quickly, her expression softened and a smile curved her lips.

"Fine." She shoved the clipboard toward me. "Then you can make the announcements."

"Excuse me?" I backed away, shaking my head.

"You heard me."

"No. I don't do public speaking. And I need to—"

"You'll be fine." She gave me a gentle push toward the stage. "Besides, just like you said, he's already done enough for me. It's about time you helped out, too." I opened my mouth to protest, but she cut me off. "Besides, you'll have a better view of the crowd from up there."

It was annoying. But she wasn't wrong.

Besides, it didn't look like I had much choice.

Tilley was remarkably strong for a woman her age. With

another shove, I stumbled halfway onto the stage, catching myself right before interrupting the band.

I glanced backward one more time, but Tilley simply gave me a thumbs-up and grinned.

A moment later, the band finished their song. A roar of appreciation went up from the crowd, and Tilley urged me on from the wings. "Go," she said. "You don't have much time."

I blew out a breath, and with my hands shaking, I stepped out on stage, the lights momentarily blinding me. There were some shouts from the crowd, and I heard my name a few times, but I focused on the microphone that the band leader held out for me.

"Thank you," I mouthed and gave the singer a nod before turning toward the crowd.

"Uh...hi," I started, my voice sounding too thin over the speakers, echoing back at me. A ripple of polite laughter moved through the crowd. My eyes focused on the clipboard in front of me. I worked hard to ignore the fact that everyone's eyes were on me. I preferred to be behind the scenes. I always had. Public speaking had never come easily to me. "Okay... so...um...I have a few things to say." I blew out a breath that made a loud, obnoxious noise through the microphone.

I squeezed my eyes closed for a second, and when I reopened them, I had fresh determination. "A big thank-you to the band," I said, reading off Tilley's list. "They have another set still, right after the New Year countdown, but before we get to that...don't forget to visit our vendor booths." I waved in the direction of the booths. "And of course, a big thank-you to all our volunteers who help make these events possible."

There was another cheer from the crowd.

I stuttered through the rest of my bullet points, my throat dry and my nerves completely shredded. And then I glanced up—

Grayson.

He stood at the back of the crowd, his dark gaze locked on me like I was the only one there.

Something in me steadied.

My fingers loosened a little on the clipboard, and I let it fall to my side. The rest of the words I was supposed to say evaporated. What came out instead was the truth.

"In case you didn't know…" My voice trembled. "I'm not leaving."

The crowd erupted into more cheers and whistles, no doubt thinking it was part of the announcements. I swallowed hard and pressed on, my eyes never leaving Grayson.

"I came back to Trickle Creek for my grandma, but somewhere along the way, I realized that my being here was about more than just her. It was about me. This town…this place…" My throat tightened, but I forced the words out. "It's a part of me. It always has been. I know that now, more than ever. And *you*, Grayson Lyons…"

The plaza went still. The cheers faded into a stunned hush, but I only half noticed.

I drew in a shaky breath, my voice dropping lower, meant only for him despite the fact that I still held the microphone and the entire town could hear me clearly. "I love you. I never stopped."

Grayson

"I LOVE YOU. I NEVER STOPPED."

Her voice carried across the plaza, soft but sure, slicing straight through the buzz of the crowd and directly to my heart.

For a second, I couldn't move. I couldn't breathe. All I could do was stand frozen in place for what felt like forever, but was probably only seconds.

Even from a distance, I could see her close her eyes for a moment and drop her head, like she wasn't sure I'd come to her or turn away. Like maybe she was bracing herself for me to do what I'd done before: run.

But not this time.

Not again.

I'd let her go. More than once. Hell, I'd pushed her away. And now, she was on the stage, with the entire town watching, telling me what I'd been waiting years to hear.

Exactly what I should have told her years ago.

My legs finally obeyed, carrying me forward into the crowd that magically parted as I moved past. I vaguely noticed as neighbors and friends slapped me on the shoulder, wished me well and called words of encouragement as I moved across the plaza to my girl.

My girl.

Harper.

She always had been, and she always would be, my girl.

My love.

My life.

She'd stopped talking and simply held the microphone, her eyes locked on mine as I reached the edge of the small stage. I didn't bother with the stairs. I hauled myself up onto the structure, breathless, with the entire town roaring their encouragement behind me.

"I've been looking for you all night," I said, my voice raw and low, just for her, but carrying over the speakers anyway. I reached for her free hand, pulling her close.

"You found me."

I certainly did. "You beat me to it."

"To what?"

"You think you're the only one with something to say tonight?"

Shouts of encouragement rang out from the crowd behind

us. Harper tensed. I squeezed her hand to keep her focus on me, where it belonged, not on the crowd hanging on our every word. I remembered how she never liked to be the center of attention. Too late for that now.

"Harper Bennett," I continued, "I love you." Such simple words, but they meant everything. "In fact, I can't remember a time in my life when you weren't the first thing I think about in the morning, and the last thing I think about before I fall asleep. You have all the minutes in between, too."

Her eyes softened and glistened with unshed tears.

"Losing you once almost destroyed me, and while I might be a slow learner sometimes, I'm not going to make that mistake again. I can't. Because, no matter where in the world you are, or where you want to be, I want to be there with you. Forever."

Her breath hitched, but I wasn't done. "Harper, I am madly, desperately in love with you and no matter how much time or space there is between us, that will never change. You're it for me. You're mine. You always have been."

The crowd cheered but it was merely background noise, because this was only for her.

Tears slipped down her cheek, but she didn't bother to wipe them away. "Grayson, I—"

"*Ten!*"

The countdown chant began.

Stunned, I half turned to see the projector screen at the back of the stage displaying the New Year's countdown.

"Tell me I'm yours, too."

"*Nine…*"

Harper nodded. "You know I am."

"*Eight…*"

"I always have been."

I knew it to be true. Part of me had always known it. But hearing it from her mouth hit different.

"*Seven…*"

I released her hand long enough to reach into my pocket. My fingers wrapped around the silver ring I'd been carrying with me for the last few days.

"*Six…*"

Her breath caught when she saw it glisten in the stage lights.

It wasn't just a ring. It was *her* ring.

"*Five…*"

Her hand trembled as I pulled her mittens off and slid the ring on her finger, where it belonged.

"*Four…*"

"This time I'm asking you to keep it."

"*Three…*"

Her smile wrecked me.

"*Two…*"

"Forever, Grayson."

"*One! Happy New Year.*"

Fireworks exploded above us, the crowd erupting with cheers and celebration for the new year—or for us. I didn't know. And I didn't care.

The only thing that mattered was Harper. I kissed her under the exploding sky, confident in whatever the new year would bring as long as I had the love of my life in my arms, exactly where she had always belonged.

Harper

THE TINY AMETHYST sparkled like a five-carat diamond on my finger as Grayson led me out of the spotlight. Finally. I'd never spent so much time on a stage in my life. Let alone during one of the most emotional moments of my life.

"Better?" he asked the second he'd handed the microphone

back to the lead singer and we'd retreated safely down the stage steps.

"So much." I smiled with relief and let him pull me into his arms again. "For so many reasons." When I tilted my head up to look at him, my heart swelled.

This was real.

This was mine.

Grayson was mine.

Finally and forever.

I reached up to cup his cheek, cool from the cold, and pulled him down to my lips.

When I opened my eyes again, the world had carried on around us. The band had started playing again, the crowd was singing and celebrating, and Grayson was still looking at me as if I were the only person there.

"Finally!" Tilley Beckett appeared from nowhere, her clipboard once more in her hand.

I belatedly remembered dropping it on the stage at some point, but like a boomerang, it had found its way back to her.

"I knew it!" she declared. "I don't care what the two of you said about it being pretend. There was nothing pretend about…this." She waved between us with her clipboard. "I think I speak for the whole town when I say that we couldn't be happier for you two, right?"

The small crowd that was still paying attention to us, instead of the band, roared their approval.

"Best part of the night."

"I knew there was more to it!"

"It's about time."

My cheeks burned, but I knew my hometown well enough to know that there wasn't going to be any escape. Especially not when we'd been so public, intentionally or unintentionally, about it all.

She gave us each a quick hug and a kiss on the cheek

before bustling off to deal with some other emergency, just as Reid pushed his way through the crowd with Avery at his side.

He stopped short in front of us, his eyes locked on his twin in some unspoken communication until finally he nodded and pulled Grayson into a tight, back-slapping hug. "I'm glad you both got over yourselves, brother."

Grayson stepped back. "Me too, Reid. Me too."

Reid hugged me next. "Thank you for finally putting him out of his misery, Harper. I don't think I could have lived with his moping around for another fifteen years."

I laughed. "Happy to help."

We accepted more hugs and congratulations before Charli appeared with Symon at her side with baby Poppy, fast asleep in the carrier on his chest. My old friend pulled me in for a tight hug. "What did I say, huh?" she whispered in my ear. "Sometimes those second chances are worth everything."

"You're not wrong," I told her, but was unable to say anything more because at that moment, the rest of the Lyons brothers appeared. Quinn wiggled herself free from Ethan and Delaney and threw herself at her uncle.

Grayson squeezed her tight. "I'm sorry I was such a grump, kiddo."

"It's okay, Uncle Gray." She waved him away. "Love does funny things to people." She rolled her eyes. "Which is why I'm never going to let it happen to me." Everyone laughed, and she rolled her eyes again, harder, before turning to me. "That was epic," she squealed. "Way better than the fireworks."

"Although I'd say there were plenty of fireworks on the stage."

I looked over Quinn's shoulder to see Grandma, bundled up in her parka, watching with careful eyes.

"Grandma." I stepped through the others to pull her into my arms. Fresh tears slipped down my cheeks as I held her and shared the moment with the most important woman in my world.

"That's enough crying," she said after a moment with a pat on my back. Despite her gruff words, I saw the tears on her own cheeks. "It's a happy occasion. You're in love, your New Year's feast was a massive hit, and we're all together. I can't think of any better reason to celebrate."

I couldn't agree more.

The noise of the plaza blurred around me. The cheers, the laughter, the teasing—all of it fell away. All I could focus on was the man beside me, his hand warm and steady, grounding me through all the chaos.

For so long, I'd thought the life I wanted had been out there. Far away from this town and these people, across oceans —or on them, in some port, chasing menus and adventures that were never truly mine. But here, in the biting cold, half frozen, surrounded by friends and neighbors, with Grayson Lyons at my side, I finally saw it all clearly.

It had been here all along. I just needed to stop running long enough to see it.

Grayson's mouth brushed my temple, his voice low and for me alone. "This is fun and all," he murmured, his breath warming my skin, "but I don't plan on sharing you with the whole damn town all night."

A shiver skated down my spine.

He pulled back just enough to look into my eyes, his expression fierce and full of intent. "I'm taking you home."

The words weren't a question, but a promise. And I didn't hesitate.

Chapter 25

NEW YEAR'S DAY

Harper

I could have stayed wrapped in Grayson's arms all day long. But as happy as I was, I knew the bubble would be popped eventually, and there were things that I'd already been putting off for far too long.

I hung my coat by the door and slipped off my boots, my heart pounding harder than it should have been. After everything I'd already done—the plaza, the crowd, and the microphone—having a frank conversation with my grandma shouldn't be sending me into a panic.

But it had to be done. It was long past time I knew the truth.

I found her in her chair by the window, her new soft blanket over her lap, a cup of tea in her hands, looking suspiciously...healthy.

"Good morning, dear," she said without turning. "I trust you had a lovely evening."

My cheeks heated, but I was not going to be swayed from

my mission. "Grandma." I moved across the room. "We need to talk."

She turned to me then, peering over the top of her mug. "Sounds serious."

"It is." I perched on the arm of the couch, my nerves twisting in my stomach. I didn't know what I was going to hear, but I knew I wasn't going to like it. I blew out a breath. "How sick are you, really? I know you don't want to talk about it, but I need to know."

I resisted the urge to hold my breath while I waited for her answer.

She blew across her tea, radiating calm. "Harper, I'm eighty-two. Everything creaks and hurts. Be more specific."

"Grandma." I narrowed my eyes. "Enough. You called me, remember? You told me you weren't well."

"I do remember," she said simply. "You were finishing up your last charter, and I called to let you know I'd been to the doctor."

"Right." I swallowed hard, trying not to get frustrated. "You said you weren't well."

"No." She held up a finger. "I said I wasn't *feeling* well," she clarified. "Isn't that why one goes to the doctor in the first place?"

My frustration was growing, but there was something else going on, too. "Wait," I said slowly. "Are you not really sick?"

Grandma waved a dismissive hand. "Oh, honey. It's just a bit of reflux, is all. The doctor says if I lay off the fried onions and red wine, I'll outlive everyone in town."

"Wait." I blinked. "Reflux?"

"Mm-hmm." She took another sip of her tea. "It's really quite unpleasant."

"I'm sure it is," I said, my words clipped. "But you let me think—" My voice broke, half anger, half relief.

"Sweetheart, I don't think I *let* you think anything." Her

voice was sweet, but her smile was devilish. "But when you assumed… Well, I didn't see the harm in letting you think it was a bit worse than it was. Besides, you wouldn't have come home otherwise. And it was *way* past time you did. And you most definitely wouldn't have let yourself fall into that boy again without a little nudge."

"But you manipulated me." I shook my head, still unable to fully comprehend what she'd done.

"I just gave you a little push in the right direction, that's all." She fluttered her lashes at me with such exaggerated innocence that I had to laugh.

"See?" she said when she noticed me laughing. "You can't even pretend you're not grateful."

I shook my head. "Okay, okay. I guess I am grateful," I conceded. "I guess." I swallowed hard. "You're impossible."

"That's nothing new." She set her mug down and reached for my hand. Her touch was warm and steady against mine. "You found your way home, Harper. That's all I ever wanted for you."

I squeezed her fingers, my chest aching in that good, overwhelming way. She was impossible, it was true. But she was also right.

I was home.

And I didn't plan to leave anytime soon.

Grayson

AS IT DID for many people, the first day of a new year had always felt like a fresh start for me. A blank slate. But this time, walking through the plaza on the morning of a brand-new year, full of potential and opportunity, the future felt brighter than ever.

There were still so many questions and unknowns about

what was going to happen, but the one thing I knew for sure was that I loved Harper and she loved me. As long as I had her, I had everything. All the rest of it would be figured out with time.

The other thing I knew was that I was done waiting around for life to happen to me instead of making things happen for myself. That strategy had almost cost me the love of my life, again. No more.

New year. New me.

Or something like that.

The plaza always looked different the morning after a big celebration, but the distinction was particularly noticeable the day after New Year's. With all the people gone, it felt extra quiet. Decorations dropped, strings of lights tangled in piles waiting to be boxed up for another year—so much for putting them away neater this year. I shook my head with a smile, knowing I'd be the one to untangle them in less than a year.

A handful of cleanup volunteers worked in the frosty morning to dismantle the stage and put everything away until the next celebration that Tilley was no doubt already cooking up.

My boots crunched over the frost and ice as I walked through it all, more determined than I'd felt in weeks.

I spotted Ollie on a bench outside the Bean Bag, just as I knew I would. He was a man of routine. Which was why I also knew that was a paper bag of cinnamon twists that sat beside him, and in his hand, the steam that was rising from the cup contained his other morning indulgence. Coffee, two sugars and two creams.

Don't tell Doris, his wife of almost fifty years.

"Morning, Ollie."

He looked up and nodded when he saw me. "Happy New Year, Grayson."

"Got a minute?" I skipped the pleasantries. It was long past time I got down to business.

"You know I do." He picked up the bag and scooted over on the bench to make room for me, but I remained standing.

"Have you signed the papers with Homeworks yet?" I got right to the point.

His face flickered with a moment of confusion before he shook his head. "Not yet," he said.

Two words that gave me a flash of hope.

"Why are you asking?" His eyes narrowed, crinkling even deeper around the edges.

"Sell it to me," I said before I could talk myself out of it again.

He lifted his brows, but he didn't look as surprised as I would have expected. "I didn't know you were interested," he said after a moment.

"I was. I am." I took a beat and inhaled slowly. "I waited too long to tell you, and then there was never a right time, and when you told me that Homeworks had made you an offer, well, I knew I couldn't compete, so I just…it doesn't matter." I shook my head clear. "What matters is I'm telling you now. I'd like to buy the hardware store, Ollie. Don't count me out. Please."

Finished saying what I needed to, I exhaled completely, blowing out the stress I'd been holding onto.

Ollie was quiet for a moment. He took his time taking a sip of his coffee and rustled around in the bag of cinnamon twists for a pastry before finally looking up at me. "Homeworks has made me a very generous offer, you know?"

I nodded. I didn't need to know the specifics of the offer to know it would be more than I could manage. "I'm sure they did, Ollie. And I know that security is important for you." He leveled me with his gaze, but I wasn't done. "I also know that you built that store from the ground up," I continued. "I've seen the photos and I've heard the stories about how your first storefront was little more than a shed in a back alley."

He sat back; I had his full attention.

"You put your whole life into that store, Ollie, and you built it into the thriving business it is today." I also knew I had something to do with that in recent years, but it didn't need to be mentioned. "Yes, Homeworks can offer you more money than I can. They'll come in and put their shiny sign on the front of the building. They'll standardize everything inside and there'll be clean, neat shelves with matching bins and glossy posters on the wall. Just like every other Homeworks store in this country. But you know what they can't offer?"

Ollie set his coffee down and crossed his arms over his chest. I couldn't read him. I couldn't tell whether I'd lost him or hooked him, so I carried on.

"Homeworks will never know that Bill Bensen buys ten gallons of dark oak stain for his fence every two years, but he'll forget and try to order the light. Every time. A cold corporation will never know that Mrs. Woods has done all her own home repairs since her divorce three years ago, and when her ex-husband moved out, he took all their tools, so sometimes she needs to borrow something to get the job done."

My boss opened his mouth to speak, but I wasn't finished. "This town and the people in it deserve more than that, Ollie. They've given you years of patronage. You wouldn't be where you are without them—don't you think they deserve that personal touch?"

He nodded. "They do."

"Then sell it to me, Ollie. I can't offer you top dollar. That's not a secret. But I can promise you that the legacy you built in Trickle Creek will continue. I'll work hard to make sure the business you built remains a trusted one in this town. I've been running things with that same focus for the last few years. All I'm asking is that you give me the chance to keep doing that."

Finally finished, I blew out a breath and waited.

The older man was quiet for a long time. Slowly, he took a bite of his cinnamon twist and chewed thoughtfully for a few minutes before finally speaking. "It sounds like you've put some thought into this, Grayson."

I nodded.

"You know," Ollie continued, "when I told Doris about our conversation the other day, she was pretty upset with me."

"Really? Why?" That surprised me. Doris never had much to do with the business, and I'd only seen her in the store a handful of times. She was a nice lady and was always very friendly and kind to me, but to be honest, I was surprised that she'd noticed what the store meant to me.

He nodded. "She's a very observant woman, my Doris. It didn't go unnoticed by her that you were the only reason I've been able to focus on my recovery and take this unofficial early retirement over the last few years. She's very thankful, Grayson."

That touched me unexpectedly.

"Which is why she was very upset with me when I told her I hadn't even offered you the option to buy the store."

"What?"

Ollie nodded, unaware of my genuine surprise. "She really was," he continued. "Especially when I told her I was going to accept the offer from Homeworks. In fact, she feels very much the same way you do." He chuckled a little bit and shook his head. "And you know what, you both make very valid points. I just assumed you weren't interested."

"I've learned a lot about the danger of assuming things lately," I said, shaking my head.

"You're not wrong, Grayson. I should have just asked you straight out."

A flicker of hope lit up deep inside. "I don't know what they offered you, Ollie. But I have a solid business plan, some savings, and I think the bank will give me a loan. Even so, I don't think I can come close to their—"

"Oh no." He stopped me. "You won't be able to offer me what they did."

My stomach sank.

"But money isn't everything." He shrugged. "And I'll tell you what…"

I watched and waited.

"Part of me always hoped you'd be the one to take over the store."

"Really?"

He laughed. "Of course. I don't have a son of my own, and my girls couldn't have cared less about this hardware business. They never did. Took after their mother, really."

"So you're saying…"

"What I'm saying, Grayson, is that as long as you have some financing lined up, and a solid plan, the way you say you do…"

I nodded. "I do."

"I have no doubt." He pushed himself slowly to his feet. "Then I'd say I'm sure we can work something out."

"What about Homeworks?"

"What about them?" He shrugged. "I haven't signed anything yet. I'm sure they'll find some other small town with a store they can get their franchise hands on. But it won't be mine. What do you say?" He held out his hand.

I stared at it for a second before clasping it in my own and pulling the older man in for a hug.

He was shaking his head when he pulled away. "Like I said, I always hoped you'd be the one to take over things. I guess you just needed a little push."

A shaky laugh escaped me. "That seems to be a theme in my life lately."

For the first time, Ollie grinned. "Good. Then consider this your official push. Why don't we sit down tomorrow and look at the details?"

My shoulders sagged, relief rushing through me so fast my knees almost buckled. "Thank you, Ollie. You won't regret this."

Ollie picked up his coffee and bag of snacks and, with a wink, said, "Something tells me I won't."

Chapter 26

Harper

By the time I made it downstairs to the kitchen, Kevin was already hard at work.

"Do you ever rest?" I joined him at the stove to see what smelled so good. "You do know we're closed today, right?"

My new head chef laughed and offered me a spoon to taste the delicious soup he was stirring. "I know, but I woke up with an idea for a roasted vegetable soup that I think will be perfect for a lunch special this week. It's supposed to be a chilly one."

I took the spoon and dipped it into the soup, blowing on it gently before putting it to my lips. My eyes squeezed shut as the flavors hit my tongue. "This is amazing, Kevin. We're definitely making this a special."

"I'm glad you like it."

"I love it." I tossed the spoon into the sink and assessed the kitchen I'd grown up working in. It was hard to believe that I'd come full circle after so many years. It felt right.

"Last night was a huge success," I said after a moment. "I don't think Willa's Whisk has ever pulled off a feast like that."

"It was pretty incredible," Kevin agreed. "Everyone I talked to afterward told me how much they enjoyed it and can't wait for the next event."

I wasn't surprised; I'd received the same feedback. And even if I hadn't, I experienced it. What we'd done in the restaurant had been fantastic. It felt good to be creative in the kitchen again.

"We'll definitely have to start brainstorming about the next one."

Kevin pointed his ladle in my direction. "So, you haven't changed your mind? You're staying?"

"Of course she's staying." Grandma burst through the doors to join us. Now that I knew she wasn't sick at all, she looked even younger and healthier than ever. "And I can't wait to see what she does with this place. Are you sure you're up for the challenge of working for her, Kevin?"

"Am I up for it?" Kevin laughed. "I welcome it."

"You're probably sick of all my old fuddy-duddy recipes." Grandma waved an arm in his direction.

"Not at all, Willa." Kevin wrapped an arm around her shoulders and squeezed gently. "You know I love the classics. But this granddaughter of yours, she's something special. I can't wait to see what she comes up with."

"She certainly is special." Grandma smiled warmly at me. "And the first thing she'll need to come up with is a name for the place."

"Wait. What?" Her words caught me off guard. "What do you mean, a name? It's Willa's Whisk."

"It *was* Willa's Whisk," she said simply. "But you can't call the place *Willa's*." She shook her head and wrinkled her nose. "Not when it's *Harper's*."

I glanced at Kevin as if he might hold the answers, but he simply shrugged before excusing himself from the kitchen.

"Grandma, what are you talking about? It's *Harper's?*"

"Exactly what it sounds like." She pulled a legal envelope I hadn't noticed before off the shelf and handed it to me. "I had the papers drawn up a few days ago. Right after you told me you were staying."

With a shaking hand, I took the envelope, but didn't open it. "Papers?"

Grandma gave me an exceedingly patient smile. "Ownership papers, Harper." She nodded toward the envelope. "The restaurant officially and legally belongs to you. Make it your own."

"But...what..." Finally, I slid the papers out of the envelope and saw the documents with my own eyes. But still, it was hard to register what they really meant.

"Grandma. This is too—"

"It was always meant to be yours, sweetheart. Willa's Whisk gave me such a great life. A full life. But my time here is done." She laughed and quickly held up a hand. "And no, I don't mean my time *time* is done. My time in the restaurant business is done."

I shook my head and couldn't help but chuckle.

"Watching the way you followed your dreams has been inspiring, dear. And I think it's time I did a bit more of that myself."

I tilted my head. Grandma had never spoken of her dreams. Maybe it was naive or self-absorbed of me, but I'd never stopped to think about what more she might want out of life. "What does that mean?"

Her smile was radiant and untroubled. "It means I'm ready to do a bit more traveling of my own. Visiting you over the years, I got to see all kinds of beautiful places, but I'm not done. I think I'd like to take some cooking classes in Italy. Learn to make pasta the old-fashioned way. And eat all the gelato." She winked. "And maybe drink some wine, too. After that, we'll see. But I plan on giving you some space to create your own dreams now."

My heart filled, and the emotion overwhelmed me, making words impossible. Tears slipped from my eyes, and I shook my head until she laughed again and pulled me into a tight hug.

"Oh, Harper."

"It sounds amazing," I said finally. "And I'm going to miss you, but I'm so happy for you."

"And you, dear." She pulled back, holding me at arm's length. "I can't wait to see what you do with the place. But one thing I know for sure is that this town is so lucky to have you back and all the delicious food they're about to get from you."

Her faith in me wrapped tighter than the hug she'd just given, and as I tucked the envelope against my chest, one thought echoed louder than the rest. This wasn't just my home again. It was my future. The place I belonged, with the people I belonged with.

Grayson

THE BREWERY BUZZED with holiday energy. The après crowd was starting to file through the doors after a full day on the ski hill. Peaks & Brews had been a huge success from the moment Ethan had opened the doors.

Fortunately, Brody had already secured a corner table and was halfway through a pint when I slid into the chair across from him.

"You look like a happy man, brother." Brody raised his glass. "Congratulations."

I froze, and it took me a minute to realize he was talking about fixing things with Harper, and not the hardware store. Of course, I couldn't wait to tell all my brothers that news, but only after the love of my life heard it first.

"I am, Brody. I am."

"It's good to see, Gray. Really." Brody poured me a pint from the jug sitting in front of him. "Is there something else going on?" He eyed me suspiciously. "You look like a man who has a secret to spill."

I laughed and raised my glass to my lips, shrugging.

Brody shook his head. "You care to share?"

"I do." I turned to look at the door and saw Harper outside, crossing the plaza. "But not yet. She gets to hear it first." I put the glass down and pushed up from the table.

Brody studied me for a second, but to his credit, he just nodded and tipped his glass. "Fair enough."

I returned his nod and moved through the crowd to greet Harper.

"Hey there, beautiful."

Before she had a chance to slip out of her coat, I kissed her deeply. It had only been a few hours since I'd seen her, but it had been too long as far as I was concerned.

"You look excited." She grinned up at me, a little breathless, like she, too, had something to tell me.

"I am." I took her hand and led her through the room, looking for a quiet spot to talk. I gave Ethan, who was behind the bar, a glance, and he nodded, gesturing me into the back room.

The moment we were alone, we turned to each other.

"I have something to tell you."

"I have news."

We spoke at the same time.

I laughed. "You first."

"Are you sure?"

I could sense the same glow of excitement I was feeling coming off her. I nodded. "Go ahead."

Her eyes shimmered as she reached into her coat and pulled out an envelope. "Grandma gave me the restaurant."

"What?"

Harper nodded. "Officially. She wants me to rebrand it and make it mine." Her breath caught, but her smile didn't waver. "I have so many ideas and…" She exhaled hard. "It's overwhelming in the best way."

"It's incredible." I cupped her cheeks and kissed her deeply. "You're going to be amazing, my love."

Harper pulled back a little, concern on her face. I knew her well enough to know exactly what she was thinking. No doubt she was trying to temper her excitement for my benefit. We'd only briefly discussed the situation of the hardware store the night before. Long enough for me to tell her that I'd been too late in making my offer to Ollie.

"Grayson, I know that—"

"Let me tell you my news." I stopped her.

She nodded and waited, leaning in closer.

"I'm going to buy the store," I blurted. "I found Ollie this morning and told him that while I couldn't offer him the same kind of money, I could offer his store a solid future in this town and the type of service that Homeworks could never provide."

Her mouth fell open. "Really?"

"Yup," I told her. "Trickle Creek deserves more than a white-washed big-box store, and he agreed."

"He did?"

"Yup," I said again. "We're going to meet tomorrow and finalize things, but it's mine, Harper." I had to blink hard to keep the tears at bay. "It's all happening."

"It really is." She still looked stunned as she reached for me and wrapped her arms around me. "And I couldn't be any happier."

I kissed her again. Longer and deeper this time before realizing Brody, and no doubt the rest of the family, were all waiting for us.

"Wait," I said, thinking of one more thing we hadn't

discussed. "What about Willa? Your grandma…is she giving you the restaurant because…" I let the sentence trail away, unwilling to say the words out loud. I knew how worried Harper was about her.

"No." Harper shook her head as she understood what I was saying. "It's not like that at all. In fact, she's going to travel."

"Travel?"

Harper laughed. "Because she's not sick." She rolled her eyes, but I still wasn't totally following. "She just let me believe that so I'd come home."

"Ohh." I put the pieces together. "Diabolical."

"Right?" Harper laughed again. "And I can't be all that mad since I also told a little white lie. And look how that worked out." She leaned forward and gave me another kiss.

"I'm certainly not complaining," I told her. "But you know, I'm pretty sure Willa knew what was going on the entire time. Did you know she was responsible for my volunteer appreciation gift?" I used air quotes. "She wanted us to have a little bit of alone time."

Harper let out a low whistle and shook her head. "Wow. She's good."

"She sure is." I looped my arm through hers. "Are you ready to share our happy news?"

Her mouth dropped open. "You make it sound like we're having a baby."

Her words shocked me. But only for a moment. "Not yet, muffin." I winked. "Why don't we take one thing at a time?"

"Ha! That's not—"

"What's this about a baby?" Ethan chose that moment to burst into the back room. "Did I just hear what I think I heard?"

Harper shook her head fiercely and held up her hand. "Settle down."

"No way. Your baby and our baby will grow up together," Ethan continued. "That's cause for celebration if I ever heard one."

"Whoa!" I put a hand on my brother's shoulder. "No one here is having a baby. Except you and Delaney," I added quickly. "But we do have news."

Ethan's smile dipped momentarily, but once more lit up at the mention of something else to celebrate.

"Come on, let's share with everyone all at once, so no one can spread any baby rumors." Harper shot a look at Ethan and then looked back at me with wide eyes before laughing.

By the time we got back to the table, everyone else had joined Brody. The table was full, with Reid and Avery cuddled along the back wall, Lauren snuggled suspiciously close to Brody, and Delaney and Quinn perched on stools. Even Preston had made it on time. He was still in his ski gear, dusted with snow, but he was there.

Ethan followed us to the table with two fresh jugs of beer that Brody immediately started pouring.

"So?" he prompted once all the glasses were poured and everyone had a glass, Quinn and Delaney with sparkling apple juice instead of beer. "What's just as exciting as a baby, but *isn't* a baby?"

"A baby?" Lauren's mouth dropped.

Harper and I replied in unison: "No!" and "Stop!"

"No baby," I said firmly. "Stop it before a rumor really gets going."

My brother laughed, but I ignored him and looked at Harper. "Do you want to go first or should I?"

Harper's eyes sparkled as she looked around the table at the expectant faces, then back at me. "Go ahead."

I squeezed her hand, took a steadying breath, and lifted my glass. "Ollie and I talked this morning. The hardware store is going to be mine."

The table erupted in cheers and clinking glasses.

Reid leaned over and smacked me on the shoulder. "Well deserved, brother. It's about fuc—" He stopped himself, looking to Quinn, who was waiting to pin him down with some money for her swear jar. "It's about time," he finished with a grin.

Before the noise died down, Harper lifted her glass. "And Grandma gave me the restaurant. Willa's Whisk is officially mine to run and rebrand."

Once more, everyone cheered, and there was more celebrating.

"That's amazing, Harper." Preston pulled her in for a quick hug.

"Will we still be able to get that yummy lasagna?" Quinn asked seriously.

"I'm sure I'll keep the lasagna on the menu."

"Phew!"

Everyone laughed.

There were more cheers, clinking and celebrating as we toasted to family and the promise of an exciting new year. I slipped my arm around Harper and pulled her close.

For the first time in a long time, I didn't feel like I was simply surviving in this town—I was building a future in it.

With the love of my life by my side.

Finally.

Epilouge

Harper

The last of the dishes had just gone out. The special chocolate lava cakes with a raspberry coulis and a dusting of powdered sugar had been the perfect touch of simple and elegant. It was only after Erin walked through the swinging doors to deliver the final cakes that I could exhale properly.

"We did it, boss." Kevin came to lean against the counter next to me. "Again."

"Again." I laughed a little. "These special dinners are starting to be a bit of a trend. That's two in two months."

"The customers love them," Kevin said with a satisfied smirk. "You sold out in minutes. I think word is going to get out that Wander & Whisk is the place to be for a special occasion."

Wander & Whisk.

Hearing the new name of the restaurant—*my* restaurant—still made my heart skip a little. Of course, the rebrand was still pretty new. The special Valentine's Day meal had been the official launch of the new brand. The custom-made wooden sign Reid made for me had been hung outside less than twenty-four hours earlier.

"That sounds pretty good."

"That you were sold out in minutes?" Kevin teased, with a gentle elbow to my ribs.

"The name." I grinned at him. "This place is really mine."

"It sure is." He pulled the towel from the string in his apron and wiped his hands before shoving up from the counter and moving to the stove to start to clean up. "And I couldn't be happier to be part of it, Harper. You've got something pretty special going here."

I sat in the glow of his praise and soaked in the moment, knowing he was right. I *did* have something very special here. And it wasn't just the restaurant. It was all of it.

Trickle Creek.

Grayson.

There was no doubt in my mind that I'd made the right choice in staying. The last six weeks had been a whirlwind as I put into practice all the ideas for the restaurant I'd been thinking and dreaming of. And Grayson had been full-on as well. The sale of the hardware shop was finally official, and soon the doors would open for the grand opening of Lyons Hardware. But as busy as we'd been, every minute of it had felt exactly right.

Tears pricked at my eyes as I looked around the room, taking it all in, when the kitchen door swung open and Grayson walked in.

"Knock, knock." His eyes scanned the kitchen, lighting up when they landed on me. "Is this a good time?"

"It's the perfect time." I crossed the room and greeted him with a kiss. "Happy Valentine's Day. I'm sorry we didn't get to spend the day together."

He dismissed my apology with a wave. "Are you kidding?

You had kind of a lot going on." He turned to take in the state of the kitchen. The part-time staff had already started on the cleanup, but there was no hiding the chaos Kevin and I had created. "How did it go?"

"Great," I answered honestly. "I can't wait to hear what the customers thought."

"I can tell you that," Erin said, joining us in the kitchen. "All rave reviews," she continued. "And every single plate was practically licked clean. You did it again."

I beamed, my heart swelling with pride.

"I had no doubt." Grayson pulled me in close. "Because you are amazing and your food is incredible. Trickle Creek is lucky to have you back."

I closed my eyes and sank into his kiss, completely uncaring who else was in the room.

"I'm lucky to have you back," Grayson said when he pulled away. "And I know we said no gifts, but—"

Grayson took a step back and produced a gift bag I hadn't noticed before.

"Gray." I held up my hand. "Just being together is—"

"I know. I know."

His grin was so boyish and handsome, I couldn't help but laugh.

"But it's just a little thing."

I tilted my head, not buying it.

"Trust me," he said. "It's perfect."

I wasn't going to win the argument, so I took the bag, pulled the tissue paper out, reached in and pulled out a…

"A whisk?" Obviously, I had plenty of whisks in the kitchen, but this one was shiny and gold and…perfect.

"Now that this place is officially Wander & Whisk, I thought it was only right to have your very own whisk to hang next to Willa's whisk."

Again, my eyes filled with tears. This time at his immense

thoughtfulness. When the rebranding of the restaurant was complete, I took Grandma's favorite whisk out of the kitchen and had Reid build a shadow box to preserve it so it could forever hang in a place of honor in the dining room. A reminder of where I'd come from and where it had all begun.

"It's so perfect." I dropped the whisk back into the bag and reached for Grayson, but he stopped me.

"You didn't even take it out of the bag," he said. "You need to see it all."

Again, I tilted my head, giving him a questioning look. I'd seen enough. It was a beautiful whisk. How much more to it could there be?

Without further argument, I did as he asked and once more reached into the bag, this time pulling my gift all the way free. It was only then that I saw the satin ribbon tied to the bottom, and hanging from the ribbon was a—

"Oh!" My hand flew to my mouth when I realized what I was looking at. "Grayson, I—"

Grayson

THE RING SPARKLED in the kitchen light, but I wasn't looking at the gold and diamond jewelry I'd picked out weeks ago. I only had eyes for the love of my life, who was still holding the whisk up in the air, letting the ring dangle from the ribbon.

I took it from her and untied the ribbon before sinking to one knee on the tile floor. From somewhere behind me, I heard Erin, or someone else, gasp as they realized what was about to happen, but I didn't take my eyes off Harper.

Her hands covered her mouth, her eyes wide and filled with tears as she watched and waited.

I wouldn't make her wait too long. "Harper." I reached for her left hand and the silver ring I'd put on her hand for the first time when we were kids. "When I gave you this ring back, I told you I hoped you would never take it off again." I took a moment to look at the simple design. The perfect purple stone. It represented so much. And it always would. "But I lied," I continued. "Because I do hope you take it off."

She gasped a little and swallowed back a sob. Her hand shook in mine, but I couldn't stop.

I held up the engagement ring with the cushion-cut diamond, set in a platinum band. "Because this is the ring I hope you never take off." I took a moment to catch my breath and ground myself. "I have spent my entire life loving you, Harper Bennett, and that will never change because I plan on spending the rest of my life growing and learning with you, building the life we both want, together. Will you make me the happiest man in the world and do me the honor of being my wife?"

With the words finally out, I blew out a breath.

"Grayson. I…" She shook her head, and for a moment, my breath caught in my throat. "I…this is so…oh… I mean…I can't wait to marry you," Harper said in a tumble of words. "Yes!" she cried. "Yes. Yes. Yes. Of course I'll marry you."

Before I could slide the ring onto her finger, she dropped to her knees on the floor with me and, with a shaking hand, took the silver ring from her left hand and moved it to her right hand.

I pressed a kiss to the amethyst, thankful I'd kept it all these years, before turning my attention to Harper's other hand.

We were both shaking as I slipped the engagement ring onto her finger. A perfect fit.

"It's beautiful."

"You're beautiful."

I pulled her in for a kiss and lifted us both to our feet in the same move, needing to hold her properly. My fiancée.

My love.

My future.

A chorus of cheers and congratulations rose up behind us. With Harper still in my arms, we turned to see Kevin, Erin, some of the part-time staff, and of course, Willa, watching us.

Earlier in the day, I'd visited Willa and asked her for Harper's hand in marriage. It was an outdated tradition, and I of course already knew what she'd say, but Willa appreciated the gesture. And I knew it would be important to Harper that her grandmother was there to witness the moment.

"Congratulations, you two," Erin said.

Kevin clapped and whooped. "Incredible."

But it was Willa who walked slowly toward us, tears in her eyes, arms outstretched for a big hug. "I couldn't be happier for you both," she said as we embraced. "I just love you both so much."

After a few moments, Erin interrupted. "I think this calls for a bottle of bubbly."

"Yes!" Willa pulled away and swiped at her eyes. "Everyone out to the dining room for a toast."

The others moved first, but Harper pulled me back before we could follow.

"I love you, Grayson Lyons," she said simply.

I cupped her cheeks in my hands and held her gently before pressing my forehead to hers. "Wherever this life takes us," I pulled back to look in her eyes, "I will always be by your side. Because there will never be even one second of my life where I don't love you, Harper."

We stayed that way for a minute, soaking in the moment and everything it meant, before we heard the cork pop in the other room. "We should get out there and celebrate properly."

With a laugh, hand in hand, we joined the others to raise a glass to toast to us and our future.

We moved out to the dining room bar, where Willa already had a bottle of prosecco and a tray full of glasses.

There were still a handful of diners, finishing up their meals. Including, I noticed belatedly, my brother Brody and Lauren tucked into a corner table.

"What are those two doing?" Harper asked before I could say anything. "I thought they weren't together."

"They're not." I shook my head. "And from what I understand, Lauren is on some sort of dating quest, but apparently it's tradition for the two of them to spend Valentine's Day together."

"Hmm." Harper shook her head.

"Maybe we should get Willa to give them a little nudge? She seems to have a way of bringing people together."

I winked at her, and Willa shrugged. "Say the word, and I'll go work my magic."

"Later," I said firmly. "Tonight is about us." I took a glass that Erin had poured and handed it to my fiancée as everyone else took one and raised it for a toast.

"To Wander & Whisk," I started. "The hardware store, and of course, more importantly…to…" My throat tightened as I looked at Harper. "To forever."

"Forever," Harper echoed, clinking her glass against mine before we each took a sip.

I kissed her temple and held her close. She'd been my first love. My only love. And now, standing in her restaurant, hearing the people we cared about cheering around us, I knew she'd be my last love, too.

"Oh, I almost forgot." Harper turned to face me. "I actually have something for you, too." She reached into the inside pocket of her chef's coat and produced an envelope.

I narrowed my eyes. "I thought we said no gifts."

She shrugged. "I think you'll agree that it's completely perfect." She wiggled her left hand. "Especially now."

With a laugh and a shake of my head, I tore open the envelope and pulled out a room key. "Don't tell me this is for the lodge?" I raised an eyebrow, remembering exactly how our night had gone the last time we'd stayed there.

She nodded with a smug smile. "For tonight."

"Tonight?"

"I thought maybe our first Valentine's Day as a *real* couple deserved some memories. Besides, I never got a chance to try out that big bathtub last time."

A low growl slipped from my throat as I pulled her close. "Careful, sweetheart. If you keep spoiling me like this, I'll never let you out of my sight."

Her eyes danced as she tugged me toward the door. "Come on then, that bathtub won't fill itself."

I laughed, sweeping her close for one more kiss.

This wasn't a show. This wasn't pretend.

Finally, this was us.

Forever.

Join Harper and Grayson for their special Valentine's night.
Keep reading for that scene!

Bonus Scene

Harper

It was late by the time we got to our suite at the lodge. I should have been exhausted after such a complicated dinner service, but the prospect of spending a luxurious night with Grayson—with my fiancé—had me wide awake.

I was still getting used to the idea of being engaged. The ring on my left hand felt surreal, but also perfect. Part of me always knew, even when we were a world apart, that the two of us would end up together. We were meant for each other.

I twirled the ring around on my left hand and held up my right hand to compare rings. They were both beautiful and absolutely perfect.

"Harper?" Grayson poked his head out of the bathroom, damp hair curling at his temple. "Are you coming?"

The sight of him standing there, sleeves rolled up and collar undone, stole my breath. For a second, I stared, the two rings glinting in the low firelight. Solid proof that this wasn't just a dream.

"I'm coming," I whispered, slipping out of my shoes and padding across the carpet toward him.

The bathroom was warm, steamy, and scented with lavender from the bubbles foaming high in the oversized tub. He'd lit candles too; the entire scene looked like it was out of a movie.

"This is incredible, Gray."

"I may have gone a little bit overboard with the bubbles."

"No such thing." I laughed as bubbles fell to the tile floor. "Thank you for doing this for me."

"I'd do a lot more than that for you," he murmured, his mouth brushing mine in a kiss that was slow, certain, and full of promise.

My dress slid down my shoulders, each touch of his hands deliberate, reverent. He moved like he had all night. Like I was a precious gift to unwrap. Like I was his.

When he finally eased me into the hot water and stepped in after me, I sank back against his chest. His arms banded tightly around me, holding me in place. Bubbles clung to my skin and floated in the air around our heads.

Under the water, he found my left hand and lifted it to admire the ring he'd put there. "I know this started out as a pretend love story," he whispered, rough against my ear. "But there was nothing pretend about the way I felt about you. Ever."

My body tingled with the truth of his words. Because I felt exactly the same way.

"And this." He kissed my hand. "This is the realest thing I've ever had, Harper."

I curled my fingers through his and leaned back against his chest, content with everything we had.

After a few moments, I sighed. "This was a very good idea."

His lips brushed the sensitive spot just beneath my ear. "The very best idea."

Heat pooled low in my belly as his hands skimmed over me, fingers splaying wide as if he was reminding himself I were real. When he cupped my breasts, teasing lightly, my body arched into him without hesitation.

"Grayson…" The sound came out breathless and full of need.

"Tell me you're mine," he growled against my skin, his voice barely constrained.

"I'm yours," I gasped. "I couldn't leave you if I tried."

His moan vibrated through my back, and then his mouth was on me, kissing, tasting and worshiping me. His fingers slid lower, parting me beneath the water, stroking until every nerve was alive. I twisted against him, clinging to his arms as he coaxed the pleasure from my body.

When release tore through me, I shattered in his arms, water splashing over the edge to the tiles below. I pressed up hard against his chest, my cries swallowed by his kisses as he held me tight.

The next thing I knew, I was in his arms as he lifted me from the bath as if I weighed nothing. He carried me across the suite, dripping water on the floor until he laid me on the bed.

"Grayson," I muttered. "The sheets will—"

"I don't care. I can't wait any longer."

His need coiled fresh heat deep inside me.

"God, you're beautiful," he rasped, kneeling between my thighs. His hands stroked over my damp skin, which once more had me arching into his touch, needing more.

He dipped his head, his mouth following the touch of his fingers. Heat spread through me as his lips closed around my bud, teasing and sucking until I was once more on the edge of release.

I threaded my fingers through his hair and tugged as my breath hitched.

"Tell me what you want," he whispered, lifting his head slightly.

"You," I gasped. "Always you."

His mouth once more found my hot core, slow and devastating until I was writhing beneath him. My body trembled, my pleasure cresting hard and fast, his name pulled from my lips in a broken cry.

I was still shaking and breathless when he rose over me, his mouth capturing mine in a kiss, the taste of me on his lips.

"Look at me." His forehead rested on mine. "I need to see you."

My eyes fluttered open, my body still vibrating as he pushed his girth inside me. Slow and deep, he filled every part of me completely.

Every thrust, every kiss was stronger and deeper than ever before, filled with the years of love and longing that we'd never stopped feeling for each other.

"Mine," Grayson groaned, his lips brushing my ear. "You've always been mine."

"Always," I whispered back, wrapping myself around him. "It's always been you."

The words undid him. His pace quickened. More desperate, laced with need, dragging me with him until we both shattered together, clinging and gasping.

After, we collapsed into the soft pillows, tangled together. My chest rose and fell against his as I fought to catch my breath, my hand finding his and linking our fingers tightly together.

I was home.

And it felt amazing.

Jess Anderson has always been in control—until she leaves her fiancé at the altar and escapes to a remote mountain cabin.
The last person she expects to find is Preston Lyons— her biggest critic and the man who's made it clear they'll never be on the same side. Preston's story is next in *Only for Tonight*.

About the Author

Elena Aitken is a USA Today Bestselling Author of more than sixty romance and women's fiction novels. The mother of 'grown up' twins, Elena now lives with her very own mountain man in the heart of the very mountains she writes about. She can often be found with her toes in the lake and a glass of wine in her hand, dreaming up her next book and working on her own happily ever after.

To learn more about Elena:
www.elenaaitken.com
elena@elenaaitken.com